Early 1900,s

"The Flickering Candle"

80,921 words

BY SYLVIA JACKSON CLARK
Copyright April 19th 2014

THANKS AND LOVE TO JOY JACKSON HURST

AND DAWN JACKSON GOLDING

FOR FRONT COVER, AND PATIENCE

AND JUST BEING THERE!

LOVE AS ALWAYS TO MY BOYS.

*THANKS TO PAUL FOR TECHNICAL
ASSISTANCE
HAPPY DAYS TO ALL AT HINCKLEY
SCRIBBLERS
KEEP A PEN HANDY AT ALL TIMES!
READ MY BOOK AND BE CONTENT.*

*BEST REGARDS TO CAROL AND DOUG
MOGANO*

*GLAD TO HAVE YOU BACK PHILLIP
AND RUBY. MC.CORMAC
ALL MY WORK COMES WITH
DEDICATION AND LOVE.*

SYLVIA

"The Flickering Candle"
Sylvia Jackson Clark

Copyright 19.4.2014   80,921 words

To Olive
one of the first ten books
Sylvia Jackson Clark.

Hope you enjoy

Prologue

In life we look for kindness, love, passion and respect, we do not always find it. Doors are locked, love misunderstood, the wrong and rocky road has to be endured. How can we survive? Is happiness so far away, should we never find it? We try, and that is what makes the difference. We all count, what we do counts. What we say counts.

Chapter One

He back handed her across the face, she reeled back, his mood was grim his face harsh, her cheek had the imprint of his fingers.

"Get up woman, or I will really hit you."

Four children stood watching as their mother was slapped and punched, falling again and again to the ground.

"Please I beg of you don't hit me anymore."

She caught on to the leg of his trousers, appealing, so fragile.

"Hit you, I am not hitting you, this is just a taste of what you will get if you back answer me once more."

His teeth clenched, saying,

"You poor thing"

Mimicking false reaction,

"Did daddy hurt you; get out of my sight take those brats away with you."

The children whimpered standing in a huddle, tears running down dirty faces leaving a trail, noses running inflamed from the bitter cold they were being forced to live in.

Sara didn't move, had he finished his rampage, she didn't want him to start on the kids, no telling what lengths he would go to *when things didn't suit him.*

"Get up to this table, where I can see you, all of you."

They feverishly moved to the table.

Sidling around the table he went to Sara putting his arm around her shoulders as she sat, Sara went rigid. No love in the way he treated her, now he wanted her.

"Come on love don't be like that, let bygones be bygones."

In front of the kids, at the table, he slid his hand inside her blouse. Sara drew back, Bill could feel the rejection.

"Now then get up them stairs, you are my wife, refusal will get you nowhere, I am entitled to what is mine."

Saying or doing anything was out of her field, not wanting to feel his fists again, she humoured him.

"Let me go upstairs then, I can't while you are in the way. He grinned, he had taught her a lesson, he was glad she remembered it.

"Go on then I will follow you, now you are having another child I can play with you all I want to, can't get pregnant twice can you."

A self satisfied grin spread across his face.

His words defiled her; he didn't give a damn for her welfare, or her kids. She went upstairs to the bedroom, as she did she locked the

door behind her, putting a heavy blanket box with the chair wedged under the door knob.
"You lousy little bitch."
Bill hollowed, as he tried the bedroom door.
Sara went icy cold would the chair added to the lock, be enough to keep Bill away from her? She looked around the room, there was another box if she could haul it over to the door, and it was very heavy. That would keep him out tonight, lowly beast as he was, this was one night he was not going to manhandle her. Sara trembling all over, hoped he hadn't realised the kids were not in bed, if he started on them she would have to submit.
"You can go to hell, I will soon find me a woman, your efforts are pathetic anyway, go and get lost, take your bloody kids with you."
Sara listened carefully to his feet tripping downstairs, mumbling to himself about her shortcomings, she didn't care; she had won for the moment, Bill, thank God had missed the golden opportunity of starting on the kids. As soon as she could they would be in their beds with their door safely locked too. Sara heard the door slam, she waited for a moment, just to see if the coast was clear, then tiptoed downstairs, furtively looking, making double sure he had gone out. Secretly she hoped he had disappeared for good.

Knowing as far as he would have got was the nearest boozer. Maybe if they were lucky Bill would have enough to drink, so that when he returned he would fall asleep. She had to make sure he was gone.

Sara heard the front door slam, furtively she went on to the landing and step by step down the stairs, yes he had gone. Hurrying to the kitchen she went to her children,

"Come on my dears,"

Her arms went out to embrace them. Now she spoke quietly,

"He doesn't mean it."

She defended her husband Bill because he was the father of her children, much to her regret, wanting to ease the pressure in their minds having witnessed his temper, not only this time, many times before. Sara didn't even know what she had supposed to have done Bill could go off at the deep end with very little cause she shuddered, wiping her face where the blood was trickling down. Being quiet, not too sure he had gone out of hearing distance .Tentatively she went to the front door, opening it looking around and listening, there was no sound, beckoning the children they all stepped into the hall passage.

"Go upstairs, all of you, lock your bedroom

door, I will make sure Dad has gone, then you can come down again for something to eat, don't cry any more, I am all right, I am really sorry." She dropped a kiss on each head as she ushered them to go.

Life was hard, Bill a colliery worker down the mines most of his daily hours, money in short supply, and pit workers didn't have a good wage. Almost all of the time having his pit clothes on trouser legs tied with a bit of string where the long sock finished, rough clothes, pit shirt as black as the miner himself. A coal face worker, with marks and scratches all over his back from the pit props, also jagged coal. When in better temperament Sara would search his skin where he could not do it for himself, looking for any injury that had gone septic, at the same time giving the skin a good scrub. The pit dust perpetrated everywhere. There being no pit baths, no indoor washing facility, the tin bath on the hearth did the job. That is when the time presented itself. It was not uncommon for Bill to fall asleep in his chair, waking only to do another shift, pit black becoming usual, not unfamiliar. Sara understood a lot had to be endured, not only for her and the kids for Bill too; his way of life was not enviable. That is the only way Sara could *excuse his behaviour. A sorry state of affairs, things had got worse since Sara had told Bill about her coming child. No more children, they had agreed with each other, but she hadn't conjured the child up, it was within her, there was nothing for it other than to have the child. He blamed Sara; she had done nothing, needing love, not battering.*

"Oh! What can I do?"

Going to the kitchen sink, a yellow stone one with one tap, she bathed her injuries.

Sara sat down for a moment before calling her children for something to eat. Putting coal on the fire, to warm them all, also the soup made earlier was pulled on to the fire to heat up. Slowly her frantic behaviour mellowed.

"Come down now."

Sara called up to the children.

"I had better come up to fetch Lezzy she will be tired."

Lezzy the little one was four years old pretty as a picture, wavy hair, blue eyes.

The children were a handsome brood, it was the lack of good clothes and the fear of their Father, gave them that haunted look. Lack of regular good food made them looked pinched, and withdrawn. Sara knew she couldn't ask more of Bill, except to keep his mighty fists to himself, he drove himself into a corner, then lashed out when he could not escape, blaming anyone but himself.

Sara knew when he was likely to explode, it being the time of month he could not have relations with her. When he needed her she was expected to be there, no matter what. Sara had been told a baby would be born blind if it was conceived during a monthly period, so Sara kept Bill well away. There being no thought for herself as regards discomfort during period time, many days she endured, while nature took its course life can be very cruel, women were not supposed to be ill, woman's ailments in general were not taken seriously. Expecting the old lady next door to have the answers, Doctors were not consulted, they cost money. Many children were lost on the birthing bed due to lack of knowledge. Sara being aware of these facts tried to work it out for herself. Bill added greatly to her burden when in a frenzied rage. The only thing to do was keep out of his way. This time it had come out of the blue, she was with child, so the monthly status didn't apply.

"Sit up to the table; I will give you some warming soup."

The children still were not relaxed, being hungry though they sat up.

Everything was quieter now cheerful with the fire giving its warm glow, Sara hoped Bill would stay away, to come back in a more rational mood. Times being hard they needed to help each other, if Bill hit her she had no retreat, he could be damned cruel at times.

Chapter Two

Bill gave her less consideration, than he gave to the bawdy girls that were at the pub. He had to humour them with his physique, the good looks, the petting, buying them a drink, so that they would do as he asked. Sara was his wife he owned her, or he thought he did. He didn't have to pretty talk Sara; she was his for the taking, commanding his rights with no compassion. Until Sara came up with an answer, the bedroom door would stay locked, they were very heavy doors, would not be easy to break down. Sara knew how angry Bill must be, she was past caring. He could go to hell.

Watching the flickering candle dancing on the ceiling, not sleeping, the door downstairs slammed shut, he had returned. He bumped his way upstairs, hitting the banister and the wall with his fists. He got to the bedroom door.

"Sara, Sara, get this lock undone, I want my bed, and you're asking for it my girl. I will throw you out with the scruff of your neck, when I get my hands on you. Lazy idle good for nothing, I won't wait much longer."

"Get away from that door Bill I am never going to let you in."

"I will come in, it is within my rights!!"

"Your rights became non- existent, when you battered me with your fists."

Sara was determined never to sleep with Bill again. Every night was going to see that the door was barricaded, so she was safe. A candle on the bedside table gave her comfort, it calmed the disturbance in her aching head she would lie and watch the flame as it danced patterns on the ceiling, set against the dark of the room, the effect was soothing, and she felt more secure. Every night Sara was lying awake her mind trying to find a solution, always listening for the downstairs doors slamming one after the other. Then she knew Bill had gone to work. His door slamming shook the whole house. This was a regular performance.

Each night the same routine took place, putting her children to bed first, and then locking their bedroom door for safety, it helped Sara. She was really afraid of Bill, he had a fervent temper. There was no way of stopping him once he got started. Going to the pub, a place he spent most of his time when not at work, getting drunk, then blaming her for the money being used, saying "You want a few lessons in managing, spending money where you need not, where does the money go that I give you each week?

I like meat on my plate."

That was just it, she wasn't Sara she was "Women". How she hated that term. Mother to his four children she had become as a handy tool to be used at his leisure. Bill could be even more violent after drinking Sara trying her utmost to think of something to tame Bill down a bit, but ravishing her own body seemed the only thing that gave him satisfaction. Now she must fight back, with child again and not knowing what to do.

Bill had finished his shift, now in the pub again showing off about giving his wife a good hiding.

"Do you know said his mate George, it does them good to give them a back hander now and again need putting in their place or there is no telling what liberty's they'll take. Begrudge a bloke a pint or two, even when he has worked at the coal face every hour that God sends." "Don't worry about it Bill, you've done the right thing. Now let's have another pint, there will be more than enough weeping and wailing when we get home. The drink will take the edge off it, or it will send us to sleep altogether. Anyhow drink up, same again is it?"

"Thanks George, I'll buy the next one."

The beer was in his hand as fast as it was on

the table, gulping it down faster than he could draw breath. George remarked,

"It is still early evening Bill, I think you had better pace yourself, I don't want the job of carrying you home."

They both laughed with false enthusiasm, already the beer was doing a job, the pub was filling up, a feeling of merriment in the air, and problems had dissolved, the round wrought iron table, with the booze on it being all they cared about.

Bill readily fell in with George's suggestion, he knew he shouldn't spend the money, but hey! He was the man of the house he deserved it. Sara was always at him to do something, or to buy kids clothes, or shoes, the brats will have to wear their shoes with a bit of cardboard in the sole, always on the want. Sara could go to hell, he would find himself a girl, he would never be short of a woman, or two if the fancy struck him and it suited his humour. Did he care for Sara? He had four children by her, another one on the way much to his regret. It was the point where Bill had turned, another mouth to feed, another pair of appealing eyes trying to communicate with the man who was their Father. No he wasn't going to have it, he had needs too.

Chapter Three

Bill came home, once more from the pub, going straight upstairs, to find the door still locked, going over to the other bedroom to sleep with the kids, finding their door locked as well. Bill went downstairs, into the back yard where he was violently sick. Sara was aware of this she knew Bill so well she was glad he was sick because it took his strength he didn't have the same punch to hit her. She still kept out of his way; he was a pathetic sight, how he went daily to his 5am shift at the pit she didn't know, it being their only source of income he had to. More times than Sara could remember Bill had come home drunk and went to work in the same clothes he had worn for days, what did it matter? He just didn't care. He would come home asking for his supper, pulling her on to his knee, that wasn't all he asked for. There would follow a regular almighty row if his demands were not seen to. Sara had sunk so low, the love that once they had nowhere to be found, stuck solid in an unenviable position a sad state of affairs.

Night after night the same routine took place, Sara using all her will power to think up a solution. Leaving him, yes she could, if she knew where to go, the Workhouse offered a roof, with a meal, even that seemed enviable compared to the sex, and beatings. There were the children to be considered, so she cast that thought to one side. Perhaps she could take in washing that might cover the children's shoes and clothes, around here though no-one had money to pay for their washing to be done. In fact on a fine day the zinc Dolly Tub would be brought outside, where the clothes got a good pummelling with a Dolly, a wooden four pronged tool to swish the clothes around in the hot soapy water. The Mangle was in the yard too, it's great wooden rollers, powered by the person who was turning the handle, which in itself took a great deal of energy.

No-one seemed to know who it belonged to, they all used it. If the weather was bad, together they would haul it into the lean to shelter attached to the shed. They lived in a Quarry Cottage, eight dwellings in an "L" shaped plan, outside their front doors was a square of cobble stones, no road, to get to the road that was in use, and families had to walk along the Quarry shingle, a path still left from when the Quarry was worked. The cobblestone court yard made a good place for doing the family wash. All this Sara could do in her stride, the ladies would have a chat, sometimes fetch a cup of tea for herself and friend, leaning on the Dolly handle as she drank it, or sitting on the step, it was the fierce and many times bloody arguments from Bill, Sara could not stand. Why couldn't he look at things from Sara's point of view? He never did.

He came in again, after the pub, Sara could visualise his face red, his eyes puffed, slobbering down his chin. Sara concentrated on the flicker of her candle, while downstairs there was pandemonium, the table crockery being swept with one mighty arm sweeping across it, crashing the pots to the floor. Picking up the poker Bill shouted at the top of his voice, I am coming to bed Woman, if you don't unlock that door I will smash it down. Sara heard Bill trip on the way upstairs, an almighty clatter as his slovenly body bumped each step on the way down. Now she was listening for the sound of him getting up, was this a ruse just to get the door unlocked? After what seemed a while the familiar noise of Bill shifting himself to the yard was distinct. He would be going out for a fag she still had her candle light so lying on her back snuggled down in the sheets, breathing a sigh of relief. Still not asleep, there being no peace in her mind, she tried to think of more pleasant things. Friends with her neighbours, they felt sorry for her so tried to dismiss Bills behaviour. Still they could hardly miss the rampage that went on he was getting worse by the day, soothing words were given to Sara, with balms for her cuts and bruises, gently administered while Bill wasn't around. They knew it wasn't her fault. The Candle flickered thoughts of her place in life came to her mind as she lay watching the patterns on the ceiling.

Not all the cottages were exact in size, three or four had two bedrooms, the rest had a single bedroom, with a single room downstairs Uncle Dick's was the end Cottage with one bedroom. He wasn't anybody's Uncle, he just talked to the Kids, telling of many things, and colourful stories, he had been a commissioned soldier some years ago, been to India, his audience of boys and girls never ceased to be delighted when he told his stories, it coloured their lives. There wasn't much that fitted that bill in the way they lived. Uncle Dick also liked to colour his day to day life, he was middle aged, good humoured. All the cottagers liked him. Along with several of the other men, he kept pigs. The pig sties were around the corner of the last cottage.

Sara would go with her children when there were new piglets born. She found a soothing relief in watching the natural process of new life. The little piglets had Mother's milk, and would suckle in a row, with Mother Pig lying on her side. Sara thought how natural the process was. The large Pigs would be fed on Pig Swill, in a trough. All the neighbours contributed the left over's, and potato peelings, or cabbage leaves, stale bread going round to the sties, pouring the contents of the bucket into the trough. Calling the Pig food Swill, the Pigs soon were munching heartily. That side of things Sara could find interesting, until it came time for the owner to need some pork or bacon. The pig being chased, a knife in Dick's hand for slaughtering, the squeals of the Pig were horrific, stayed in the mind for days. The pig was halved and shared by the owners, this being the result and reward of keeping the pigs. A flitch of bacon hanging from a hook in the ceiling, covered with a Muslin cloth being a regular thing at Dicks house. Sara thought it was all barbaric yet when offered offal of kidneys or liver would be glad to accept, as it would make a good meal for the family and would of course put meat on Bill's plate!

Sara could talk to Dick, some of his ways took understanding, but he was of good solid material, if anyone had a cockerel to be killed Dick would oblige. He was good at trapping rabbits from the woods nearby, there was always something he was up to, it gave him character. Sara would go out in the autumn with the children, to pick Blackberries for jam, and Elderberries for Dick; he made wine in the copper that should have been for washing clothes. When it was matured and ready to drink it was a rich red wine with a kick. There was a bitter tang to the brew if not left to mature long enough. Only the berries were used, combing them off the stalk with a fork. A great deal of these would be needed, so Dick was always glad if anyone offered to help, a tedious job. Again it coloured a drab existence. The resulting wine was shared with neighbours. When the winds were cold and the blood run thin a glass of Dick's wine warmed the body, and cheered the soul. This small community lived together, only one that didn't fall in, of course it was Bill. He had a good obedient wife that is until he started to knock her from pillar to post. That had been the case for too long. Sara must find a resolution so that they could live in harmony.

The candle flickered, as she let her thought pattern drift into her daily living. The ceiling seemed to move, doing a merry dance her eyes grew tired. Her heart told her she was not doing the right thing by locking Bill out.

"I am his wife, when he needs me I should be here I am going to see if I can change his attitude but how? I do not know yet, but I shall give it my best shot. Sitting up in bed she blew out the candle.

Chapter four

Trying to sleep yet again, her mind wandered to the thoughts running around in it. Life in the Quarry Yard could be lived without all the grief that Bill was daily bringing. Feeling a little more relaxed now with the silence that surrounded her. Now breaking the silence was the only too familiar sound of doors banging, and the clatter of pots. Sara tensed herself. Bill was downstairs. There was peace no more. Hearing Bill coming as he climbed the stairs. Here he was at her door. "Get this bloody door unlocked Woman. How long do you think you can keep me away from your bed?"

His voice quieter now,

"Sara the kids are going to feel the buckle end of my belt, if you don't unlock your door. Oh yes, I can get into their bedroom I know it is locked, I have remembered where I put the spare keys, so your tantalising little game is over."

The blood ran cold in Sara's veins, knowing it was as he said, in reply Sara called,

"If you put a hand on a hair of their heads, you will suffer for it; I mean it so think twice."

"Threats now is it, open the door then. I will treat them kindly it is you that is stirring this

thing all up. You and your fancy idea's, you are not satisfying the need in me, you are my wife, think on girl.

The Kids were crying being terrified of what their Dad was threatening them with. They knew of Bill's anger first hand, when they watched their mother Sara as Bill beat her, they called out,

"Don't let Dad hit us. We are cold and frightened don't let him into our bedroom."

"Hear what your kids want? Only you can stop me, you know that."

Rattling the door with a vengeance Bill wouldn't be put off. Sara knew she was sunk, she was ready for him, her anger matched his, and he would not get his way entirely. She steeled herself ready to open up. The blanket boxes had to be pulled away first, so dragging the first one to free the door space, she gripped her face and bit her lip, trying to tolerate the thought of Bill coming in. Looking around there was a good heavy candle stick it paired up with the one that she used to give light and the flicker that she loved. This one had no candle. It could have done with being a bit heavier, but it would have to do, now in her hand she felt she had something to defend herself with. Pulling the other heavy box from the door she was ready.

"God Almighty woman, you're taking you're time. Get that bloody key turned and let me in."

Face to face they stood both with their share of grievance. Bill's eyes like daggers penetrating her own, which also had fire in them, they glared at each other.

"You little bitch you have led me a merry dance."

His fist swung round, and hit her full in the face, his other arm swinging into position to deliver a second blow. Sara saw what was coming, so lifted the Candlestick high and threw it into the side of Bill's head; she had a power in her that was born of disillusion and hate. Bill reeled, they delivered blow for blow, with blood spurting far and wide. They were no longer in the bedroom, just on the landing at the top of the stairs. The skirmish continued Sara was weakening, so when his fist presented itself again, she dodged it then gave Bill an almighty push that did it. Bill lost his balance to go hurtling down the stairs his body hitting each step, making a loud bump as he hit the door at the bottom. He lay silent.

Sara beside herself with remorse uttered,

"What am I going to do Dear God help me I have killed him."

Not wanting to venture down to where Bill's body lay Sara stood transfixed.

In a state of despair, Sara went weak, her legs buckled under her falling into a faint.

Coming round, everything around her was looking strange, Sara tried to stand; she could hear the kids crying. Trying to make some sense of the scene that lay before her, struggling holding on to the Banister slats, she pulled herself up. The space around her spun, she felt sick. Standing quiet trying to collect her thoughts still hoping the moment would pass. Looking downstairs, not wanting to see what was still there. It was like a bad dream, there was Bill, still lying as he was when she fainted.

"I have to get help." Sara muttered to herself.

Moving to the landing window, her thoughts all in disarray, pushing the window open. In the distance she could see Dick coming along the Quarry path towards home. His long legs soon carried him into the Quarry Yard. Sara opened the window and called out,

"Dick" her voice was weak.

"Dick.....she tried to shout louder.

Seeing him hesitate and looking around Sara waved her arms to gain Dicks attention.

"It is me, Sara, I am in trouble please will you help me?"

Dick looked to where Sara was calling.

"Need help Sara? Do you want me to come in?"

"Yes."

"Is your front door open?"

"I think it is Dick, you will find a spare key under the window ledge if you need it. Dick went in. Sara called,

"Bill has had a fall; he lies blocking the way, at the bottom of the stairs. You may need someone with you; I think his fall is serious."

"Al right Sara, don't worry, I will find someone to help me."

Dick called up to her in a matter of moments from the front door.

"Mr. Griffiths' from next door is here with me now, we are coming in."

Dick with Mr. Griffiths entered the room, going straight to the staircase door. Dick opened it very slowly Mr. Griffiths peering into the slot to see Bill lying in a huddle.

"I see no movement Dick, I think we have to call a Doctor, and contact the Police."

"Yes you're right, he isn't responding to his name, he looks purple around the mouth area did you know Bill Mr. Griffith's?"

"I made it my business not to know him Dick. The rows we have heard through the walls have been enough. Sometimes I was afraid

for Sara; she is nice enough, as are the Kids, but Bill well! I won't speak ill of him now poor chap, but I think he had it coming."

Dick lived a few doors down from Sara, so he hadn't been able to hear the constant rows that Mr. Griffiths had readily witnessed, by sight or sound living next door he could hardly miss them.

"One of us must stay, so you go Dick. You will be better at explaining and quicker, I don't walk so well these days."

Dick called up to Sara, to tell her what he was about to do, he still could only open the stair door a few inches, she was sitting on the top step of the stairs, her agony releasing in a flood of tears.

"Can you hear me Sara? I am going to fetch the Doctor, and the Police, Mr. Griffiths will be here in the living room. There is nothing that you can do."

"Alright Dick, I will go and stay with the kids in their bedroom. Try to be as quick as you can" He replied,

"Quicker the better for all concerned I think. Try to keep calm."

No sooner the word than the deed Dick's long stride along the Quarry path, that lead to the road was full of purpose, he knew when he got to the road there would be a Police man on his beat, he would contact all the right people putting the wheels in motion.

Arriving at the road, he looked around for the Policeman he could see him at the top of the hill on his way down, the pair soon met.

"Good morning Constable, sorry to say there has been a misadventure in a family who live in the Quarry Yard. You will know how to handle it."

The Policeman got out his notebook, and took all the particulars with the names of people concerned.

"You go back Sir, see that nothing is disturbed. I will contact a Doctor and get an Ambulance, with a senior Policeman too. Yes I will do that as fast as I can."

With that the pair divided to go their own way. In his stride Dick was soon back with Mr. Griffiths.

"Has he shown any sign of life?"

"No I am afraid not. I think he is dead. The pity of it is that Sara and the kids can't come downstairs until Bill's body has been moved. I can hear them crying in the bedroom. It is very upsetting. This is probably the result of one of their terrible arguments. The thing is what killed Bill? People fall downstairs it is quite common, well let's say it is not uncommon. A few bumps and bruises is the *usual injury. To die after the fall, not even trying to get up, that is what I don't understand. I keep thinking he will suddenly open his eyes, and make the effort to recover. As yet there is no sign of that happening."*

Chapter five

Sara with her head aching and the Kids crying were bewildered. Never did she think of this happening. Trying to comfort the Kids the best way she could. Folding them in her arms her words spoken quietly.

"Don't cry any more, Dad is not going to use his belt, he has fallen downstairs, and needs a Doctor. As soon as he goes into the Ambulance we will be able to go down and get a nice fire going, I will make some sweet porridge, I know you have had no sleep, so when you have ate you can come back to bed. It is almost daylight; I will sleep too if I can. We are all worn out. So sorry my dears, it is not what I wanted to happen, I love you all dearly."

Their tears turned to solemn faces as they huddled around Mam for security.

Nothing seemed real, for them to suffer like this, there had to be a reason, if there was, it was totally out of view at this moment.

Sara heard voices in the yard yes there was a Doctor arriving too, a square black official looking Horse drawn Van. The group filled the yard other neighbours now getting up from their night's sleep, to discover the tragedy.

It didn't take long to pronounce Bill was

dead, the stretcher came in and carefully transferred Bill's body into the Black Horse driven Ambulance.

Sara came downstairs shuddering as she passed the spot where Bill had been lying, she was told there would have to be a "Post Mortem," to discover the cause of death. Knowing nothing about such things she just shook her head, pretending to understand. Dick moved to her side.

"It will be alright Sara; these people are only doing what they have to do. After they have asked you a few more questions, they will leave. I will stay with you until you feel ready to be left alone."

He put a friendly arm around her shoulders and said,

"You look as though you need a Doctor yourself, your face is badly bruised you have a cut on your lip it may need a stitch. Did Bill do this to you?"

She nodded, ashamed of anyone seeing her in the state she was in. Saying she would never have Bill in her bed again only a couple of hours ago sounded strange, she got that bit right. Bill was dead; his body had now been taken away. Sara was informed for a second time there would have to be an Inquest.

A week later the result of the investigation

was told. The cause of the sudden death being a massive heart attack, brought on by the shock of the fall. Accidental death was the verdict. Sara felt that had to be right, it had all happened so fast. The frenzy he had been in prior to the fall would have brought this about. The Police were very kind towards Sara and her family. So were the neighbours, and Dick. Sara had to have time to get a future outlook, at the moment she was bewildered and depressed.

Having no skill in her hands she would have to find a paid cleaning job. There were not many people about her that would pay for cleaning.

The kids still with her kind neighbours, she sat down at the table, her head bent down to lie its heavy weight on to the table, tears poured from her she was shaking all over, shock was about to send her into oblivion once more, she struggled to keep from falling. The one good thing Bill had done was work at the Pit; it had given them all a living. Seeing things in a different light now, and wise with hindsight, knowing she should not have made such a big thing of his need for her. Now she wished she had humoured him. It may have all turned out very different. She was horrified to think that if she had played a different role, he would still be alive, with money to feed the kids. She deeply sighed. What to do? How to do it? Sara felt sick again, almost fainting as her thought pattern drifted over the bare facts of the matter. She alongside her husband pronounced guilty, the crime was the inability of lack of understanding. Nothing could undo it now. She was sunk.

A tap came at the door; this jerked her out of her gloom, she called,

"I don't want to see anyone."

Keeping quiet, hoping the person would go away, she waited a heavier knock.

"It might be important, I had better answer."

Going to see who it was, finding her dear friend Martha.

"Hello Sara just called to see you are alright, I couldn't come any sooner, what with the Doctor, and the Police, and I have been biding my time, just waiting my chance to come when the coast was clear to see you. I have been so worried."

The sane sound of her friend's voice brought on more tears.

"Come on Sara, I know all that has gone on, don't worry you don't have to spell it all out for me. A hesitant Sara said,

"Yes, hello, come in. I am afraid I am not in

the best of humour, sit down."

The two sat opposite each other. Martha looked at Sara's blown out red face, with tear marks newly evident.

"I would say Sara you need someone with you at this awful time. No good burying your head in the sand and hoping it will all go away, because it won't."

Sara burst into a flood of tears again.

"Come on now, come on, are the Kids being looked after?"

"They are with the neighbours."

Between her sobs she blurted out all her foremost fears.

"Eh, sob, eh, I have no money Martha, I don't know how I am going to get any. We'll all be in the Workhouse before very long. What am I to do?

"What are you going to do? You'll stand up and fight, that is what you will do, and if you want me to I will stand up with you, no more Workhouse talk. Your endeavour is to keep this family with you, we will find a way. Dry your tears, I am going to put the kettle on, the fire is bright it will soon boil, have you anything in the house to eat?"

"There are a few taters, and a bit of porridge."

"Then that is what I will get you, I hope you

have some tea."

"Enough to make a couple of brews Martha, thanks gel."

Martha bustled around Sara, making her presence felt, Martha had to ground Sara somehow, her friend was letting herself get out of control.

"What a shame" Martha thought and said, "I am glad I stayed at home to look after Ma and Pa, although they are long since gone. Many a time I have envied you Sara, with your own family, but now well I don't know. That which I do know is you can count on me, I haven't got much, it would mean you finding some paid work, I could look after the youngsters and pitch in with rent money, which would buy you food. Does that look like a chink of light in a dark tunnel?"

Sara's head picked up, although her eyes still were overflowing with tears.

"Oh! Martha, you would do that for me? It is a large undertaking you need more than today to think this over. I would try to get some cleaning hours that paid each week if you kept your eye on the kids it would be possible. You had better take some time to think about it, from my side I have no hesitation, and it would be an answer to my prayer. You may have second thoughts; you

have a roof over your head already. My outlook is the Workhouse roof, and being parted from my Kids. I don't know how you can offer just like that, do you really mean it?"

"Sara, I am my own keeper, I have no responsibilities, since Ma and Pa. passed on I have had my moments of loneliness. I too would get something out of it, because I would be a small part of your family, it is too late for me to think of having my own children; you could share yours with me. It has been one of my regrets. Looking after Ma and Pa. left me no time of my own to seek a partner. My days were always used in the necessary routine. I often have wondered what it would be like to have Kids around, now you can give me the chance. I would say there is gain for both of us, not just you. Now eat this porridge while it is good and hot, it will warm your insides, make you feel better. The kettle is almost boiling for tea."

"I have no milk or sugar Martha; I haven't given food a thought. Everything in my head is in a mush, which is why the neighbours took the kids to look after. I have not been capable of anything. I am my own worst enemy. I keep going over my part in this tragedy, and blame myself. Yes, I know I am

*not without blame; I can do nothing about it.
Things had got entirely out of hand, my
problem getting bigger and bigger all the
time."*

*Martha knew Sara was unloading her
mind, she knew too it was the way for Sara to
find her way back to normality. What price
normality?*

*The everyday toil brought rewards that were
not counted, taken for granted, until turmoil,
and chaos took over, only then do we see how
precious normality really is.*

"Are you friendly with the people next door?"

"Yes they are a nice couple."

*"Then I shall go and cadge a drop of milk
and a cup of sugar I won't be a minute Sara."*

*It wasn't Sara's way to borrow things she
couldn't pay back, on this occasion it would
help.*

"I will pop along right now,"

*Returning with the sugar and milk, Martha
said,*

*"Yes, she is a nice lady, she says don't worry
about returning the items, if there is anything
else she will gladly help. Can't say fairer than
that eh?"*

*The porridge had been kept warm and was
ready now they sat with a cup of steaming tea
soon everything would be calmer.*

"I want you to go and have an hour Sara, it will do you good, when you awake I will have another look at your bumps and bruises, they are still very evident. He gave you a pummelling, no doubt about that."

I can't think how you can be sad he has gone, he was a bounder. You would never have got top end of him, he wanted his own way right left and centre."

"You're right Martha, I keep thinking I should have handled the situation, week after week it never got any better, I was at my wit's end, didn't know which way to turn. I tried to keep the kids out of it, when he started to threaten them it was the last straw, the argument all stemmed from that, I had to stand my ground, what followed I had no control over, if I had to do it all again I wouldn't know how to do it differently. Did you know I am carrying another child?"

"I didn't my dear, did Bill know?"

"Yes he did, it was partly that fact that had inflamed him, another mouth to feed."

"My God Sara, I would say you have had a lucky escape, there is no telling where his violence would have ceased if he hadn't fallen. Threatening the Kids an' all, drink provoked I imagine?"

"Yes, he wasn't in his right mind, but lately

he was always the worst for drink, Honestly I wonder how he got to his pit work, the blokes must have known, bet they dreaded working with him. So much sadness, that could have been avoided, drink is an evil master, when it takes hold it spoils everything. How and why, I don't know, it is a fact I had to live with. I don't think I ever saw him sober, there were girls as well, he flaunted them in my face, told me I was no good at the game, but I had all his kids didn't I? That should have counted for something,"

Baring her soul, she carried on talking to Martha, it was good to just tell someone.

"I think rather than going to lie down now, I would like to collect the kids, they must be very upset to say the least. Then when they go to bed so will I. Please Martha do you think you could fetch me a few vegetables? I could make a satisfying soup that I hope will settle the Kids down."

"Of course, I will, the greengrocer is only on the corner, we will have that on the fire simmering in no time. Shall I bring just a general mix of greens and some taters?"

"Yes please, I feel quite a bit easier now, it is good to have you Martha. I was in such torment, didn't know how to get free of it, and then you turned up on my step. It will take

time, but now you are with me I can judge with a clearer mind, taking things one at a time I will get back to being myself again,"
"Do you want any more of this tea Sara?"
"No, tip it into the slop bucket then you get off for the veggies."

Chapter six

Martha reached the shop, a lady talking to the shop keeper was saying about the incident.

"Bad do down at the Quarry Yard, isn't it? Can't tell me the wife had nothing to do with it. She probably seen her chance to be rid of him, not that you can blame her, drunken wretch that he was. Drink and other women was all he wanted. He is paying for it now, bet she will be in a bit of a mess for money, perhaps she will find company of the male kind, if you get my meaning. Having kids to feed she'll have to do something to put brass in her pocket."

The shop keeper stood up for Sara saying,

"I am saying nothing, he probably got what he deserved, Sara is a customer here, and I don't want to pick her bones. The girl has enough to get on with, doesn't she?"

"Oh, I am not saying that she doesn't, it just seems mighty peculiar to me, and how it all happened, wish I had been a fly on the wall at the time,"

"Fact is sometimes stranger than fiction, don't you find?"

As she turned and walked out the shop keeper said,

"I must get on and serve this lady now. Hello,

what can I get for you?"
Martha abruptly said,
"I want some mixed vegetables, and taters, by the way I am glad you didn't dish the dirt with that nosey old woman, Sara has a lot to deal with, she herself isn't well, and I am staying with her. If I hear anyone else having a go, I won't be responsible for my actions, leave her to sort her life out, and don't pick and probe. All will be well shortly."
"Of course, you could see I wouldn't join in with the previous customer, I wish Sara all the best; you won't find me dishing the dirt."
"That's all right then, I'll be off now, get these taters on to boil."
The shopping basket lumped on to her stomach, to support the weight, Martha walked haughtily away.

The kids returned; glad to be back with Ma. The stew was simmering on the fire, it smelled good. They all sat to the table and enjoyed the meal. At bedtime Sara tucked them in, kissing each of them with warmth to convey her love. Sara went downstairs to speak to Martha.
"I shall go to bed myself now Martha, if that is alright with you."
Sitting in a comfortable chair, her comely body filling the space, Martha nodded, her

lovely face, with brown eyes, brown hair with a touch of grey had a doleful expression. The day had been long and wearing, she just wasn't used to looking after a family. Ten years older than Sara, with no knowledge, it would take some getting used to, Sara, being comparatively young, Sara's kids had come so quick, it had taken the vibrant edge off Sara's appearance, also the beatings that Bill had dished out. Her face always bruised or her eyes were blacked. Her neighbours had long since stopped asking her about bruises. They knew who the guilty culprit was. All trying to give Sara a moral boost, but words are futile when the sting from Bill's fist had been delivered.

Upstairs Sara went, carrying a new candle, it flickered as she carefully put it on the bedside table, undressed into bed, and she lay quietly.

Peace, the silence that surrounded her, the pitch black room lit only by the one candle. Lying between the sheets, looking up at the ceiling, the candle caught by a breath of draft, flickered a little dance with its story on to the ceiling, Sara, had many times related a fiction that went with the moment, now at last in peace, no door locked, no listening to Bills clatter as he moved around in a drunken stupor downstairs, his anger conveying itself widely, his mood apparent.

Guilty, yes, that was her feeling, because Bill was now down in the Morgue, stiff and cold. Thoughts drifted around her mind until out of exhaustion she fell asleep.

Sara spoke to the Youngsters explaining the idea that Martha had come up with the night before to the Kids, this meant no more strapping, and a much softer existence. The nine year old boy greeted the information with a smile, saying,

"Don't worry Ma, I am the man in the house now, when I am ten I can get a job down the pit, then there is Jack, he will follow me and do the same. It is only the first couple of years you would have to find work. If Martha is going to cook, I would think we could be happy. Dad never gave us his time or his love, so we won't be missing it.

Sara listened and said,

"I am so sorry for all that has happened Charlie, but I can't do anything about it now. What you have just told me eases my mind; we will learn how to go on a bit at a time. When I can I shall look for paid work. Martha is going to pay board money, so that will pay the rent and buy simple food until we get organised."

She sighed deeply, at the moment it was all just words, and it was easy to say things, when it came to doing the deeds it would all be put to the test.

In the afternoon tidying around the Cottage, Sara was feeling pinched.

"I feel giddy and sick Martha, I don't know whether it is all the events that have taken place, sorry I just have to lie down."

"Go upstairs Sara, you need rest and a cup of tea, I will bring you one when I have got little 'Lezzy down."

Sitting on Sara's bed Martha spoke softly to her.

"Have you anything to suggest something is wrong."

"It is just as I said, this fuzzy giddy feeling, and tightness in my lower parts."

"I will leave you to rest then; I'll give you a couple of hours, and then tap your door."

Martha left, went downstairs, sat quietly thinking.

"How can I give Sara the entirety she will need? Telling her I confidently will is just words to calm her down. Martha, my gal! You have a large task before you."

It was her turn to sigh, she needed to be strong.

The two hours passed quickly enough

because Martha herself had dropped off in her chair, the toddler hadn't made a sound, the quiet almost too good to be true. The kettle had been simmering on the fire. Now Martha had done a bit of shopping there was tea, milk and sugar, so trying to rouse herself as well as Sara, another pot of tea was made.

"Sara, Sara, she tapped the bedroom door, can I come in?"

A dreary muffled voice answered,

"Yes come in."

Going over to the bed Martha could see Sara was still bleary eyed.

"Feeling a bit better now dear?"

"Well yes, but my body is pouring with sweat."

Martha pulled the sheets back to let some cool air in. She had a shock, the sheets underneath Sara were covered with blood, Martha had never seen this before, and it panicked her,

"Sara my dear girl, you are bleeding, what has happened?"

"Don't distress yourself Martha, I have been getting pain in my lower parts, this blood means I am probably going to lose my baby. I must ask you to go and fetch old Genny Silk she will know what to do."

"Where does Genny Silk live Sara? Will you

be alright while I fetch her?"

Martha was out of her depth, but she recognised emergency.

"Just go along the Quarry Yard path, till you come to the proper Road, then look for 221, a small terraced house, Genny has tended me before, so just tell her I need her right now, be quick Martha, the pain is getting stronger I need help."

Martha at once turned to the door went downstairs as quick as she could. Putting her head in next door to tell Charlie to go and keep an eye on little Lezzy as she had to fetch Genny. The boy seemed to know what was going on, and immediately went back to his own home.

Martha found Genny's house, and told her to come quick, fearing Sara would bleed to death. Genny said,

"Calm down my dear, this sounds like a miscarriage, Sara is young and strong, and she will survive."

Genny picked up her black bag and a couple of clean towels. Taking some clean towels in case there were only soiled ones available. Always she would do her best to see Mother and child had a fair chance. More than that was in the lap of the Gods. They were soon on their way.

Arriving just in time to see the tiny form expelled on to the bed, poor little might, Genny knew she couldn't have saved the baby Sara was too far into the labour when she had arrived, she was very lucky to have saved Sara.

There was a strange sadness in the room, there was no baby now. Sara knew it was for the best, responsibilities surrounded her, glad also that Martha was living in; the other Kids would be looked after Sara needn't worry. Knowing a recovery time would have to be observed, taking that into account Sara reckoned she would be up and about in a month's time, two months on would likely see her in a paid job. Now with the baby gone she would have more chance. She was not expected to attend Bill's funeral, it being a Pauper's funeral that took place in a few days time. Having no wish to talk about the sad affair, feeling she had side stepped this without losing respect. Time, she had to have time to many problems would see her flat on her back for a much longer period. Having to learn how to depend on someone other than herself wasn't easy. Sara always looking for inner strength was quite put out when she was laid useless. It had to be for the moment. Genny Silk, a kind old soul was coming every other day, leaving instruction with Martha, as to Sara's condition. There had been a lot of blood loss, Sara being very weak, Bills sudden death, and previous upheaval all had weakened her. Martha now in the thick of things had not lost her intent, yet finding everything a heavy load to carry, they would go on.

"See who that is at the door Charlie."

Dick stood there cap in hand inquiring about Sara.

"I haven't seen Sara for days; hope you don't mind telling me how she is."

"Not at all, I am only too glad you have called."

Martha went on to speak to her caller.

"It is Dick isn't it?"

"Yes I am Martha; I shall be doing my best for Sara, and the Youngsters in the future, step inside Dick."

"I am glad to see Sara is in good hands I have been worried about her, but didn't want to push in."

"You can push in all that you would like, I am sometimes out of my depth with this lot, I am doing all I can. Never having to look after a family before I find my judgement sometimes a little stretched. Then again Sara is so glad that I am here it makes up for my

shortcomings.

They both smiled, Martha noticed how the smile had lit up Dick's face, not young but not old either. A forthright handsome appeal, Martha knew straight away he was the kind you could depend on.

"Sara is in bed, she has lost her baby and she must rest." Dick said,

"There was another one on the way then was there? In Sara's position I would think in the long run it will be to her advantage. Tell her I will attend Bill's funeral, so that at least there will be one mourner, maybe a couple of his drinking pals, he wasn't very popular.

It might help Sara if she knows we are here to help all we can."

"Are you married then Dick?"

No, I meant myself and other neighbours that care. Times can be very hard if there is no one to talk to. Many a problem in the past has found its way to my door, so don't hesitate if you need me." Good news for Martha, a strong and willing hand would be there if needed.

"I will take my leave of you Martha; give Sara my best will you." Dick went his way.

Martha went up to see Sara, finding her awake she went over to the bed, lifted her hand and held it dearly, comforting her good friend, she said,

"I thought you were going to die. I have brought a bowl of water and cloth to take the sweat from your brow. I had no way of telling how bad you really were. I have never seen a baby born, or a miscarriage. When Genny was beside you I thought I should be doing something to help, but didn't know what. I was well and truly out of my depth, please forgive me."

"Sara's weak voice answered,

"Don't worry Martha, you did as I asked, and went for Genny, it was your speed in doing just that, you helped save my life, I will never be able to thank you enough, all the work downstairs too, I couldn't be in better hands."

Martha could see Sara had been forcing her voice, and she had had enough of talking so Martha said,

"You sleep now Sara, I will take care of the kids, and the jobs to do around the place."

She walked quietly out of the room, eager to set a balance between all of them.

Chapter seven

It had been six weeks since Sara's miscarriage; she was getting her strength back, and her smile. It was time for her to look for work. Sara wasn't adept in any special work; all her efforts had gone into having her Babies and looking after them. Sara had not much to offer an employer when it came to paid work.

"Martha, she called."

Martha was pegging washing on the line to dry.

"Yes what is it? I will be in very shortly, nearly done."

Sara went out to her,

"I am going a little walk, just along the Quarry path, I will take the little Lezzy, I want to feel normal again, there has been so much going on I have lost my bearings.

"You go; it will do you good to see your neighbours, telling them you are much better now. Yes Sara, you can talk, not like when Bill was here stopping you, keeping all behind closed doors, the bounder!"

Yes it was true Bill hadn't given her an inch of freedom, he wanted her to stay put, to live with the door locked to "Nosey Parkers" as he called them.

Sara walked speaking to the people she

passed asking her how she was. Picking little 'Lezzy up, she said

"Come on little darling I will take you to see the baby Piglets."

Sara retraced her steps, passing her own cottage, and round the corner to where the Pig sties were kept.

"Look how they are gathering around Mother Pig; she looks after them as I look after you." The four year old her eyes wide laughed, look Mammy that little one has got pushed out.

"Don't worry your head about that dear; Mother Pig will look after all her Piglets, as I look after all of you. Time for home now throw a kiss.

Dick's loud voice broke into their talk.

"Well hello there Sara, how good it is to see you.

He cupped the little Lezzy's chin saying,

How you are growing up, you're as pretty as a picture."

His rough hand tousled the blonde little head. Sara's offspring all had been born blonde, growing darker as the years went by, at the age of seven all had the dark brown hair and blue eyes that Sara herself had. She was glad it was that way, at times she thought as the Lads got older their Fathers features were *beginning to show. She didn't want that, and would deny the fact if anyone remarked about it, she wanted none of them to feature Bill, his memory in her mind needed erasing, it pleased Sara now if there was nothing to remind her of their Father.*

"I have heard you are looking for work Sara, yes the paid kind, what would you like to do?"

"That is just it Dick, I have had no job before, so I have to take just what I can get, I suppose it has to be cleaning, I know how to do that."

"I know a couple of gels that work at the "Danbury Hall" shall I tell them to keep their ears open, in case a spot you can fill turns up?"

"That's kind of you Dick, yes do that for me. Do you know these gels names?"

"Yes, it is Alice, and the other Rosa. I deliver fresh vegetables and meat to the Hall regularly.

Perhaps you would like to come with me to meet them, they are not posh at all, one is about 20yrs, and the other about 24yrs, and I believe they have worked at the Hall for some time. They are always there to help lift the goods from the cart into the kitchen."

"I keep saying yes Dick, it would be a help if

I knew someone to show me the ropes, so yes again, I will come with you on your next delivery."

"That will be this Friday; mind you it will be early in the morning, before 6am, the gentry like all the bits and pieces tied up, before breakfast, and all the necessary mucky jobs done too, I think they like to pretend there is no such thing as dirty work, not so, the early morning servants have seen to it that the dirty work is done."

Sara went excitedly to Martha,

"I have made the first move towards getting a job Martha; I am so pleased I went out because I saw Dick, as always he seems to find the right way, so I am going with him to deliver his order to the Hall on Friday before 6am."

"Hold on, hold on, going where to deliver what?"

"Sorry Martha, I am so happy to be moving in the right direction, my words are not making sense. Yes I am going to the Hall to see two gels' that already work there, get a look in to see if I could do the menial jobs that may be offered. Yes again, Dick is going to take me."

"That's a bit of luck Sara; will you be able to go into the Hall to see what the Kitchens are

like?"

"Dick seems to think I will, he says the gentry don't get up till all the dirty work has been done, so there will be no-one around."

"Oh Sara, take in as much as you can, I would love to see the Hall in its finery, even in the Kitchen, a totally different way of life I am sure, you can come home and we will sit to have all the detail you can pick up pulled over the coals. I do hope you get in to work, there are endless things we could talk about, and look now I am getting excited!"

The week dragged a little, waiting for Friday to come. Here was Dick; it was 5.15am, just getting light when Sara stepped up to get in the seat beside Dick.

"Giddy up old horse, Dick called to his trusty friend, Dick and his horse had a way of knowing each other, the horse being dependable. Dick would consider old Dobbin, never drove him too fast or too far, the horse sensed from the little whisper when standing still, the gentle pat, that Dick was happy with him. It worked it gave each of them a feeling of security. Today he had Sara on board a tinge of gladness in this occasion.

The "Tower" loomed up before them, the gates were locked.

Dick had to get down from the cart to see the

gate keeper he had to allow him in.

"Delivering Dick? The weeks go so fast it is hard to think how all the stuff gets used.

The gate keeper unhooked a huge key that was hanging on the wall beside other keys, so unlocked the gates. Sara was fascinated and said,

"Goodness Dick, you can't get in here in a hurry can you, is the Hall a long way up the drive?"

Sara was looking at the long tree lined drive, couldn't see any sign of a Hall, the drive seemed to go on forever.

"Yes, bet it is more than a mile to it."

Sara was thinking how she would be able to walk that far if she got a job, it would be a daunting task, and she turned towards Dick saying.

"Even if I managed to get a job, how would I get to the Hall? The walk to the "Tower" would be enough, but this to drive to follow on, I know I wouldn't make it."

"You wouldn't have to, a Horse and Cart would be here to pick you and a few others up, you would have to get yourself to the Tower, and then carried in the cart up to the Hall, and I am not saying it would be easy, the cart leaves to go at 5.30am. It would mean your day would start leaving home about

5am. Fridays I will offer you a lift, which is the best I can do, my week fits a tight schedule, and I am sorry I can't be more helpful.

"That's alright Dick, I can do that, it was thinking I had to walk the drive to the Hall as well as getting to the Tower."

The morning was turning into a sunny day, the ride to the Hall Sara enjoyed, looking all around her at the grandeur of the place. Walking many times past the Tower, yet never once wondered what the Hall was like, it being a no go area to her. Now she may become part of the place, it was a strange feeling. All her life had been behind closed doors. What lay beyond she could only wonder at. Good or bad, it had to be faced. This morning it was good, there was Dick beside her, so she faced whatever came with confidence. Not that she wasn't wondering what Alice and Rosa would be like. Would they take to her? It didn't matter, she wanted money for her and her kids to live, and this was one way she may get it.

Chapter eight

Pulling up at the back of the Hall, eager faces greeted her and Dick.

"Dick" Alice said with a smile. What you bought for us today?"

"Some good pork freshly slaughtered." Alice replied,

"The Missus will be pleased; she said it was about time for a killing."

"Yes he was a slippery one too, had me down on the ground a few times, he's here now, I have bought half of the meat and half of the offal, I will bring it in, go away from the cart while I carry it, as it is heavy."

"Who might you be then?"

Alice didn't like Sara in on the scene.

"I am Sara; I am looking for work, Dick will you tell Alice about me? Sorry Alice I am not too sure of myself."

Dick in a nutshell related Sara's purpose. Once Alice knew she wasn't being threatened by Sara's presence, she became friendlier.

"I don't think they want any extra staff now, soon maybe, as the summer rolls in Lord and Lady Gerald give Open Air Parties, they do then need extra help."

"I was looking for a regular job, but would not be able to board; I can clean, and do a bit of cooking. I didn't think there would be anything today, I have come with Dick to see the Hall, and I have never seen it before."

"That's alright then, I will fetch Rosa, she works with me, you can say hello to her."

"Sara, is it? Rosa is my name, work you want is it?"

Rosa broke out into a lovely smile, Sara knew right away how likeable Rosa seemed, Alice being a bit short when she first met Sara, had given the wrong impression, she had seemed brittle in her manor.

"Perhaps you would like to see inside the kitchen Sara."

"I would really like that, if you have the time."

Stepping into the reception part of a vast kitchen Sara was overwhelmed, all the space, a central Table, where vegetables were being prepared, pots and pans of every description, ladles, sieves rolling pins, a huge fire that lit up and warmed the room, complete with black kettle gently simmering, on the black leaded range that had ovens included. Table of wood that needed scrubbing, a floor of red tile, that too would need scrubbing. Copper pans held on hooks on the wall, shining, Sara didn't find anything to dread, in a kitchen like this who would mind working. Her rough road with Bill had no comparison to what life *could offer her now.*

"I must go, Dick made for the door, and I will be here next week, keep your ears open for Sara won't you."

With that Sara got up on the cart seat beside Dick, waving her goodbyes.

I am glad that is over, and I have done nothing!"

"It was bound to be hard for you the little time you have spent out with people, you will get better at it the more of yourself you give. What did you make of Alice and Rosa?"

"Well it is a first meeting, it wasn't long to judge people on, but they both gave me a welcome, perhaps Rosa was the friendlier."

"Well Rosa is the eldest, she is 24, and Alice is 21 and more flippant.

You will soon get to know them if you can find a place there.

"It is all so new to me Dick; the Quarry Yard has been my only look at life, if you had told me about the Hall I probably would have cast it away without a second thought, thinking I never needed to know about such places, how strange life can be."

"Yes strange and cruel, we must remember it wasn't meant to be like that, it is the big wigs wanting to put us down, no time for the man who has to work his tail end off, or starve.

When we get hungry we need to eat, that is when money takes on a very earthy reality."

Dick got down from his position behind the horse, and then went to help Sara; she thought this was very gallant of him. The light was dropping into a dusky hue, everything being quiet Sara said

"Thanks Dick I am so glad you took me, I have a better idea of the Hall now that I have seen it, and I shall go to bed early to see it all in my mind's eye again."

"Martha, it's me I am back."

"Not before time I say, you have been gone a good part of the day."

"Sorry, I have been learning about the Hall, met Alice and Rosa, they are two maids that work in the kitchen. You should see it Martha, very grand, the walls of the kitchen are bedecked with Copper pots and pans of all description, beautiful jelly moulds, great big ones, I suppose that is for when company is staying. To me everything was over sized, you could fit this place in the broom cupboard."

"Do you think they will find you work?"

"I can't tell at this moment, I didn't see any house keeper, or Cook, there was no man in charge, the two girls are going to listen out for me, and then tell Dick, he will then let me *know, he delivers regularly on Fridays, and he won't let me down.*

"I have just got little Lezzy down, Charlie is playing dominoes next door, Jack should be in any minute. What will you have to eat?"

"Is there any Cheese in the pantry?"

"Yes, it may have got a bit stale."

Martha went to get the Cheese.

"I don't know what you will make of this Sara."

Placing it on the table, brought a knife out of the drawer, and commenced scraping the mould from the cheese."

"It will do, I will toast some bread on the fire, and grate the cheese on it. I wouldn't bother at all, but I have only had an apple all day, so I am hungry."

The two chatted about the Hall, Martha glad enough to see Sara in such good humour. Bringing her out of her doldrums hadn't been easy. Now she was satisfied Sara would soon be strong again.

Martha didn't mind at all being the one to look after the kids, it was a big change for her, her lonely life was no more, and she liked the feeling of being depended on, the kids had taken to her as well.

Once more it was bedtime, Martha had a piece of toast, but no thanks she didn't want any cheese, fancying she could see maggots writhing in it!

Next day was kept for shopping, down to the market to pick up a bargain or two.

"Shall we both go this week Martha?"

"Yes if you feel well enough, Mrs. Griffiths will look after the young 'un's, we needn't be too long, is there anything we are completely out of?"

"Yes, candles suppose we have burned more than usual, what with one thing or the other. Even the kids have asked for one to go to bed. It is after Bill dying on the stairs, it has unnerved them, mind you I creep in when they have gone to sleep, to bring the candle out, they would only have to get out of bed to use the pot, to catch the candle, or knock it over, then we would all be in more trouble. Trouble is not going to be sort after, better safe than sorry eh?"

Martha nodded her head in agreement, saying,

"Trouble comes so easily without looking for it. Must look on the bright side, it isn't easy. We'll get there Sara don't you fret."

Chapter nine

Sara finding herself in the town with Martha felt very daring; Bill would not have allowed her to do any such thing. Still she couldn't believe she only had herself and the kids to answer for. The day was dry, not a lot of sunshine, a good shopping day. The stalls were bedecked with all manner of things to eat, the men shouting their wares.

"Look love, two pound for a penny, sweet as a nut so they are, shiny as the smile on your face, come on give us a kiss, we like our pretty girls so we do. No harm meant love wouldn't touch a hair on your head."

They hurried by, trying not to be alarmed at the punter's patter. Grinning at each other as they stopped by a stall with a Lady merchant, no way did they want all the fuss, but had to admit it was interesting. It was what made the market different to the greengrocer's shop. Atmosphere, and jostle, a bag with a bargain, the wicker baskets they carried would be full at the end of their trip.

The meat stall would have pig's liver, heart and kidneys, cheap enough. The shoulders and leg cuts were dearer, a shoulder of pork if cut in two could make some lovely baked potatoes, and some fat also to drain off as dripping. It was made to go a long way. The meat a bit fatty, they needed all the fat they could get to store in their bodies to keep out the winter cold.

Every piece was used, with no waste. Of course it wasn't as good as Dick's Pig, but Dick only slaughtered about three times a year, then all the neighbours wanted some, so the market was the sensible alternative.

"Look Martha," Sara pointed to the shop window.

The window had models dressed in the latest fashion, beads and sequins, frills and lace, Sara was taking it all in, beguiled by the colours and patterns.

"Is that what Ladies wear? Those sorts of dresses Martha?

"Not our sort, that's for sure, I suppose there is a middle class that can afford the price, I have heard of the husband taking the wife to a dance, a collective band plays music to dance to, I don't recall anybody having been to one, people don't know how other people exist. They would not have to seek work, married to men with a pile of money. They trip the light fantastic. Look at the shoes to go with the dress, we would break our necks in them, one slip on the Cobblestones that would mean a broken leg, they are not made for use, just ornament, gingerly they show themselves *off, just to get the husband a good business deal, or the like. Come on Sara, enough day dreaming.*

Through the crowd they weaved there way, picking up fruit when they found it hard to resist, considering the price. The Kids would eagerly look in the baskets on their return home; there was always something they could have in their hand to munch on.

The walk home tired them both, the baskets being full and heavy. The thought of different food in the cupboard made it worthwhile.

Next day, Sara had taken the little Lezzy for a walk, on returning she went upstairs to put on a working dress, and some soft shoes. Hearing Martha call,

"Sara, Dick called while you were out."

"Did he leave any message?"

"Yes he did, oh! Come downstairs it is like talking to a brick wall."

"Here I am what was it that Dick wanted?"

"He has made arrangements for you to go with him to the Hall on Friday."

"What do I have to do that for?

"You have to see Miss Olivine."

"What a strange name, I am not likely to forget that am I?"

"Don't be flippant, you have to go looking the best that you can, she is interviewing you for

a job."

Sara drew in a long breath and gulped.

"That has been quick, thought it would be a week or so before I heard. That has given me collywobbles... Pull the kettle over the fire; I could do with a cup of tea."

Martha laughed, saying,

"They are not going to hang you, just interview you. Bet you'll go into the main part of the Hall, don't think they do interviews in the kitchen."

Sara had a couple or so days to prepare. She sorted out what few clothes she had, a black ankle length dress was chosen, it was what she called her funeral dress, it being homemade and plain, black button boots too.

"I could put that lace handkerchief in the little pocket at the top; it wouldn't look so sombre then" The handkerchief had been given her many Christmas's ago, it had never seen the light of day, it was time it got used. A coat would have to be worn, as it would be early morning, she could leave that in Dick's cart, and nobody would see it then.

"That's it then the plainer the better surely, Sara now had her clothes ready.

Friday came around, Dick was at the door.

"Won't be a moment Dick, just seeing if I look alright."

Sara stood with her chosen dress and shoes on, trying to see her reflexion through a large mirror that was pitted it had a crack straight down the centre. Not the clearest of images. Her dark hair was now tied into a bun at the back of her head, giving the white handkerchief a tweak, she decided she was ready. Tiptoe downstairs, so as not to wake the whole house. Excitement was the feeling that held her.

"Here at last Dick, sorry I kept you waiting."

"We have plenty of time so don't worry, it is a fine morning as I hoped it would be. Let's get on the road, and see this job done, bet you haven't had much sleep eh? Are you nervous?"

Don't know what you mean Dick; I have never been to a job interview before, so I don't know how you are supposed to feel. I know I want to say all the right things, but I can only speak the truth. I feel a bit sick, I suppose that is what you call nerves isn't it? I call it my collywobbles."

They both laughed at this, and then they were on their way. The interview was for 8am. But Dick had his merchandise to unload, money to be exchanged. The hour before seeing Miss Olivine would quickly pass.

Arriving, Rosa and Alice were at the door.

"Hello Sara, we have a cup of tea ready to brew, we thought you might need one."

"Thanks very much, I will have one, I have to see Miss Olivine, what is she like?" Rosa said,

"Very straight laced and proper, she has been head over the female staff for many years. She is formal and to the point. Not to be messed about. She will see through any act you might put on, wants only girls that are prepared to work to a high standard. Does that answer your question?" Sara's face went a shade of grey.

"Yes it does, I don't know how I will get on, the description you have given me doesn't leave much margin for error, and however, I can only be myself. I am not one for airs and graces, so here's hoping I say the right things.

An upstairs maid came to show Sara down a corridor, telling her to sit outside a very heavy door; Sara felt the atmosphere heavy and daunting.

Miss Olivine opened the door after just a few minutes.

"Come in girl, sit down."

She offered Sara a huge chair, which Sara sat on just at the very edge.

Sara looking at Miss Olivine could see she

*was a firm mistress, stern, carried herself
straight as a stick, and was as thin as a stick.
A full length dark brown dress, button boots,
hair parted down the centre to make a wound
plait each side of her head, it looked like
earmuffs, but yes it was her own greying hair.
Formal and unyielding eyes that looked right
through you, no gentle welcome, not a sign of
a smile.*

"Where do you live girl?"

"In a cottage, in the Ford."

*"Have you any special attributes that single's
you out from other girls?"*

*"No ma'am, I am afraid not but I am a good
cleaner."*

Do you think you are good at anything else?

*"The simple truth is I have no choice, it is
work or be hungry."*

*"Have you been living on your own very
long?*

*"No I was looking after mother and father
until they died.*

"Were they ill very long?"

*Sara looked up sharply, now she was telling
lies, if only she could tell Miss Olivine the
plain truth, about Bill and his fists, his
temper and his drinking. No she couldn't.
She was so ashamed of all that had gone on.
Miss Olivine wouldn't give her a job if she*

thought there was any question of drink being involved. She may think Bill and Sara had been a drinking couple, so Sara kept quiet.

"Would you want to live in?

"No I would need to be home in the evenings."

"Why must you get home?

"I keep livestock in the yard, they have to be fed."

Miss Olivine was so abrupt and clipped with her questions! They were fired at Sara; she had no time to give a proper reply. Beginning to feel overpowered by this dominant woman, feeling she was shrinking into the huge chair, wishing the interview would soon be over. The palms of her hands were sweating; her feet began to fidget under her chair, this bombardment of questions fired at her. Not wanting to answer any more, her mouth dry, her voice hesitant and fragile. Did she want the job? It was now debatable, what she felt like saying couldn't be said it would place her down with the riff raff.

"You can go now, be here at 6am.sharp on Monday. I will hire you as Kitchen Skivvy, till we know what you are made of, your duties will be to get out and clean the ashes from the previous day, lay new paper and wood ready

to be lit when needed, this needs to be done in the upper bedrooms as well as the ground floor rooms. You will have to do this when the occupant gets up and leaves the room vacant, make the beds. At this time you will also empty the chamber pots and wash out. The first fire to tend is the range in the kitchen, Cook likes that shining and ready, with the fire built earlier so there is heat to cook breakfast, and scrub the red tiled floor. If you have any spare time it is to be used cleaning the silver, and shining the copper saucepans, or polishing the glassware. Mind! You start at 6am, till 12pm, one half hour for a cup of tea, then on again till 4pm not going a minute before your time. Sundays off, your wage will be two and sixpence a week. I will stand no chattering or otherwise messing about with the other Maids. Is that clear to you? Keep out of the upstairs Maid's way; they have a different set of work and rules Sara stunned nodded.

"We will provide your clothes for work, you may go now. Goodbye Sara."

Miss Olivine abruptly got up opened the door, Sara left with a look of concern on her face. Wanting to cry but tears didn't come; she was desperate to get home. Once home that night her front dropped. Saying to

Martha,

"Oh Martha, my God, I don't know what to do."

"What is wrong then Sara?"

"That dreadful woman up at the Hall, she has made me feel like the dirt beneath her feet, I cannot tell you how she belittles a person, you don't get a word in your own defence."

"Come on now, we'll talk about it, see if there is anything to be done."

"Like what, I could never like her, I am no match for her, and she would find fault in her own mother."

"It is the outside world Sara, you are not accustomed to other people, only knowing this small world in the Quarry Yard, you'll see, a couple of months and you will know how to handle this Lady."

"Lady, she is a monster, old spinster, brittle and not loved, I will never do anything right for her, never a smile, and her face is like steel. Why do people have to be like that?"

"'Cos they don't know any different, that's why."

Martha moved around the table, and put her arms around Sara, who at once let her tears flow, burying her head into Martha's bosom, her friend's kindness left nothing wanting.

Always she was there to help in any way she could.

Chapter ten

Sara laid thinking in bed, how Dick had waited patiently for her in the Hall's back porch, he had asked her when she got back, "Did you get a job Sara?"

Sara had been quiet felt more like crying than rejoicing. The heavy heart she had was near to the feeling she was just trying to get rid of. Looking back he must have thought her very rude, she would put matters right in the morning, for one day though she'd had enough.

Sara again left the cottage at 5am the following Monday morning full of apprehension. Going over, and over, what Miss Olivine's had said.

"I should have a spring in my step, this is the job I have been praying for, new ground now to discover, and it has been my fervent wish these past few months, now I can't put myself into action can I do all that has been asked of me?"

It was half hour's walk from the Quarry Yard to the round Tower, and then a Cart would be waiting to pick her up, along with the other day workers. Wishing she felt stronger, that was part of her trouble, since miss- carrying her baby, along with the previous troubles, she was still not up to things in general, her *tears came easily, she had lost her confidence.*

"Ah! There is the cart at least I am on time."

Three other workers got into the back, they looked like farm labourers. Sara had to be helped to get up into the cart. None of them spoke. They soon arrived at the Hall. Today Miss Olivine was there to meet her.

"Come on no dawdling, you get in the Kitchen girl, you Alice and Rosa go to the jobs you have been allotted."

By the time they arrived in the kitchen Alice and Rosa had already started their day, Alice being occupied with a jowl, that had flour, and other ingredients placed around it, ready to make their daily bread. Rosa had bread held with a toasting fork up to the fire, ready to pass to the upstairs maid to take Milady fresh buttered toast. Milady always had toast early before she even got dressed just a habit now.

Alice passed Sara a pile of clothing.

"You can go in the cloakroom to change,"

Sara was wondering if the clothes would fit her, she took them and went the way she was shown.

Pulling the dress over her head, she now knew they would fit, the clothes were about as shapeless as you could get, and hung on her bones. No style. For on top of the dress a hessian apron was provided. Miss Olivine said,

"First day Sara, see that you remember your duties as discussed last week, get a mop and bucket Alice. Sara can do the floor first, it is not usual to use mop and bucket, Milady likes the floor clean. I shall expect you to get down on your hands and knees with a scrubbing brush hereafter."

Miss Olivine turned abruptly and left.

"She has got one on her today, yes Miss Olivine, no Miss Olivine, some days you can't please her any which way, crabby old spinster."

"Shush Alice; she'll give you crabby old spinster, if she hears you.

She won't hear me, her plaits are braided over her ears, wonder she hears anything at all."

The three of them gave a cautious grin all being glad to be left alone.

"Here Sara, your bucket and mop for the red tile, do them well because she will be back to inspect."

Sara got on, the floor seemed enormous, and the suds had to be changed several times. It would seem twice as big when scrubbing it.

At least the job was done; Rosa thought Sara

had made a good job of it, saying,

"Alice and I done the ash and black leaded the range before you arrived. So you can get on with polishing the silver, that is until Milord and Lady vacate the bedrooms, then you can go in to make their beds and clean out the fire ash, set another fire, ready for later on in the day, they don't want it lit until late afternoon. Next bring down the pots empty them in the sluice, wash them and return them back under the beds, you'll soon get the hang of it."

Sara looked at the formidable pile of silver placed at the end of the table.

"Have I got to clean all of those?" Her hand pointed towards the silver cutlery.

"Just get on with some Sara; you will leave what you can't do until you have seen to the bedroom duties."

The day stretched out before Sara like a ten mile hike.

I have just heard the upstairs occupants down in the breakfast room, you can go upstairs now Sara, leave the silver that is still to do, until later, take off your hessian apron. Rosa gave Sara a winning smile, it helped.

Sara was longing to go home, her first day, and she had only done half of that. Before Sara went upstairs she flopped down into the nearest chair, legs aching, feet hurting, tired to the point of exhaustion.

"What's up with you then?" Alice said, with hands on her hips.

"Caught you having a snooze then haven't I?"

"No I am not having a snooze as you call it, but I just had to sit for a minute, I am tired out, and not yet half way through my day, I can't help it"

"Trouble with you Ford girls, you don't know what work is."

Alice spitefully spoke, a cutting edge to her voice."

"Hey! Mind what you are saying Alice, Sara's very new to her duties don't forget she has to learn from scratch.

Rosa had quickly jumped to Sara's defence.

"Well she has someone a friend she says to look after her own cottage, lucky she can afford it I say."

Rosa looked at Alice.

"What has gotten into you today, go and put the kettle on, it is about time for Sara's 30min. break, can't say I am not ready for mine, it has seemed a long morning, now no more upset, we must get on with each other, we all have too much work to do, Miss Olivine sees to that, petty quibbling is not *going to help any of us.*

The day wore on all doing the jobs set for them. Sara was so glad when the cart came to take her to the Round Tower, she would soon be home.

Alice and Rosa had said,

"Goodnight see you tomorrow" Sara readily forgave Alice, we all say things in the heat of the moment, a couple of weeks they would be getting to know each other, then a softer approach would be applied.

"Alice I am so vexed with you, why on earth did you have a go at Sara you know how she must feel, I couldn't believe it myself when I listened to your onslaught, slang as well, you know we are not allowed to use slang in the house, or anywhere else for that matter.

Decorum must be maintained, I want you to apologise when Sara gets here in the morning. "Alice do you remember the day you started in this kitchen?

How glad you were that I was here to look after you?"

Alice bowed her head, she knew all the things that Rosa was saying were true, she didn't know why she had done it, not the usual Alice at all, replying to Rosa she said,

"It had just got on my pip, Sara this, Sara that, we all have to work you know."

Alice closed the conversation, not wanting to aggravate Rosa any more.

Chapter eleven

Sara had got off the cart at the Round Towers, hastily she took her leave. As soon as she got to the bottom of the hill, she would be on the Quarry Walk; never had it seemed so inviting. Into her cottage she went.

"Back at last Martha," the kettle was singing on the hob of the black leaded grate, the fire was burning bright, the table set for tea."

"What's it been like Sara? I have been thinking about you all day, yes you could even say I have missed you."

"I have missed you Martha, everything has to be precise and polished a different life altogether, I was desperate for the day to be over."

"That is because it was your first day; once you get into a routine it will be better. Can't expect that to happen for a while, in the meantime don't worry, do your duties to the best of your abilities, when you have done that, learn to walk away. It is the only way to be when facing a new beginning. Even I coming to work with this family have felt utterly bewildered, especially the first week or two. Slowly the realisation of routine took over my fear, and I have developed an understanding, with the cottage and with the kids. Really it didn't come easy. More than

once I thought of coming to tell you that I couldn't cope, but you were too poorly, I didn't want to give you anything further to worry about. I got through it, taking the "Bull by the horns," I came out the winner."

"Oh dear Martha, I am so sorry I didn't recognise your plight. How selfish not to have understood the job I had given you was so great. I am truly sorry."

"Don't worry about it Sara, I am only telling you so that it eases your burden, give yourself time to adjust. Now we will have that cup of tea, and let's see you smile. We have liver and onions for tea, bet you are hungry."

Both bustled around the table, making the room give a welcome to sit and eat.

The rest of Sara's first week heavy with work passed, the weeks turned into months, and then a change occurred at the Hall. Miss Olivine came into the Kitchen.

"I want to see all of you girls in the study; tidy yourselves first, do your hair. I want you to be presentable." Miss Olivine left. Her nose in the air.

"What do you think she has up her sleeve Rosa?"

"I dread to think, I pray it is not like the last time, you were not here Sara when this happened before, I am not going to say what, *it might be totally different today, and I don't want you to worry."*

Sara looked at them both wide eyed saying,
"Is it a dark secret then? Why shouldn't I be told?"

"Look Olivine wants us in the study, no more, we have to comply with her order, or we will be dismissed."

Each girl made her appearance acceptable. Standing at the study door Rosa gently tapped on it.

"Come in,"

This reminded Sara of her interview, she felt herself go cold.

"Well now girls, I know you will be pleased, because I am going to raise your money by two shillings a week. More than you ever dreamed of earning."

The girls looked at each other, why should Miss Olivine do this? There had to be a catch.

"Will our duties change Ma'am?"

"Yes slightly, I will come straight to the point, you know the two Sons of this family are away at college, well they are now coming home. It will be your duty to see to their needs. I know you Cottage girls are familiar with the rules of life and you will accept your position gladly. You will not think it strange to entertain the gentlemen; they are about

your own age. You will be called on at random, any time, I am just advising you at this moment to be prepared."

Rosa went white; Alice and Sara didn't quite know how to take this news.

"You can go now, that will be all for the moment, back to your duties. You will be earning more for your extra duties. I trust you will make the effort, and receive compliments from the young men. If you don't we can always get more kitchen staff."

Having been quiet on the way back to the kitchen, arriving not having said a word, each took a chair and sat down.

"What do you make of that Rosa?"

"I don't quite know what to think, I have been here longer than you two, it has happened before. The last time the boys were involved, it was just a case of broadening their horizons. Any questions they came up with, even personal, either I or the head butler had to demonstrate or teach the two of them, if we didn't know the answer, it would mean finding out, and relaying the needed knowledge. I hated it, but the money was good." Alice said,

"That's all very well, they are much older now, and have a good education behind them. So what on earth do they want us for?"

Sara, listening to the conversation, couldn't add her views, dark thoughts were running through her mind she said,

"How old are they now?"

Don't know exact, about mid twenties I think, Vincent is the elder one.

"How old are you Sara?" Rosa asked,

"I am 27yrs. old"

"That doesn't make any difference when you are here; your age is of no consequence."

"That's you the eldest 27yr., you Alice 21yr. and me24yrs."

"I don't like the sound of what this is leading up to."

Sara felt her skin bristle.

"Now don't start jumping to conclusions, I think we had better get on with our work, we will soon see."

Rosa tied on her apron and looked around to see where she had left off.

Sara was immediately afraid, two extra shillings! Sara was more familiar with the ways of men, these two coming home were men, what were the needs that Miss Olivine had stated? Alice and Rosa getting on with their own work didn't say anything, all were trying to think for themselves, an uneasy quiet fell on the room.

Home in the cottage that evening, Sara was

confiding in her friend. Martha saying,

"It could be something quite simple, but as you say you will have to wait and see. I tell you what Sara, when it comes to your turn take a hat pin hidden in your cap, it could come in very handy in a tight spot.

"Who would have thought that this could happen in such a well regulated family, just shows you never know, that is just it though, we are only surmising you know."

The days passed in the same way, except their money had been raised. No-one had been called upon to meet the demands of Richard or Vincent, although the girls knew they had arrived. They talked about it between themselves, still not coming up with an answer. In the evening in the cottage Martha asked too, saying,

"It seems funny to me, Miss Olivine wouldn't be the one to give you extra money for nothing would she?" Sara replied, "Oh I know that, I have never met such a disgruntled woman, we get no praise for our efforts, she is so matter of fact, walking around the Hall with her nose up in the air, as if she is Lady of all she surveys. I keep well out of her way, do my job and leave it at that.

Chapter twelve

Sara now found herself discussing the question of the raise with Dick,

"We haven't been asked to attend anyone yet Dick, and the longer it goes on the more worried I get."

"Worrying will get you nowhere, you should know that, I am afraid I don't know much about the ways of Lords and Ladies, I plod along, keeping myself to myself, best way if you ask me."

"Yes I agree, but it has taken over in my judgement of things, it is as you say stalemate, what you don't know, you shouldn't guess eh?"

"No indeed, now I must take my leave, have my Pigs to feed, they get restless if I don't keep to a time, see even they have standards. Tell Martha I will be by in the morning, where is she anyway?"

"Just gone to fetch some meat for stewing, it goes a long way in the stew pot, get plenty of vegetables in the pot then it serves us all." Dick said,

"A good friend Martha can't see why she didn't marry."

"It was because she stayed at home to look after her Mum and Dad. When they passed on she was getting on in years, didn't think *anybody would be the slightest bit interested. As you say, I can think of many a one that would be proud to call her wife. As it happens she is helping me, and I am selfish enough to be glad about that."*

"Goodnight Sara, I will pick you up on Friday." Dick took his leave with a wave.

Sara sat down, and tried once more to shed some light on her position, still she was in the dark. Martha came in,

"Hello, I am back, a bit late to put this on for today, tomorrow I will slow cook it, it will be ready for when you get home."

Next day rapidly came, Sara setting about her walk to the "Round Tower."

Thinking what this day would bring, it was a miserable morning, drizzle damp, and dark skies Sara would be glad to be in the warm, the Kitchen was always warm; the fires had to be lit early for cooking purpose. Sara beginning to be less worried about her duties in general, it was just this special duty that she could not get out of her mind. Rosa greeted her.

"Hello Sara, quite foggy this morning, we are glad we haven't got to go out in it. Are your clothes wet?"

"Not really, it is the mist more than the rain, I am glad to be out of it, is there a cup of tea

going?" Alice said,

"We'll soon make one, nobody around this time of day; I can even put my feet up, see."

Alice demonstrated the fact, dragging a second chair that reached her leg length and promptly popping her feet up.

"Now then Alice, stop it, you are too risky in what you do, Miss Olivine could be anywhere, at any time. Don't want the sack do you?" Rosa corrected Alice.

Alice pulled a face saying,

"Can't do anything because of this and that, we have to live a little you know."

Sara looked quietly on, filling the bucket with hot water from the kettle, finding the soap and scrubbing brush, ready to do the floor.

"Little miss perfect eh? Do everything you have been told to do. They might give you a red star in your prayer book"

Alice had to have last word!" Sara replied

"I will be half done before you have started, can't see the point of sitting around waiting to be told off before the day has hardly begun."

Rosa, held her peace, she was not taking sides.

Lunch break already, toast on the fork before the fire, lots of butter.

There always was plenty of plain food to be

had in the pantry. Good job their jobs were partly done, because Miss Olivine came into the Kitchen. She couldn't reprimand the girls; it was their lunch half hour.

"I have a request from Mister Richard; he would like one of you to go to his room at 2pm. I will leave it up to you who will go I shall expect satisfaction, so will he."

What was that supposed to mean?

Olivine left them to sort out who would go.

"I think I had better go, I am the eldest I shall know how to conduct myself."

"You're brave, Alice grinned, sure of your ground are you?"

"No not really, I can give as good as I get, hoping there will be no animosity, someone has to go first, my years put me at the top of the list, although Sara is really the eldest but Sara is still new so it falls to me I believe, I don't want to go. Mr Richard hmmm has he changed these past few years?"

Rosa thought a lot about her visit, decided Mr Richard was a man now. How should she deal with him? Then a positive thought crossed her mind, and she went to the medicine cabinet to put something in her pocket.

"I am going now, Sara, do you know I have no idea what Mr Richard will want of me, I *suppose I am about to find out."*

The room that was Richards was at the top of the stairs, Rosa didn't know whether to be excited or quiet, a feeling of uncertainty rumbling inside her. She tapped the door,

"Come in, ah! It is Rosa."

"Yes sir, Miss Olivine said you wanted me to spend some time with you."

"Quite right, so sit down and we will brush up on the time I have been away." Rosa said

"Nothing much has happened to me sir, I do as Miss Olivine tells me, and the days turn into weeks, and now the weeks into years, it is a long time since you lived here Sir."

Their chat went on, nothing happened; all the while Rosa was on guard, watching Richard's every move, waiting for. Well what was she waiting for? This was a perfectly adult conversation, nothing more. Anticipation had swamped Rosa, what had she expected him to do, or say?

One hour later Rosa was back in the Kitchen.

"Well, what did he say?

Alice expected a story. Rosa didn't want to disappoint, so she made up a plausible tale.

"Oh, we talked about lots of things, he tried to hold my hand a couple of times, but I refrained, I think I have the measure of him now, he won't find me easy to get."

Sara spoke up,
"I would have been terrified; I don't want to go to either of their rooms I feel danger there."
"Don't be silly, Alice laughed, they won't eat you."
Sara had been in circumstantial situations that Alice and Rosa didn't know of, in her heart, and considering the tell tale scars on her body, she knew just what a man could do, brutal and unrelenting, she thought of Bill, it made her shudder. Vowing never again, she dropped the subject and went on with the silver polishing; hoping Rosa and Alice wouldn't talk about it anymore.
"There is going to be a garden party stated Alice."
Who always seemed to get the news Rosa asked,
"Who's invited anybody important?
"It is an open day, with flags and balloons, on the lawns, I think some side shows are attending, there will be a small children's fair, and raffles, I expect we will be in the waitress's quarter, we can still have some fun, there will be ice cream cornets, and candy floss. I hope the weather stays fine, I suppose it is in the name of some charity or other, maybe the Workhouse children will benefit. I

hope so; they get very little in their lives."
*Again Sara shuddered, thinking that is where
she and her children would have ended up if
it wasn't for Martha. Sara was thinking,*
*"I should have told the truth, and told Alice
and Rosa about my background. How to tell
two complete strangers though, they might
think it was all her doing, so she had kept
quiet. Thinking the least said the better. Even
down to the fact of her not being married,
using her maiden name, she wanted nothing
of the stigma that followed after Bill had died.
A new start, without the baggage, no she
didn't mean her children, they had suffered
too, the Hall didn't need to know she had
children; she did her job to the very best of
her ability, so why look for trouble?*

Chapter thirteen

When Sara got back home things had come to light in her own mind, about how she had not been straight forward, telling Miss Olivine, as little as she dared. She spoke to Martha.

"I have got something on my mind Martha."

"What is that then Sara, can I help at all?"

"When I went to the Hall to get my job, I lied about me being married, and also where I lived, not telling of the Children either. I didn't want my name to come from my marriage with Bill. There has been so much gossip, I didn't want myself to be any part of it, so I invented a new me. In the Hall things have changed there is now the two sons' returned to stay, we have to obey Miss Olivine, and tend their needs. I am so afraid of what "their needs" means. I also have to keep the lie valid; it is making me feel very down.

"You can hardly change your story now Sara, it would be instant dismissal, I can understand yourself approach, I wish I had a clever answer, but I don't."

"Wasn't I silly Martha, I needed the job, I thought I wouldn't get it with such a past as mine."

"I know what you mean Sara, I think you will

have to brazen it out now, they would dismiss you anyway if you do a turn around and tell the truth, and maybe no-one ever needs to know. They would have to have a reason to delve into your past now, so don't give them one. Keep quiet and stay calm, do your job as well as you can they will have no reason to interfere if you do that."

"Thanks Martha, I feel better now that you know, I will be able to tell you if anything amiss happens, I am very grateful, not only for this, there have been so many things to say thank you for, the Workhouse would have been our next stop if it wasn't for your kindness."

"I enjoy what I do for you Sara, I judge myself to be part of this family now, I am proud of your children, and would do anything for them. They trust me, I will never be able to take the love that they have for you, but I am happy to receive the respect they show to me. Don't forget I had no-one when I cum' to you, I was turning into a lonely old spinster, that was my outlook, couldn't think of a thing that would change the course of my life, then you came along, I was needed again, it has made a big difference to me. See, we don't owe each other a thing, our mutual benefit is good, so let's stay as we are,

each getting the best that is offered from life. Keep the kid's happy between us. Hey! What a speech, get the teapot filled Sara, my mouth is dry as a bone.

They laughed, and got on with getting the tea on the table for when the Kid's came in.
"Young Lezzy is still asleep upstairs, better fetch her down, else she won't sleep tonight."
Martha went to get Lezzy, Sara was so happy to have Martha, who else would indeed take on this heavy burden, four children to look after, Sara working 6am. Until 4pm, then when she did get home she was fit for nothing, having one half hour's break, which wasn't very much, out of ten hours work. Even then there was the time she used to get there and back.

The three kitchen girls working all together on the table were getting all the required common cutlery into an acceptable state, ready for the open day. They were able to have a girly conversation quietly of course; if Miss Olivine came near enough to hear them they would be severely reprimanded.
Alice started the conversation, saying,
"Don't know why they get this common cutlery out, I suppose they think it is good enough for the riff raff."
"What do they sell that needs cutlery Rosa?"

Sara asked,

"Well they roast a pig, but that goes into batches, and ate holding in the hand, a knife may be required, then there are soups, which by the way Cook won't make, we have to make the soup, are you any good at making soup for the five thousand Sara?"

"I did make soup for my parents but only in small quantities. I wouldn't know how much it would take for a large crowd."

"We'll teach you, we make just two choices, one tomato, and one Vegetable, the gardener gives us home grown, so we don't have to worry about where to buy. Although I say it myself the outcome is generally good. I suppose it is because the stock is made from garden produce, we season it to spice it up a bit, it sells out. Spoons are all that is needed, and of course bowls, which are bought in for this purpose. I must say most people drink it straight from the bowl, Manners makes Man they say, but on open day it is a free for all, people let their hair down and relax, anyway many people would do the same in their own home. If it happens to be a cloudy day especially if a wind is blowing the soup is very popular."

"I will try some myself, Sara joined in; you have made me feel hungry, how long to our break? Is there any bread to use up for toast?"

"We can find a bit of that Sara, and if we can't find stale we'll have a bit of the new, the job has to have a few perks hasn't it?"

They smiled in unison, going quiet once more, as Miss Olivine was staring at them.

"Get on with your work girls, no time to chat, there are plenty more jobs waiting for you when you have finished that one."

They knew that, so being fast was not the ideal way for them cos as soon as they had finished one job another would loom up in front of them. As soon as Miss Olivine left the girls chuckled, and started to talk once more, Sara wanted to know more about open day she asked,

"Can any-one come into the ground? Or do people have to pay?"

Rosa replied,

"There is one penny to pay for each family, the payment is low because the Hall depends on getting the ground full, relying on sales at the various stalls, and selling food. Why does it concern you?"

Sara caught her breath and said,

"It doesn't concern me, I am just curios."

Inside she was building up a fear, what if someone recognised her, and spoke about the

Quarry Yard, or her Kids, she thought,
"I will have to avoid mingling as much as I can. I will blame it on not being comfortable in crowds, it is a feeble excuse, but it will have to do. I have to keep away from anyone who knows my past, it is only one day, if I tread carefully I will be alright, my secret will be kept."

Finishing their jobs they each went their separate ways. Sara had the upstairs fires to lay ready, extra work had delayed the time for this job to be done, and she must be quick.
"This is the last one," Sara said to herself, no-one will know I was late, Going to open the door to leave, she bumped into a Gentleman, he opened the door just as she opened the door, both wanting the same space, embarrassment, Sara had her dust pan and brush in hand, carrying a coal bucket with the other one. He had found her flying around trying to fit her jobs in.
"Oh Sir, please do excuse me, I am sorry to be late doing this job."
"I nearly knocked you flying dear Lady, are you alright?"
"Yes Sir, no harm done, it was just a surprise to us both, wanting the same spot at the same time, may I go now Sir?"
"If you are sure that I have not hurt you, yes

of course you can go, are you new here?"

"Not entirely I have been here for about a year now, it is because you have not been here, you have just arrived home to stay, and you haven't seen me before."

"Better tell me your name then."

"Sara, Sir, I will be more careful next time."

She brushed passed him, and took herself downstairs, being mad at herself for creating a scene, her apron was soiled her countenance ruffled and blushing she thought,

"What a first impression to make."

In the kitchen she told Alice and Rosa what had happened.

"Was it Mr. Richard or Mr. Vincent?"

"I think it was Mr. Vincent, he looked older, he wasn't angry, in fact he didn't tell me off at all. Me! I was good and properly annoyed, with myself of course."

Chapter Fourteen

The open day came, all the staff well dressed, and doing their personal jobs.

"You say you don't like mingling in the crowd Sara, so you can stay on the terrace and sell the soup, Alice and me, we love to mingle, I have had my bottom pinched many a time, and enjoyed the engaging look that follows it, isn't that right Alice?"

"You Rosa, openly invite those pinches, the Men think it is part of the amusement to flirt with the Maids, it is harmless enough, unless the wife or girlfriend catches him at it, then he soon turns into the gallant escort again."

"Not for me, Sara said, men are evil; I don't trust any of them. There's one thing on a man's mind that is how to get into your knickers."

Rosa and Alice made a mock up of looking shocked.

"How could you say a thing like that Sara, it is nature's way of keeping us all interested in an otherwise dull and colourless life."

"You'll think again if you get caught for a baby, I don't know how you dare." Sara said.
Rosa replied,

"We like living on the edge a little, it puts a little spice in the mix, we are always careful."

"Well careful or not, you do not have a law of

your own, so think on while you are safe."

Rosa and Alice chuckled at the seriousness of Sara's warning; they were still not taking a blind bit of notice, well with Rosa it was just words, she had every cause to avoid men.

The grounds were crowded, the sun in a blue sky, everyone smiling and stopping to chat, the Coconut shy had a good crowd around it.

"Four balls for a halfpenny, knock one off and it is yours to take home, cut it up amongst the kids, does their teeth good to munch on a chunk of coconut, crack it with a hammer, that's Dad's job, take the fun home with you, gather your family round and make your own amusement."

The vendor went on and on tempting the folk to part with their coppers. There was the odd Coconut knocked off, and true to his word the happy family had it to carry around with them. This advertised the stall, and the fairness of the play. Always the profit went to the Man shouting his wares; he in turn had to give up half of his takings to the charity involved, this being the Workhouse Children. The ones that threw the balls and didn't win had the thrill of trying. At the end of the day it was all fair and square.

Sara had been quite busy filling soup

bowls the soup was in demand. Much to her surprise, for the day was warm with a lovely breeze.

Thinking there would not be many who would want soup on a day like this. Trying the soup for herself she had to say it was spicy and delicious. Many would have this soup as a substitute for dinner, it was full bodied, and satisfying.

The mother of the family knew when her brood had that inside of them it would mean less cooking in the Kitchen on their arrival home.

Sara couldn't lose her anxious feeling. Thinking she had seen a familiar face, the day had gone well, but Sara, for one, was glad to have it over.

In the Quarry yard cottages all was well, Dick and Martha getting along forming a firm friendship. Often Martha would invite Dick to spend the last hour of the day with her the Kids would be in bed. It was a satisfying conclusion for them both, many a secret would come to light as they sat chatting, they trusted each other so said just what pleased them to convey, not having to guard their words. Martha told Dick about Sara and her lies at the interview.

"You know Martha you can't blame her can

you? Look at the merry dance Bill has lead her. Sara was the one I thought I would be picking up off the floor dead."

I agree, but it has left her with a problem she has to mind her tongue all the while, in case she says the wrong thing."

"Best not get into deep conversation with anyone then, it won't be easy."

Dick had a serious look on his face. Martha replied,

"Exactly what I told her, I feel it is a tall order too, Sara has learned enough by now to look after herself, do not go worrying unduly Dick. You have enough looking after her kids alongside me."

Dick smiled and said,

"I have told her I enjoy looking after them, I have their respect and I am proud of that. Let's change the subject, I have thought of something special Martha."

Dick was trying to drop the talk about Sara.

"What's that then Dick? I like the sound of special."

Her face broadened into a wide smile, her inviting cosy look Dick thought was very genuine.

"How about we go and collect Elderberries to make us some wine?"

"Wine, never had any, what's it taste like?"

"On a cold winters night you can do yourself a lot of good by drinking a glass of Elderberry Wine, it increases the fire in your blood, helps keep chilblains away, you actually feel it's warmth as it goes down, of course being home-made it is very potent. If we can't find enough berries the old apple tree comes in handy, there is always some good falling's from that to be used, they go well with elder makes a slightly lighter wine."

"Well Dick you sound as if you know about the wine, have you made it before?"

"Yes I have, still got half a dozen bottles or so matured ready to drink; I thought we could open a couple of those at Christmas. Stocks are getting low so it is time to make a fresh brew thought this time you would enjoy doing it with me. Our neighbours keep any suitable bottles for me; they get to have a bottle of wine to keep as a thank-you. What do you think me darlin?"

"It would be a real down to earth experience; I will help all I can. You'll have to let me know when you will want me; I can get one of the older boys to keep their eyes on the young uns do we have to walk far?" Martha said, thinking of her poor feet.

"I will take my Horse and Cart, a ride on that wouldn't hurt you, into the country side,

along the lanes, we can then decide where the best picking is. Keeping the cart in sight we could pick berries to our hearts content as we went along I would move the cart keeping it in sight.

Very often Elder trees grow in side by side, I bet we get a worthwhile picking between us, going back to the cart each time so that we haven't too many to carry, they do weigh heavy after a while, you need such a lot. I think they are ready to pick now after all the sunny days they have just had to ripen. We want them a good black colour, the Apples will provide the acid, I keep my yeast, use a tiny bit of stalk for tannin, and then there is only sugar to buy. Some people make elderflower wine,
I have found this too messy; the flowers hold tiny insects too."
"Oh! You do know your wine I wouldn't have a clue how to begin."
"I will teach you, Dick said with a grin and a twinkle in his eye. Better get round my own shack Martha, the time has gone so quickly tonight. I am glad I spoke up about the wine, I didn't know what you would think, I am not a drinking man but a glass of wine on the right occasion fits the bill. Making it between us will be a pleasure, and twice as exciting,

are you looking forward to it?"

"Indeed I am, I thought at my age I had tried most things that had been made in the Kitchen, and this is new to me. Also I am looking forward to trying the one you have saved for Christmas, can't wait to try it."

Martha's face was aglow.

"Goodnight then Martha, if you want me for anything I'll be around."

"Thanks Dick, it is good to know."

He left feeling in good spirit, life was not over for Martha and himself, they were at a beginning not an end.

Chapter fifteen

Next day seeing Sara, Martha told her of what Dick was planning.

"I am really looking forward to it, you won't mind if I leave Lezzy with the boys for a couple of hours will you?"

"Of course not, it would help take away the awful guilty feeling I get now and again. You and Dick get on very well then?"

"Yes we do, he is a kind and thoughtful Man, and I know we are both getting on a bit but we speak each other's language if you know what I mean."

Yes both Martha and Dick had the slang of the Ford, it was endearing in Sara's eyes. Being up at the Hall Sara had learned to drop the local twang although she found herself slipping up now and again. Everything was so straight laced now. At this moment she found herself envying Martha and Dick. If Bill had only been half the man as Dick was there would have been a far happier Sara, and Bill would still be alive.

"Has there been any more information about Mr, Richard or Mr. Vincent?"

Martha looked hesitant as she asked, she didn't want Sara to think she had to keep things to herself, Martha knew Sara needed someone to confide in so she encouraged her to be open.

"No nothing at all, in fact I wondered if they were still around. I know that is silly because I have to empty their chamber pots every day, wishful thinking I suppose."

"You keep well clear of them Sara, do what you have to and no more, that sort of unattached male gets what he can where he can, if you take my meaning."

"I know only too well Martha; I shudder every time I let it pass through my mind. It does pass through my mind though, and brings back vivid memories of Bill and his orders, am I to be plagued all my life. I thought time would distance the past, as yet it hasn't. I am scared if a man even looks at me. I chose to stay on the terrace at the open day. I wasn't so vulnerable there the nearness to the Hall seemed to me protection. I didn't want to walk amongst the people."

"Dear Sara I am sorry indeed to hear you say that. I know even I am warning you off, but there must be a few good Men left around."

"It is finding them Martha, they are few and far between, you can't judge a man by his looks, and so how are you to know?"

"Yes you have to be with a Man daily to know him, you do have a job on your hands, somehow though I think you know if he is for *you, perhaps you have yet to meet, now there is a pleasant thought, try to think on those lines Sara, if love comes looking he will find you."*

Martha was doing her best to change Sara's outlook, what's more it may be true, who knows?

When Dick gave Sara a ride in his goods cart that Friday Sara casually talked about what Martha had said,

"It seems Martha and you are getting on well Dick."

"We see eye to eye about most things, I make myself available to her. I think of your Kids Sara, so try to make Martha's life as easy as possible. Just lately though I must say we have talked on subjects nearer to our own hearts rather than the kids. Being straight forward as I am, I have found the same quality in Martha; we have built a trust in each other."

"I am pleased for you both Dick, don't let my Kids stand in your way."

"Of course not Sara, Martha and me we soon sort them out, don't you worry, and they are quite attached to Martha."

Sara felt herself cringe, they were her brood, knowing Martha was a substitute and was getting on so well oddly did little to please her, after a depressive sigh she went on,

"I only wish I could look after them myself, I have to have money to clothe and feed them, Martha pays towards the rent she is as good as gold, I really don't know any other way to make things work."

"Let some time slip away" Dick said. Things will change you are a very attractive woman you have youth on your side, don't despair, you haven't got over your ordeal with Bill yet, it must be coming up for a year since that happened. Terrible for you, Martha and me, we realise your distress, we are both here for you."

There it was again "Martha and me" and "we are both here for you" it all sounded a foregone conclusion. Where do I fit in Sara thought?

They arrived at the Tower gates, as the Horse trotted along the drive Sara had a sudden cold revulsion for the Hall and all her work there.

"Miss Olivine has been looking for you, she says you are late."Alice said,

"Maybe, but only a few minutes, I had a lift from Dick this morning he is always on time, what does she want me for anyway?"

"Don't know, usually it is after breakfast she comes with her fancy orders, have you been

up to anything?"

Alice had concern on her face; she knew only too well what to expect from Miss Olivine, she herself had been on the receiving end of the stick.

"Do you know what she wanted Rosa?"

"No I don't, she doesn't give much away does she? Her face is unreadable, she has the hard domineering look of a miserable spinster, what's more it is fixed, and I don't think I have ever seen her smile."

Rosa and Sara smiled at the description, Alice adding,

"Now she is a person that could do herself a bit of good going into a crowd, she might have had her bottom pinched, and that might have changed her destiny, you see Sara, if a man doesn't ask, he doesn't get, there has to be a way to break the ice doesn't there?"

Sara thought about what Alice had said, she would have occasion to think more about this conversation in the future. Miss Olivine didn't come again to find Sara, maybe she just forgot, Sara got out of that one!

Chapter sixteen
Dick went round to see Martha.

"The weather is good my dear, can you make time to go to pick Elderberries? They are firm and ripe, hanging like bunches of grapes, the sooner the better now."

"That's good Dick, I will see the boys and ask them if they will look after Lezzy, she won't be little for long but I'm thinking but she will still need watching. Let's see it is Tuesday, make it tomorrow or Thursday they are my best days, Thursday I think Dick it will give me better time."

"Let's hope the weather holds good then, I will pick you up about three."

"Thanks Dick I shall be looking forward to it."

It was a lovely day, the beginning of August, Dick had picked up Martha, and they were both as excited as a couple of young lovers, Martha especially, she hadn't been to collect Elderberries before.

Passed the Pool they went on towards the next village.

"This looks like a good spot Martha, can you see?"

Elderberries' hanging like black chandeliers, glorious bunches of them. Just to hand, no thorns to bother or prick. Just what Dick had in mind, he wanted to show Martha the wealth of nature that hung from the trees, theirs just for the picking. Giving Martha a steadying hand she stepped down from the cart.

"Now you take the low ones and I will reach up for the high branches."

They had a large wicker basket used generally for clothes; it was now lined with clean brown paper. Each had a small pair of scissors so to snip off the bunch at one go.

"Can you eat these as they are Dick?"

"Well they wouldn't hurt you, but they are not very palatable, they are bitter, we shall generously sugar the mash to make the wine."

"Fancy me not knowing at my age, the truth be told I had to be in for Mum and Dad, not even been country walks. Looking after things at home took most of my time, I was glad just to rest myself when I did have free time. Now it is Sara's Kids, I feel like a school kid myself learning something for the very first time. Now look am I doing this right?"

Martha held the berry bunch in her left hand cutting the main stalk with the right hand.

"Do we want the stalk Dick?"

Only a tiny bit, it will act as tannin for the wine to develop, much like the tannin you get from the dregs in the teapot, in fact you could bind the used tea- leaves into a piece of Muslin and use that."

"Will we really be able to make good wine Dick?"

"There is one big pitfall that is if the wine fly gets into the brew while it is fermenting, I use muslin and the copper lid that keeps the little blighter's out of the mash."

"Mash that is like tea as well isn't it, why do you say the copper lid?

I can see the Muslin being handy but I question the Copper lid."

"These vessels are easily sterilised, you can scrub the copper and lid, and then boil some water in it, that sterilises the vessel.

"Are you saying Dick that you brew the wine in the copper?"

"Yes that is exactly what I am saying, I don't use the copper for washing clothes, and there is only myself so I wash my clothes in the sink.

Leaving the copper for brewing, I have done this many times now, it does work."

"It is very cleverly thought out Dick, I admire you for getting to know how to do it, now I am helping you, and will I be able to help throughout the procedure?"

"Oh yes dear gel, I will teach you as we go,

then when the wine is left to ferment you can come and have a stir whenever you want. There is the bottle washing too they have to be sterile. I will be most grateful to accept your help in that. The part where we separate the pulp from the new Wine is certainly a job for two, you can hold the muslin with me it is a bit of a job on your own, I can ladle it out much easier with you to help me, by the way the pulp is referred to as mash, stop me if I am going on a bit, you will see for yourself eventually. Yes, where was I? The mash is separated from the wine; it is then useless and ready to throw into the pig bin. The yeast will have sorted that out."

"It sounds too complicated for me Dick; I never thought there was so much to be done. I won't question the outcome because you have done it before. Thanks for letting me in on your secrets, bet you don't tell everyone how to make wine."

"Too right, it is my own secret recipe, you are the privileged one, I know I can trust you we go together very well you and me Martha."

Martha knew she was blushing, what a lovely thing for him to say, and she couldn't agree more.

"We'll move up the field a bit more now; I'll go back to the cart and bring it closer to us."

"How many do we have to find Dick?"

"Well you see this basket we want that, and eight or nine more like it. When I make wine I want it to be good wine, the copper takes a bit of filling."

The day was hazy with a Sun that caressed not burned you, Hay gathered in the fields ready for winter, Blackberries in with the Elderberries, Birds flitting and singing, lazy Cattle lying in the field, this all would take up a special place in Martha's memory.

Contentment dwelt in her bosom. Hands stained, she paid no heed, this was a time to accept life and all that it was offering her.

They made their way home loaded with fruit, Martha hadn't a clue what was to be done next, but she knew Dick would be in charge so there wasn't a worry in the world for her. She had never felt like this before there had not been room in her life. Like a girl on her first date, here she was, beguiled by Dick her hero.

Arriving home, Martha got the boys to help unload, they also thought it was great fun; Martha didn't have to ask twice.

"When do we start Dick?" Martha asked,

"As soon as possible while the fruit is fresh, it was good getting the addition of Blackberries they will add a good colour and flavour. Do

you think you could spare an hour or two tonight Martha?"

"Of course, I am eager to see how you do it."

Dick was getting the copper all prepared while Martha gave the Kids their tea; it was about six before they got going again.

"Here is your bucket Martha, and here is a good wide fork, yes we have to separate the berries from the stalk and this is the best way of doing it."

Testing to find the right way Martha started.

"They are falling off quicker than I thought they would Dick, like little damsons aren't they?"

"Picking them in the dry with the bloom of the sun still on them is just right Martha, good enough to eat eh? It has been a lovely afternoon I so enjoyed you coming with me Martha."

"I enjoyed it just as much Dick, let's call this wine "Autumn Sunset" it will bring back the loveliness of the day."

Their hands working, their cheeks rosy, smiles and only good things to say to each other, their berries mounting up as into the copper they were tipped, a quiet calm reigned supreme. Building together each with the feeling of this new and gentle bond. Twilight years, a softening of all that life had thrown *at them, this was real and not to be denied the very essence of living feelings yet untold, caressing, soft a golden moment to cherish.*

Chapter seventeen

Did you have a good time yesterday Sara? Alice said,

"I sold the soup out if that is what you mean; I was surprised at how many people bought it."

"Told you didn't I, Rosa and me we are quite proud of our soup, did you try it?"

"Yes I did, it was very tasty you will have to give me the recipe."

Rosa joined in,

"I don't know about that Sara we guard our secrets, play our cards close to the chest. We never know, in keeping the recipe we have a few points in our favour to weigh up if Miss Olivine comes across rough. It pays to have a trick up your sleeve, so think on Sara."

"If you want to be mean so be it, I am sure it wouldn't hurt you to share the secret with me."

No information was slipped her way; the subject was dropped and forgot. They went about their endless duties, but as they got chance the conversation went to open day. The half hour breaks at lunch time being a golden opportunity to say more.

"Doesn't seem like you had much fun then Sara? Alice in her teasing tone said. Did you Rosa?"

"Did I what Alice? You do have such a casual way of asking I hardly know how to reply."

"Alright then I will put it bluntly, how many times did you get your bottom pinched Rosa?"

"I knew that was at the back of your mind, the answer is a fair few, I must say I like teasing the Girlfriend and I give them a cheeky look! My attitude saying, it was my bottom he wanted to pinch not yours, they stick their nose into the air, put their arm through his and drag him away post haste. I always get a smile from the gentlemen they love a bit of slap and tickle. The ladies think their men are far and away above that sort of thing. Now Alice come clean how did you fare?"

"Yes I did attract the toffee nosed few, and had my bottom pinched, that is not all."

Rosa said,

"Tell us more we want to know don't we Sara?"

"I don't think I want to know more, how much more is there to tell." Sara replied.

Alice put her hands behind her back, stood back on her plain high buttoned shoes, pouted her lips and said,

"There is a lot more."

"Well come on then give us it all Chapter and Verse."

Rosa's search for the truth had to be satisfied.

"I was going about my duties smiling, happy to be outside on such a lovely day when I noticed this fellow, no he wasn't class related, more the young farmer type. His smile and his blazon copper blonde hair enticed me, I put myself in his way hoping he would notice me, I have been dying to tell you, that is why I wanted to know about your open day."

"Come on then get on with it" Rosa said.

Alice took on a rosy eyed look.

"As I said before I was interrupted by Rosa, for the next hour I looked for his head bobbing up and down in the crowd, his copper bronze hair was unmistakable, and every time I looked my legs went weak. He must have sensed what I was doing, so the next hour he followed me. I was thrilled, it was as if we had known each other forever, all the while I was trying to find a way to actually meet and touch, I was obsessed, he had such a power over me."

"Did you meet?" Sara said.

"You are too impatient Sara, and you Rosa, let me tell it how it was."

"You are keeping us in suspense Alice" said Rosa.

"It was like that though, I want to convey the deep meaning of this encounter, and it made a big impression on me."

Sara and Rosa sat alert not wanting to miss a moment of this tale.

"It was getting towards the end of the afternoon, the crowd now thinning and drawing back towards the Hall. There he was beckoning me to towards the large Oak tree, where there was no-one about, he went, as soon as I could I followed. The tree trunk was wide, we were out of sight. His arms opened wide as he caught me to him. I was trembling and loved him more than words could ever tell. I wanted him so much he could do no wrong. It was us two with no-one else in the world. My heart was beating so fast, my face flushed I put up my hand to touch his hair, soft like a silken mass, it sent shivers all over me. Everything took on a feeling of fantasy, I could not deny his embrace I undid the top buttons of my maid's high buttoned blouse for him and felt his warm breath as he kissed my breast."

"You are worrying me now Alice, will this story soon be ended?" Rosa looked concerned.

"I shall not disappoint you Rosa" Alice went on with her story.

"My breath coming in short gasps, I held myself to him, I could feel his male hardness against my lower parts, I knew he wanted me, and what's more I desperately wanted him. I helped him pick up my skirts and take down my drawers, to reveal my naked thighs, I felt his manhood throbbing. It was so natural it had to be, he entered me, and I have never known anything as beautiful in my entire life. Quickly pulling my clothes into some semblance of order, he doing his buttons up, we so abruptly had to part. I shall endeavour to find him. I simply love him."

Rosa and Sara looked astounded; Sara first, How could you Alice! What have you done, do you know anything about this man, what is his name?"

I don't know a thing about him, no not even his name, I only know the fates flung us together, and we made love. It was a moment in time that stood still, like destiny you see."

Rosa was alarmed and said,

"You'll get destiny if Miss Olivine finds out, what's more you have risked your all for just fifteen minutes of love, where is your common sense Alice. I know we like a bit of fun but you have gone far beyond that you fool."

"Don't call me a fool Rosa; I would do it all

over again, in fact my heart longs for him."

Sara thought about herself, and the young Bill, he had taken her in much the same manner, look how that had turned out! She said,

"Well Alice it is done, I truly hope you don't come to regret it. I do not envy you the consequences; let us hope there will be none."

"Oh you are a couple of old straight laced girls jealous that's what you are, shan't tell you next time."

Sara at this point was longing to unburden herself and tell them about Bill and her four Kids, she knew she couldn't, she would lose her job, and so her income, which was vitally important to her for the support of her family. As always tears sprung to her eyes, it was the Workhouse or this job. She would not see her Kids in the workhouse; they were far better off with Martha, so she quickly dried up her tears and said nothing.

Chapter eighteen

Miss Olivine came in about two thirty,

"Mr Vincent wants to see you Sara, please go at once girl."

Sara dropped what she was doing full of apprehension went to Mr. Vincent's room, tapping lightly and straightening her dress she waited,

"Come in,"

Sara went in,

"Miss Olivine says you wanted to see me Sir" she dipped her little curtsey.

"Ah yes, it is my little Sara, did you bruise from the collision we had the other day?"

"No Sir, I am still sorry about that."

"You needn't be, if all is well it can be forgotten."

"Thank you Sir."

"What I wanted you for, is to come a stroll around the garden on this lovely afternoon. I know you finish at four, we have over an hour, is that alright with you Sara?"

Sara was so relieved she beamed a smile at him, a walk in the garden she could do with ease, even naming a few plants to keep his interest. They went down the terrace steps, now walking on the lawns there was very little conversation, both just strolling, with no orders or confusion.

"I think the public gave the lawns a bit of heavy use, still they will survive, grass soon gets it's cared for look back." Vincent politely said,

"Yes Sir, the flowers are better for the Sun they had yesterday."

"Are you familiar with the Flower names Sara?"

"I know some, I haven't a Flower garden at home so I haven't had occasion to remember them Sir."

"That's you and me then, what would you say to us both learning them together? We could walk then and see how the Polly blobs with the correct name were doing."

"I would like that very much Sir, there are some lovely flowers in bloom at this moment, and I suppose being August they will soon be over."

"No they will last some time yet, sometimes we get weather to keep them going until the early frosts sets in. I will go to look in the Library, there is a wealth of books in there, Father keeps it well stocked, he will have a smile when he learns what I want the Library keys for, he still thinks of us as his boys, of course forgetting boys grow up to be men. I think we should have two books, one for you, and one for me, we could exchange

information then, a challenge you might say."

Sara at this moment could only think of the work it would release her from. Flowers and their names being a much better option than scrubbing the floor or cleaning the Silver, she smiled to herself saying,

"I know that one's name Sir."

"What are they then Sara?"

"It is called a buttercup, I know it because it grows wild around the place where I live, and I think it is a weed, and look here it is growing amongst the grass."

"Well so it is that is our first named finding, weed or not it is still a flower. Next time we will find more, we will have the books to identify a few."

There was going to be a next time, Sara felt her mood change, looking forward not dreading that next time, in fact Vincent seemed quite a decent fellow. Guessing his age to be about thirty she wasn't overpowered by him, he affected her but pleasantly so, they had things in common, she wanted to know him better. It was all too soon Four o'clock; the cart would be waiting, to take Sara back to the Tower, from whence she would walk her way home. In her pocket she had placed some buttercups folded in her handkerchief, being very careful not to break them for these were to be pressed for the book, thinking Mr. Vincent would like that.

Arriving home Martha awaited any news from Sara, a cup of tea together and a chat. Most often Martha had been in all day, so Sara's news was welcomed. Seeing that Sara's mood had lightened, Martha was eager to get the tea poured. Sara said,

"I was so surprised today Mr Vincent took me out with him for a walk, I have been dreading this encounter, I needn't have done, and Vincent is pleasant and easy to get on with. We talked about Books and Flowers, we are going to get to know the names of the Flowers at the Hall, I know it sounds almost ridiculous, we enjoyed each other's company, I was elated, he also said next time, so he will send for me again. I shall go with a spring in my step. Have we got any old books anywhere Martha?"

"What do you want old books for? No I don't think so, slip along to Dicks; I think he will have some."

Going the few steps to Dicks Cottage, Sara suddenly felt silly what would Dick think about her new obsession?

"Hello Dick, I have come to ask if you have any old books I could have for flower

pressing, the weightier the better.

"Not took to reading have you? No time I expect, Flower pressing eh? What's bought this on?"

"Don't laugh; it is what I am asked to do with Mr. Vincent. He took me a walk around the Gardens; we found neither of us knew the Flower names."

"Well that is a hobby for the gentry; he's asked you to study it with him has he?"

"No, not study just a companion."

Sara's story came out for the second time.

"I never thought these would get used said Dick,

The rummage through the untidy rubbish that lay around produced two weighty books. "How will these do?"

"Very well I would think."

"You take them then, I won't miss them, no I don't want them back you can show me the pressings when you have a few. I can see you are enjoying the time you spend at the Hall, somewhat anyway, see not all gentry are alike. This Mr. Vincent seems to be one of the good sort, you are lucky Sara."

Her heart was lighter than it had been for a long time, it would make maybe a new beginning.

<u>*Chapter nineteen*</u>

It was sweltering hot, Rosa, Alice, and Sara all did their jobs under duress the sweat running in beads down their faces stinging the eyes.

"Whew! I will be glad when the sun goes down, this weather is not at all usual, the grass is brown with sunburn, the Gardens are looking tired."

Rosa was looking tired too as she commented about the heat. Alice looked the worse for wear saying,

"Let's have a break; it is too hot to work."

Sara and Rosa knew they shouldn't but needed a break as much as Alice. They all took a kitchen chair and went to sit by the open door, this was in shade, they thanked goodness for it. A light breeze eddied its way down the cold stone of the building.

"Lovely! Alice said unbuttoning her blouse. Hitching her ankle length skirts up to reveal darned lisle stockings and billowing off white pantaloons, with lace so worn it would unravel in one pull of the cotton that held it. Wish we were sitting on the sand with the sea water tickling our toes, some people can."

"Not for the likes of thee dear, said Rosa, anyway the heat would be unbearable, we would all want large Sun hats, and there

would be no shade. Fancy us three in Sun hats and bathing costumes that would be a sight for sore eyes. I think I will take my chances in the shade of the Hall. I never did like the idea of a beach hut, never know who has been there before you" Again I say, looking at the pair of them sitting beside her, not for the likes of thee."

Sara asked "Does anyone want a drink of water?"

They dare not make tea for this was not there break time. If Miss Olivine caught them it would be "domino" for all.

Rosa said,

"I hope Cook is doing something cold today, jelly and blancmange would be nice, and that is if she can get it to set on the pantry thrall."

The slab in the pantry was very useful on days like today.

Alice seconded this, and then they all went quiet, taking in the cool air that bounced off the stone of the Hall.

"Are you alright Alice?"

"What do you mean Rosa?"

"You know full well what I mean, alright then. Is the monthly to time?"

"Oh you Rosa, I have told you I am fine."

Rosa meaningfully said,

"Only wanting to help Alice I have worried

about you."

"Better get back to work Sara said, before Miss Olivine spots us, one thing for today jobs are going to take a back seat, and it will be "a lick and a promise" today."

They each went back to their different jobs, reluctant in doing so. In the nick of time too Miss Olivine appeared as she always did out of nowhere.

"Rosa, Mr. Richard wants to see you."

Rosa went straight to the Medicine Cabinet reaching in on tip toe then taking out an item that went into her pocket. This was twice Sara had seen her do this. What could she want from in there? It puzzled Sara."

"Come in, Mr Richard called, hello Rosa, how is my pretty little Maid today?

"Quiet well Sir except that the heat seems to be overpowering today."

"Yes it is hot, perhaps you would like to loosen your blouse, and take off your boots?"

"No Sir I am alright as I am."

Richard felt the snub in her voice, so tried to make amends saying,

"Perhaps then I should ring for some iced tea, or would you sooner have a glass of wine?"

"Iced tea would be nice Sir."

Pulling the bell rope cord Richard ordered

iced tea, saying,

"Please bring a plate of cakes too,"

"Now Rosa would you like to sit out on the Terrace? The sun is slanting to give a little shade out there, and we can come back in if it is still too hot."

"Whatever you say Sir, shade outside is preferred."

"Afraid of the Sun drying your lovely pale skin are you? Pity I haven't got a parasol handy, as for me I thrive on the tan the sun gives me; the bronzed look is what I aim for. Don't worry we will sit in the shade."

The upstairs Maid brought iced tea and cakes, her expression puzzled seeing Mr. Richard with Rosa.

"That will be all; I will ring if I need anything more."

They strolled on to the terrace; he took her arm to help her over the small step that was part of the French door.

"I have had my eye on you for some time Rosa, I think of you as more than a Kitchen Maid."

"Oh yes Rosa thought, what is that supposed to mean?"

"Have you a fondness for me Rosa my dear?"

Now what did she have to say, butter him up and risk the consequences? Or stay as ice cold as the tea, she decided to put a dampener down, she said,

"I was well acquainted with you when you were a boy, so the feeling of knowing you well is still alive. I am sure it is enough of a background for us two to be friend's Sir."

She knew it was not what he wanted to hear but it was respectful and honest it would have to suffice. The talk between them followed her suggestion it was all that she could offer.

Again Rosa went back to the kitchen and returned the item back into the medicine cabinet. Sara was dying to know what it was it wasn't her business to ask so once more she kept her own council.

Alice sat that evening looking despondent.

"What's up Alice, are you melting in this heat?"

"It's not just that Rosa, I am pinning for my red haired lover."

"You can stop that then, he probably doesn't come from around these parts it was Open Day you know. Answer me Alice if you can; are you alright from that moment of madness that took you so completely?"

"If you mean am I having a baby I can't tell you,"

"Surely you should know by now Alice?"

Rosa turned to look at Alice full faced trying

to read her expression.

"Don't look at me like that Rosa as a matter of fact how are you getting on with Mr. Richard does he make demands on your charms?"

"No he doesn't and no I am not with child, even if I was I would know who its Father is."

"Much good that would do you he would never marry a Kitchen Maid." Alice said.

"Let's stop now before we tear each other to bit's."

"You started it Rosa; I was quite content with my daydreams. I really do want to see him again; I shall ask anyone I think might know him as soon as an opportunity presents itself. Is it impossible love at first sight?"

"You are trying to prove the impossible Alice, who am I to say, or was it just a mad misread infatuation?"

"I shall only be happy when I prove to you it was the former that I want to be with him forever, it is my idea of bliss."

They each went quiet again wondering where this would all end; the future was not theirs to see.

Alice as good as her word asked everyone she came into contact with describing the young man in question. It became a more pressing *detail for now she knew she was with child. Wanting the baby not telling a soul not even Sara or Rosa knowing what solution they would advise, Rosa would take her to a place where they got rid of such mistakes. Where hooks and needles were used and nothing said afterwards. Alice already loved this child; she wanted the baby mistake or no mistake, this child was to be born from the man she loved. She would find him one day.*

Martha was going to Dick's each day, together they stirred the wine slowly adding dissolved sugar.

"This is already fragrant Dick. Hmm, the bouquet filled the air."

"It is going to be a good un Martha what with the prime state we harvested the berries, and the loving care we have both administered to it, we shall have to name this wine."

"What a lovely idea Dick, shall we name it now or wait till it is nearer being done? Didn't we say "Autumn Sunset" would be a good name?"

"Well it is like a baby's name, going through the options, then settling for the most appropriate, so say what you would like to call it then we can change it if we want to."

"This is really exciting Dick, I shall start to think of names right away."

"You will find if you do Martha your mind won't be on the daily drudge, instead the names will be flitting through your mind so your work will be done in no time at all. Every one you think of will be the best, so jot them down so we can choose together our very favourite."

"Oh I would like that Dick, how long before this Wine will be ready."

"Hold on Martha, Wine takes a long time; it will stay in the copper for a long time after we have taken all the starting mash out, we do that by passing it through Muslin so the liquid looks comparatively clear. The liquid goes back into the copper, with dissolved sugar and water; this gets topped up as we go this will take us through next winter. Elderberry wine takes a lot of maturing, but that is why most of it gets drank before it is properly ready."

"Well I never! All that time and effort I should think Dick the few bottles you have stored will be mature."

"You think right Martha, although there is always a small residue left at the bottom of the bottle so we stand them out on a frosty night so that which has settled stays at the bottom, as a matter of fact it is this Yeast that has settled as a residue that is kept to start the

next mash off. I keep to the bottoms to start the next lot good wine good yeast, some would pay a rare old penny for a bit of that, the more times the cycle goes on the stronger the next Wine is, takes an old un to know the tricks of the trade. There is many a glass had a hand in keeping the drinker warm on a bitter cold night. It has its medicinal uses you know. You can do the same using gooseberries, they are commonly grown around these parts, they make a sparkling wine, crisp and uncommon, in our way we call it "Poor man's Champagne" how's that for something new eh?"

Dick was enjoying relating his tale to Martha; he had never had anyone to be close enough to be interested. Yes there was Sara, who a long time ago picked elderberries for him, but she would be out with the Kids then popped them in on her way back, he was always pleased to get them. Sara never had anything to do with making the Wine. This time it was totally different Martha was so keen and revitalised the flame that was essential between two likeminded people. Dick looked forward to the time he would spend with Martha each day. Thinking,

"The older I get the softer I get, I don't know what has come over me, I must admit I like

the feeling, I am just another silly old devil, not to worry, life was getting so repetitious this change is what I needed. Martha and me will be drinking this wine together for many a year, that thought makes me smile."

He had surprised himself his outlook was beginning to be for two, not one!

"Better go now Dick I have the taters to peel, by the way Sara seems to be in a bit better humour just lately."

"I thought so too she came for the books for the flower pressings and seemed to have cottoned on to the idea, that is a refreshing first it will do her good, take her mind into a different direction. Alright Martha I am keeping you, better let you go, I tend to think you have only me to look to, not so is it?"

Martha went back to her own place albeit reluctantly.

Sara rushed in her face reddened with the heat.

"Mr Vincent asked for me again today Martha, and look what he gave me."

Martha looked expecting to see a small trinket; no it was a book with flowers on the cover.

"How beautiful is that Martha, it is going to hold each flower we find and name. Mr Vincent has found another book, with *pictures about nature. We can pick the flower then go to the book to see what its name is. The book I have is to hold the pressed flower with the name, the heavy books Dick found me will do the job of pressing I am looking now for some absorbent paper."*

"You mean tissue paper Sara; I haven't got any you will have to try next door Mrs. Griffiths family bring her small gifts now and again, they could well have been wrapped in the paper you now need. Go and see her while I get this dinner ready."

"I want some right now, look at these marigolds their orange colour glows like the sun, to keep their colour as well as I can they need pressing straight away."

"I can't give you what I haven't got, said Martha; off with you next door you may be lucky."

Sara went explaining the need for the tissue,

"Yes dear I think I have some, it came as wrapping around a gift I had on my birthday."

She went upstairs coming down with the tissue in her hand.

"It is only plain white Sara, will it do?"

"Very well thank you, if you come across anymore, or know where I could get some I would be obliged."

"I'll do that for you Sara, then on a cold winter's night you can come and sit with me for an hour and show me, it will remind me of the Summer Sun, when Mr. Griffiths sits dozing in his chair, I would like to have your company."

Happily Sara went back home, her tissue paper carried carefully as you would if it was precious. It was precious to her.

"What are you going to press today then Sara?" Martha enquired.

"I have these lovely rose petals, look at the colour."

The colour was deep rich pink.

"Then I want to get a page display from these marigolds, a spray would show them off."

"Why don't you press the whole rose Sara?"

We didn't like to pick it from the plant it was in its full glory, so we chose one that had started to fall; they are still very fresh I have the rose stamen as well. It is called Pretty Betty, isn't that a lovely name?"

Martha agreed, wondering at the change in Sara, it was for her good so Martha didn't ask too many questions.

Chapter twenty
Back at the Hall all was going on in the usual daily manner. Although Rosa thought Alice was looking a bit pale and tired. She never drew attention to this, supposing the same could be said about herself or Sara. It was the weekly drudge day after day of housekeeping, same day in same day out. There was very little to relieve the boredom. Sara had her flowers to think about, her mind while doing her job wasn't occupied with the job in hand, no she let it drift out into the Garden

The colour and interest made a tapestry of delight. Mr Vincent often came into her thoughts too Sara knew it was hopeless, to think of him in any way other than her employer was out of the question. He was so kind treated her as an equal, after her experience with Bill this really pleased her, beginning to feel whole a Woman in her own right, with

Opinion's that were listened to, could it last? Sara wanted it to. When she was asked for by Mr. Vincent a delight filled her. Alice and Rosa were a bit suspicious about the regularity of these occasions, especially when it left more work for them to get done. They didn't say anything, pot calling the kettle and so on. The thing they had to do was look after each other, that's what Alice had come out with anyway She was right!

It had been twelve weeks since Open Day, there were always periods of time like this nothing to look forward to, the days dragged, nothing much happening.

Next day at breakfast they were all talking together when Alice suddenly jumped up rushing out of the room, her hand tightly clasped over her mouth. Sara said,

"What on earth is the matter with her Rosa?"

"I don't know, perhaps she has swallowed something down the wrong way and it is choking her, she looked sick."

"She looked sick, that's it she is being sick, now we have it Sara."

Rosa then went post haste after Alice.

Reaching the toilet room Rosa could hear Alice, she didn't need twice telling what the matter was.

"Come on Alice, deny it now, you're with Child aren't you?"

Alice couldn't say anything; she was bringing up all of her breakfast. Rosa waited, when Alice had calmed down Rosa said,

"I am right aren't I? Is this the result of your blue eyed boy, your secret love?"

Alice started to cry, a sob sobbing despairing cry, it was difficult to distinguish her words.

"I, I, can't keep it to myself any longer sob, sob, I don't know what to do. Sob, sob, I am in such a mess Rosa."

"Why didn't you tell me before, I could have been more help to you earlier. Come on now Alice, all this sobbing will not solve your problem, does anyone else know?"

Alice sniffed her tears up her nose.

"Where is your handkerchief? Oh here have mine. Please Alice pull yourself together, if Miss Olivine catches us she will drag your secret out of you, count on it."

Alice knew Rosa was right and did her best to calm down. Rosa trying to think of a solution was not having much success.

"Look dry your tears let's get back to the Kitchen, you can tell Sara it was something that you ate that had upset you. That is until we can see our way clear and there is a solution at hand."

"I must tell you Rosa, I would dearly love to keep this baby I was hoping by some chance I would find the Father, try as I have I cannot find anyone that fits the very specific description. It is a face you would not forget easily, with his reddish blonde hair and blue eyes. There surely can't be many that can be described like that."

"Forget everything just now Alice, just stay

calm, we won't make things worse than they are. I am not going to chastise you anymore, the deed is done what you want is a way out. I will search for an answer, be ready to comply, it is for your own sake."

Alice went quietly back to her work, hoping the answer Rosa had spoken of was not an abortion.

"I don't want an abortion Rosa" her voice frantic once more.

"You don't know what you want at this moment, you got yourself in, now you have to get yourself out by fair means or foul, it is the name of the game Alice. We all have to play by the same rules. Let us drop this conversation now or the whole Hall will know."

Alice thought "I still might find my lover, the depth of feeling is different to the sort Rosa is implying. He wanted me as I wanted him, he would want the child too, if only I could find him. Somewhere perhaps very near he is living his orderly daily round, but where?

Chapter twenty-one

Rosa told Sara Alice was not well, Sara saying,

"I will do all I can to help her with her duties, will she be over it shortly?"

"I depends Sara, I am going to take Alice to see a Doctor, and then we might know."

The "Doctor" Rosa had in mind was for abortion Finding the cash was not going to be easy, Rosa was almost as worried as Alice, this coming Sunday they both had the day off, Rosa had to find cash quickly, it was the sooner the better. Knowing Alice would not be easy to persuade, money or the lack of it being another stumbling block. For Rosa there was only one thing to do that being to ask for her wages to be paid early. Full well she knew how this would be received, there was no other way, she asked for an appointment to see the Head Cook who also gave them their wage once a month. Going to see Cook Rosa's mouth was dry, she could hardly string two words together, and in she went.

"Hello Rosa, what brings you to see me?"

"I have to ask for my wage to be paid two weeks early Cook."

"Dear me, you know our Lady doesn't hold with that kind of thing, what is so urgent

Rosa?"

"I have an Aunt who is sick, I plan for Alice and me to visit her, there is a Stage Coach that leaves on Sunday, as we have Sunday off I thought it would be the best time to go. Of course the fare is the problem, I also would like to take flowers or chocolate, it will be an expensive outing."

As Rosa lied she felt her colour rise, she was desperate to get out of the room.

"Where does this Aunt live?"

"In Coventry, a fair distance,"

"I will see Milady, and then I will tell you Rosa.

"Thank you."

"You can go back to your work now; I will let you know in good time Rosa."

"I have done it" Rosa declared, her next move was to get Alice to comply, telling Alice about her fib lightened the atmosphere, Alice didn't want to go but Rosa had gone to such lengths to help her, getting the money together Alice could not refuse.

Sunday arrived, Rosa had her money, the Sun was up and except this major blot on the landscape all was well. They had asked Dick to take them as far as the Tower, they would walk from there.

The strong feeling of apprehension that they

felt was unreal, like a dream, or more like a nightmare. Trying to keep a conversation between them became impossible. Alice was going against her every natural feeling as she walked forward into this unknown territory. Fear, Love Guilt, apprehension overwhelmed her. Every step took her nearer to the fate designed for her. Why had she agreed with Rosa to do this awful deed? More terrible than ending her own life, for this baby inside of her depended solely on her judgment, the babe hadn't asked to be born now it depended on Alice to give it life, and Alice was going to kill it, or more to the point the Doctor was going to kill it. Thoughts rushed through Alice's mind, feeling sick and giddy they arrived at the destination. Alice looked at the house that Rosa had pointed out, white net curtains that had turned yellow with age. Windows unclean, the whole appearance of slap dash method made Alice cringe, if the woman hadn't spotted them and come out to greet them Alice was sure she would have run away as far as she could get.

"Come in my dears" a Lady with a double chin and a fat bottom greeted them.

"I am prepared for you; leave your coats on the stand."

Rosa and Alice did as they were told,

although Rosa couldn't see why she should take her coat off.

"Now it is Alice I need to examine isn't it? Take off your boots and drawers I think I can manage if you just hitch up your skirts."

Alice complied with the request.

"Get up on this couch I need to examine you first, the woman steered Alice to the place she wanted her to be.

"That's right, no names you understand, hitch up your skirts a little higher please."

Alice lay on the couch, her brown stockings complete with black garters looked a sight nothing romantic there then?

Alice could now see the evil instruments laid out ready and cringed, even the bit of cloth on the tray they were placed on was grubby.

This woman was going to destroy the beautiful baby that lay inside of her. Not knowing what else to do, Alice slipped her discarded clothes into a pile on the floor.

The woman said,

"Relax now so that I can examine you."

Relax no, Alice would not relax the tension that held her fixed was the only protest she could make. Inevitably the examination took place.

The woman pushed up her sleeve, parted Alice's legs and thrust her grubby hand inside of Alice's private parts not being caring in any way, her right hand inside, and her left hand on the top of Alice's stomach. Pushing and moving, prodding then putting her ear on to the top as well as her hand, she appeared to be listening. This invasive action was too much for Alice saying to the woman,

"Just get on with it before I change my mind, I am a person, I have feelings, not a thing to be mauled with."

This startled the woman, very rare did anyone give her a bit if lip, in her mind she was doing this silly girl a favour.

"I still have to examine you further internally, it is for your own good, if you relaxed I could do this quicker, tensed up as you are I can't feel what there is in there."

Alice felt the rebuff, thinking,

"Doesn't she know the pressure she is putting on me, I can barely breath, it is more than I can face. Let it be over soon she prayed what am I doing here?

At last the woman straightened up.

"I have some bad news to tell you, this baby is far too formed to be aborted. If I attempt it I may kill you girl, why have you left it so long, this should have been done weeks ago. I don't want a dead Mother and a dead Baby on my hands. Get dressed you can go now."

Alice shouldn't have been but she was jubilant.

"I still have my baby, and I will keep it until it lies in my arms, someday I will find my love, I know deep inside of me that this is right."
Rosa looked at her saying,

"Well Alice, I don't know where we go from here, we'll have to think of something."
Alice dressed they both were ready to leave when the woman said,

"That will be a half crown that you owe me."
Alice and Rosa looked at each other, the woman hadn't done anything. The look was recognised so the Lady said,

"This payment is for advice and examination I don't work for nothing you know."
They paid and left, this woman had only told them what they already knew, they didn't want it verified only rectified. This she hadn't done.

Another path they would have to follow, they decided to tell Sara she might have a solution. Money spent the only thing left to do go back to the Hall, both weary and tired. The final walk down to the Hall seemed miles usually they had a lift on the cart but the cart wasn't there. The tree lined drive was very picturesque, the two walking in the distance pathetic little figures still with the problem in their minds.

Chapter twenty-two

Mr. Vincent greeted them saying,

"My dears you look hot and bothered, it is not the weather for long walks, rest is what you need I have been looking for Sara.

"We all get Sunday off Sir."

"Of course silly me no wonder I couldn't find her anywhere. I will leave you two in peace then."

He left the room.

Immediately they sat down Rosa saying,

"I will put the kettle on, it is a cup of tea we need. A wasted effort Alice, what did you think about it all?"

"I felt well and truly cornered Rosa, if the truth be known I hated having her dirty hands on me at all. Next thing I want to do is go to the wash room and give myself a good scrub with plenty of soapy water. I am sorry Rosa that I have involved you in all of my trouble. Now it seems I have to rope Sara in."

Rosa felt herself overcome Alice wasn't any trouble to her; they were as close as two peas in a pod, working day in day out in each other's shadow. Alice could feel the stress in Rosa so she went over to her putting her arm around her shoulders, dropping a kiss on the top of her hair. Rosa said,

"I am alright Alice, I feel I have been a bit

pushy with you lately, thinking quite honestly about your condition, it is a very natural one, we were meant to conceive and bring children into being, it is part of being a woman you have done nothing wrong."

Alice felt her eyes tingle with tears.

"Dear Rosa thinking about me and my baby, it is circumstance that is making this turn into a problem."

The tea was made Rosa found some cake in the cupboard, neither of them had any appetite for a meal. Alice had been to wash while Rosa made the tea, now they sat in comparative comfort with very little more to say.

Sara came in Monday morning, she sat and listened while the truth was told saying,

"I don't really know about these things I can give you no immediate answer. I am so sorry Alice, how torn you must feel not being able to contact the Father. As Rosa is doing I will give all the help I can, at least now it is out in the open we can defend and protect you. I suppose soon it will have to be sorted with Milady, can't stop nature, there is sure to be a time when you can't conceal it any longer."

"Thank you Sara, you have already lightened my load, with you and Rosa I do not feel so much alone. I shall keep it to myself for as

long as I am able. I can't think beyond that at this moment."

They all agreed it was the immediate best solution.

Miss Olivine caught them just as they were separating, they all had to cover their tracks and look busy, she said,

"Mr Vincent wants to see Sara, please go up immediately.

Sara was so pleased, she couldn't add to that which she had already said to Alice, going into Mr. Vincent's company would divert her mind. Sara tapped the heavy door,

"Come in Sara."

Mr. Vincent sounded comfortable as he called her name, Sara preened herself at the thought, and she wanted to be someone that he felt relaxed with.

"Hello Mr Vincent, did you want me?"

"Yes Sara, I have thought about our flower collection. Sara felt her face drop."

"No no don't you worry we are still going to do it. I thought we could add to it by catching Butterflies. We could net them, then press them the same as we do with the Flowers. I know quite a few that do it, the Butterflies look stunning when pressed with the flowers."

"I would have thought butterflies would be

better left in the garden, but you seem set on the idea, so yes I would like to do that with you Sir."

"Look Sara can't we drop the formality, you don't have to say Sir, or call me Mr. Vincent, Vincent will be quite adequate. I think of you as a very pleasing friend, what do you think?"

"If that is what you would like me to do, I will Sir."

"No no, no not Sir, repeat that again Sara,"

"I will Vincent." It came quite natural.

"See that wasn't so hard to do was it?"

Sara was smiling; her whole countenance beamed, what a step he had invited her to take, feeling very proud they stepped out into the garden.

Vincent produced two large butterfly nets.

"Bet I get the first one Sara, he tripped down the terrace steps eager to begin, Sara followed him saying,

"You will be better than me; I have never held a net before."

The butterflies were educated; they didn't want to be caught. As sighted and netted it should have followed to produce a captured creature, but no, they always escaped. Laughing and running to first one place then the other they both had to give in, slumping down on the grass red faced and perspiring, but happy.

"Well Sara, I think you are right, flower collecting is not so near exhausting, we will look for flowers after we get our breath back."

Sara felt as free as a bird she thought,

"Is this me running alongside Mr Vincent carefree and content? I am to call him Vincent, what would Miss Olivine think of that when she found out, her favourite boy mixing with the riff raff, not even an upstairs Maid, a Kitchen Skivvy no less!

It was hot and humid the skies began to darken, a loud thunderclap rent the air, boulders in the heavens clashing ready to fall. It sounded like ripping and tearing, the zigzag lightening flashed.

"Sara we had better take cover it is going to pour down any minute now."

They ran into one of the huts that were scattered around for especially this purpose.

"That's better, don't think I could stand the Hall this afternoon, it will be suffocating with the heavy drapes and carpets. We will watch it rain and sit on the hut's bench, we won't get wet. We can talk while we wait for tea."

"I have to be going at four, yes there is time."

It was a new experience for Sara, there were

bench type wrought iron seats in the hut and sitting there gave a good view of the grounds. The rain added to the symphony the storm was playing. Crash and roll as the angry clouds collided with each other speaking the words loud and clear.

"Out of my way you wandering Children, I am Master of the skies, my lightening fork will pick you up and toss you into the unknown. Be humble I say, with your thoughts I will play. Listen to my song, see my sheets of rain, rip and tear, my anger will not be appeased until I have vented my entire wrath. Stay still I will give you such a show, calling on all the blackness in my realm to come to my aid, yes, you will be afraid."

Sara and Vincent sat in the enchantment of the storm. This was one to be reckoned with. Looking at each other for any sign of dismay then bursting out into frightened laughter.

"Sure you are alright with this idea Sara? I didn't realise it would be as bad as this."

"I wouldn't miss it for the world Vincent, a ringside seat no less."

The heavens opened, rain came down in great torrents hitting the paved ground around the hut with mighty force, bouncing jewels like glass beads that glanced back to look like ballet dancers standing on one tip toe precise and perfect. The parched earth enjoyed the deluge. The storm gave to the garden a look of satisfaction, all were getting the water right down to the roots, another day the Flowers would lift their heads, the Sun would come out all would be well. Whoever tended the garden would look with a smile, it would be better than ever.

"Isn't it lovely, Sara said? Just to think we would have missed all of this grandeur if we had gone indoors, I think in all my years I have never seen or heard such a perfect storm."

"It isn't over yet my dear."

As soon as he had uttered the words another thunderclap wrenched the sky, resounding on the earth, the hut shook on its foundations, yes actually they felt the earth move beneath their feet.

"That was a close one Sara, did you feel the vibration?"

"Yes I did, I must admit although this roof is only wood I am pleased it is over our heads, it frightened me and excited me at the same time. I only hope it doesn't do too much damage or break any of the flowers down."

Vincent replied,

"They are very virulent you know, they will soon pick up their heads, we shall have to *wait before we collect any for pressing they will have to be dry for that job."*

The rain still poured, they still sat taking in this natural scene placed before them, and after all they were part of it.

"I think it is going over, Vincent I don't want this moment to end,

She turned her head to look at him, their eyes met, his hand lifted her chin, and his lips touched hers, a delicate and loving gesture. Sara responded and enjoyed this momentary embrace.

That night Sara sat telling Martha she said,

"Yes I know the storm fair shook these Cottages I was glad when it was over, I get frightened when the lightened zigzags down like that, fancy you outside watching it."

"I loved every minute I felt part of me wanting it to go on Sara with starry eyes said."

"That is because you had your Vincent with you it would have been a different story if you had been on your own." Martha had said "Your Vincent" how could he be my Vincent, we are worlds apart, should it or could it be so?" Sara changed the subject saying,

"Look Martha the evening sunset."

The sun was setting like a ball of fire it mellowed wherever its rays fell. A feeling of peace also glowed from Sara she was dropping the dark clouds behind her. How far apart was Sara's life to Vincent's? Yet she knew him so well. The class barrier was only too evident, what did Vincent really want from Sara?

Morning came and so did Miss Olivine,

"You girl, I saw you running about the lawns with Mr. Vincent disgusting state of affairs. Do you dare to think you could seduce a man such as himself with a gesture and a smile? You are treading on dangerous ground girl this will stop immediately, goings on under my very nose, you are what you are, and that for you means a Kitchen Skivvy. Get on with your work girl, scrub the floor and with it scrub out any thoughts you may have of grandeur they are not for the likes of you."

Tears welled up in Sara's eyes, answering,

"I have done nothing that Mr Vincent hasn't suggested, he proposes I just follow, we collect Flowers for pressing that is all." Miss Olivine set her face and looked daggers.

"Now it is we, how easily it slips off your tongue, it is not to happen again, I will be watching you girl."

Miss Olivine took her leave without calling Sara by her name once. Sara's head hung humiliated in every respect, Rosa spoke,

"Have you been having a good time with Mr V.? If you have we will soon have two in the pudding club. You know what a mess Alice is in, is that not a big enough warning?"

Sara could tell Rosa was also angry with her, she replied,

"Nothing of that nature is going on I have merely formed a good friendship. I didn't deserve the licking I received from Miss Olivine I have been doing just as I was asked, when Mr. Vincent wants me I have to give him my undivided attention. It was Miss Olivine that gave me that order."

Alice agreed saying,

"That's right I was here when she told you Sara. I have been wondering why I am not sent for, Mr. Richard sends for Rosa, Mr. Vincent sends for Sara, doesn't look as though they like me. Thinking about my unborn child I can count myself lucky, I have enough problems to sort out as it is without looking for more."

They each went on with their duty, Sara on her knees scrubbing the huge kitchen floor. Her eager outlook squashed to the ground, her face sullen, and her attitude despondent. Would there ever be a time she would walk on solid ground?

Scrubbing helped funnily enough; she vented

her temper out on to the floor. Passing through her mind there were visions of her former life married to Bill. The picture was not pretty; tears stung her eyes and splashed down off the tip of her chin. The time she had spent with Vincent had been treasured moments, now Miss Olivine wanted to squash all that.

Mixed feelings of anger and resentment filled her being. Why? When life had just begun to be worth living should she let Miss Olivine pour cold water on her small dream?

Chapter twenty-three

The day was bright and sunny Dick went round to see Martha.

"Hello Martha just to say I think our Elderberry wine pulp wants straining off now. I have boiled a decent piece of muslin it is now sterile, do you think you will have time later on today?"

"I will make time Dick, but must it be right now?"

"No this evening will do us Martha the kids will have had their tea, bring Lezzy with you she is no trouble."

Lezzy could be very mischievous toddling around nicely finding all sorts of things to inspect, Martha would have to have her by her side or put her to bed.

"Here I am Dick, Sara has gone to see a friend so I have brought Lezzy in the pram she is really too big for it now but she looked very tired I think she will sleep while we get on, let's have a look at the wine Dick."

They went to the copper where the brew was still fermenting. Dick lifted the wooden lid.

"Hmm, that smells lovely. Martha said, breathing in the laden air.

The pungent heavy aroma filled the room. It was beginning to have the bitter sweet essence that told Dick all was well. Producing a ladle and half a dozen sterilised buckets he told Martha,

"You take that side of the muslin and I will hold this side. I shall ladle the mix into the centre slowly."

Martha held her muslin firmly.

"The colour is good Dick looks like the rich red ruby port that comes to the table at Christmas or occasion, can I taste it?"

"I wouldn't if I were you it needs to be sugar fed for weeks if not months all we are doing now is to remove all the pulp, it will start a new fermentation on the sugar, we dissolve the sugar in water it soon gets going again, removing the pulp helps the wine to clear at the end of the procedure, although it will want twice filtering so as it clears, we don't want cloudy wine do we?"

"It is a long job isn't it Dick, I don't think I could do it on my own, in the future I mean, I wouldn't remember all the processes."

"You would Martha, when you have done it a couple of times it becomes second nature. This is something very new to you I will always be around to give you a hand. I would like you to help Martha. I think we can safely say we have become good friends. I love to have your company I hope you feel the same."

Dick had made his first move suggesting commitment nothing more it still made Martha's heart flutter and brought the colour into her face.

They separated the pulp from the wine; Martha couldn't believe how the yeast had rendered the huge weight of berries to nothing but a bag of squash to be disposed of. Martha wondered if Dick put this in with the pig swill. Now the copper was once again sterilised, Dick did this by putting water into the bowl of it, and lighting a fire underneath it, this small quantity of water rapidly boiled so sterilising the vessel. Job done now the copper was ready to receive the liquid wine plus the syrup made with the sugar.

"There we are Martha job done."

"Dick I am almost sorry we have to leave it, I have enjoyed coming round to stir it."

"You needn't stop coming round Martha, I too have enjoyed your company. Any time you will be more than welcome."

Dick leaned over the table they sat beside and took Martha's hand.

"We make a good pair us two Martha, you are my kind of woman."

Martha blushed as a girl, she had never had men in her life, now thinking it was too late, but maybe it wasn't. Certainly Dick was the kind of man she would find pleasure in cooking for. Her thoughts stopped there, never thinking Dick would want her beside him in bed.

Martha took Lezzy back to her cottage, she had slept and been no trouble while she and Dick did the wine, being the two of them without interruption had brought a romantic element to the room, Martha being a very practical woman didn't dream, dreams were for youngsters, still she couldn't deny the very comfortable feeling of being wanted that was in her heart, Dick like a balm to her weary soul, is this what love was she questioned herself?

Chapter twenty-four

"Has anyone seen Sara?" Mr. Vincent asked Rosa and Alice.

"She leaves at 4pm. Sir,"

Oh damn, I completely forgot that, thanks I have been looking all over for her,"

He left, Rosa said,

Crickey, he is in a good mood, he has come off his high horse eh?

Alice replied,

"He is almost human, although dare I say it cos' how long for I wonder?"

"I think Sara has something to do with it, she is happier too, that is until Miss Olivine chalked her off this morning."

Rosa winked her eye saying,

"I am afraid Sara is going to get a rude awakening." Alice replied changing the subject,

"I thought Milady looked at me with a meaningful eye this morning, I held in my stomach in till I felt sick. I am not showing that much am I Rosa?"

"No I only thought the other day how well you carried, it will be ages till anyone thinks you are putting weight on, then if it happens to be the upstairs lot, the balloon will go up. I don't envy you Alice."

"I am still trying to locate my own darling,

someone must know him. I feel my fate will be decided as soon as our eyes meet. You wonder how I can love him, but I do, and long to see him." Rosa said in a meaningful manner,

"Well Alice wherever he is he knows where you are."

"He doesn't know I am carrying his baby though does he?"

"Suppose not, but if he wanted to find you he could, you are too trusting Alice. Better get on the time is slipping by, funny when we are working the time goes slow, and we chat and whoop it is gone in a flash. Do you know what cook is getting for tea?"

"Chicken, Alice said, custard to follow."

Alice liked her food, had a good appetite, besides she was eating for two now as she was always telling Rosa with a twinkle in her eye.

Sometime Alice knew she would be hauled over the coals, she was preparing for it. For this moment dealing with one day at a time was enough.

Monday came and with it Sara, who was hoping to see Vincent, he was in her mind a great deal. She tried hard not to let it be so, Vincent was the kindest man she had ever known, well, apart from Dick who was a much older man. Sara found herself wanting *to look decent, washing her maid's attire more. Keeping her hair neat, putting a little cream on her hands, using gone off dairy cream for this purpose, cosmetic cream wasn't affordable. Sara pinched her cheeks to bring the colour into them, using food colour to enhance her lips. It was all she could do, she wanted to look worthy of the attention Mr Vincent was paying her.*

A skirt rustled, Sara looked up to see Miss Olivine coming towards her.

"What now?" she thought.

"Follow me girl, Milord and Milady want to see you."

Sara's heart was thumping, she couldn't think what they wanted her for, Alice and Rosa gave a side look and a positive nod of the head to let Sara know they thought about her. Up to the main floor Sara went following Miss Olivine and keeping very quiet.

"Wait here, I will go and see if they are ready for you."

Sara felt as though she couldn't speak the air was claustrophobic feeling her mouth dry and not being able to swallow properly. Miss Olivine tapped the door and said to Sara,

"Come in and conduct yourself in a decent manner girl."

Sara thought she always conducted herself in

a decent manner, and stepped into the room. She was shown where to stand, gripping her hands together now, tacky with sweat.

"We are not going to make a great fuss about this Sara. The fact of the matter is you have been seen in intimate association with Mr. Vincent, no don't bother denying it, we know it as a fact. We have no other choice than to dismiss you. You will leave immediately after saying goodbye to Rosa and Alice."

Milady looked awesome, Sara was trembling.

"We are sorry that it has to be this way Sara, you leave us no option."

Milord stood hands clasped around his back Sara thought he did look genuinely sorry. With Milady taking the leading role drawing herself up to her best height, sticking out her chin in a definite defiance. There was nothing left for Milord to add. Miss Olivine had a smirk on her face she was jubilant. Always she had thought of Mr. Vincent as her best boy, now getting rid of any competition he would turn again to her for solace, it had all worked out with a satisfactory result.

"Come now Sara, it is time for us to leave."

Sara had not been allowed to say one thing in her defence, she was a Scullery Skivvy, and her opinion was as nothing.

Sara got as far as the kitchen then broke down into floods of tears, between sobs telling Rosa and Alice what had happened.

"Oh you poor dear, I could murder Miss Olivine, this will be all of her doing. Didn't you try to stand up for yourself Sara?" Sara replied,

"It was all over so quickly I had no time to say anything, I just wanted to get away from her as fast as I could I feel they have shamed me, I just want to tell you two there was no justice in what I was accused of. I was merely following what I had been told to do."

Rosa gave her a wise look saying,

"But you did get fond of Mr. Vincent didn't you? Why did you not realise you were just a grown up toy for him to play with?" Sara between sobs said,

"It wasn't like that, he was so genuine." The tears began to blob again.

"What is done is done, like Alice you have to learn to live with it dear."

Rosa tried to be kind, there was only her left to fall by the wayside.

Seeing the way the other two had landed flat on their face she decided to be very cautious.

Sara left with a month's wage in lieu of notice in her purse, with a heart so sad it felt it would drop with the weight of it to the floor, saying Goodbye to Alice and Rosa was not easy.

Arriving home Martha took one look at Sara and said,

"For goodness sake what is wrong?"

"Martha I have lost my job, they just dismissed me on the spot, I am so very unhappy."

"What was that about? Mr. Vincent I would think, Martha replied,"

"Yes of course, why did I think I could be on level terms with him, he was so nice, I was very flattered but didn't encourage any wrong doing between us. You must believe me Martha."

"Of course I believe you, I know you very well, it is not your style to give way to a man, I thought how happy you looked after all the trauma with Bill, and it is such a shame. Don't worry Sara, we'll find another job for you; in the meantime you have your extended wages to tide you over. Think of the times you will not have to suffer Miss Olivine, no more to scrub the dreaded kitchen floor."

Sara had to give a wee smile, Martha was right.

Sara had gone to be interviewed for a couple of jobs, but always the girls in front of her had more experience, and the wages were very poor, there were other girls there that would work for that kind of pay. So she never got a job. Then Martha had a thought,

"My cousin lives about two miles away, you wouldn't be able to come home weekdays, but weekends could be arranged off I am sure. I am making a pig's ear of this aren't I Sara? The thing is last time I saw them they were looking for a couple of new staff, they have stables, and the horses are prized and pristine. I think it would mean you being Jack of all trades but hey, there is a saying" variety is the spice of life". Would you like me to write to them? Sara replied"

"Yes I suppose so, to tell you the truth I am not enthusiastic about anything, I had only just begun to know Alice and Rosa, and of course Mr Vincent, just gelling in and I had just begun to feel part of what was going on, now I am back to square one, I can tell you it is not a nice feeling Martha."

"I will get the letter off tonight, the sooner you start the sooner you will feel better, for now don't worry."

"Thanks Martha, you are always on solid ground, would that I could be more like you."

Vincent had not been told of Sara's dismissal, the weather had been stormy and very dull so he hadn't had the occasion to send for her, thinking he would at the next best opportunity. He almost knocked Alice off her feet when coming from his room, she had been allotted Sara's job of seeing to the chambers and setting the fire to be lit later.

"Don't tell me I have done it again, he laughingly said thinking it was Sara."

"I am alright Sir I just managed to catch my balance, are you alright?

I don't fall easily, Alice is it? Where is Sara? This is her job I thought."

"It was Sir until she was dismissed a week ago."

"Dismissed what for?" He was very angry.

"Who dismissed her? Miss Olivine?"

"No Sir, well not really, I think Miss Olivine told your Mother and Father that things were going on between Sara and yourself. Then she was dismissed by them."

"What was going on?" Vincent kept repeating himself in a dilemma and not for the life of him could he make this information ring true."

He stormed up to see his Mother and Father. Bursting into the room he said with fury in his voice,

"What is all this about you getting rid of Sara? What had you found out as Alice put it? Why wasn't I informed?"

His face was blown and red, anger consumed him, and he felt like slapping his Mother and landing his Father a blow to put him to the floor.

"Sit down me boy, and calm down, it has been done for the best, you were getting attached to Sara so we were told, it couldn't be allowed to happen so we stepped in and put a stop to it."

"You are right, I was getting attached to Sara she is the sweetest girl I have ever met, what is more I shall search for her, she can't be far away, you will on this occasion not tell me what I can and can't do. I am a grown man, I will make my own decisions you better believe me there is no way you will win this one."

Vincent stormed out of the room the same anger in him, his Father said,

"My God, it is a good job we caught that in time, I have never seen him so angry, he will calm down and see that it was all for the best. I must say I thought he was going to deliver me a blow, too old for that to happen, him and me. They are as much trouble grown up as they were as children. At least their toys could be chosen with a loving eye for their safety, now their needs are beyond us, and the things they want are not bought, and could be dangerous."

Milady nodded in agreement, she was on strange ground and out of her depth. When boys become men they have their own needs, Mother can no longer kiss them better. She sighed with a huge shrug of her shoulders, tears stinging her eyes. Her Son Vincent raging at her and his Father, she didn't understand, she never would understand. Where did they lose each other? Did Vincent pay them so little regard? Sitting quietly now her hands folded on her lap. Of course she wanted the boys to be happy, but with a Kitchen Maid? That was an entirely different thing. He must look for someone of his own station she would in time be wanted to bear a Son to carry on the family name. A Kitchen girl could not be included in his selection, her heavy heart accompanied her sad face, where would this all end she wondered if Mother's love was now not enough, let them chose wisely, this was her silent prayer.

Vincent stormed off indignant at his parents intrusion, Sara had left where would he find her?
"I must find her she has become dear to me, tomorrow I will ask around, someone must surely know where she is living. The Ford isn't very big I bet they all know each other it won't be hard to track her down."

Yes tomorrow he would see Sara.

Chapter twenty-five

In the Quarry Yard positions were on the move, Martha had the reply back from her brother saying they could use one more pair of hands.

He wrote,

"I needn't see Sara, I know from what you have told me the kind of person she is. Tell her to be ready to start next Monday I will expect her, make sure Martha she has full instruction as to the position of this place we are not exactly on the main track."

Martha knew what he meant so she took Sara to one side and spread a piece of blank paper on the table.

"Now look Sara, you must get this right I am going to draw a little map for you, just so you take all the right turns, and their cottage is a bit off the main track."

They leaned over the table so that they could both see the map Martha was drawing.

"You are right Martha I would never have found it without instruction, is it a Farm?"

"No not that big, they keep a few horses in stables, a few chickens for the egg supply, a couple of pigs and a well tended field that grows produce for Market. You will find them *quite content and easy to get on with. I am sorry you can only come home at the weekend, rest assured I will take care of the Kids and their needs, I know Dick will help me if I get stuck, do you know Sara he has been a brick to me we have a lovely friendship going, I feel very at home in Dick's company."*

"I am pleased for you and Dick, I know he is easy to get on with I often thought had Bill been more like him things could have been very different. I can't change what has happened so I must get on with my life the best way I can. I must say I shall miss Rosa and Alice, and of course my time with Mr. Vincent. I am not sorry we had that lovely interlude I treasure the memory. I expect you think that is daft Martha?"

"No not at all, it is only a pity something more lasting hadn't come out of your friendship. He was the best you have had happen to you yet wasn't he?

Sara felt herself shiver, she remembered when they sat after the storm how Vincent had brushed her lips with his, how caring and thoughtful he was, no she would never forget him. Life goes on and the daily tasks cannot be ignored, it was something that never could have been, she reminded herself.

Monday morning came around soon enough, Sara dressed and waiting to say her farewell to Martha.

"Here I go Martha it will be good to get to know this couple that have offered me a place to work. I am glad they are your Kin I should know how I stand quite quickly, is your brother like you?"

"Yes he is he felt guilty when he left me to look after Ma and Pa. But at the time he had obligations and a wife to consider. I didn't put obstacles in his way it was better for him to find his own life and live it to the full. I still lived at home so the LOT fell easily into my lap. I don't regret it."

Kissing Martha on the cheek Sara must leave it was a long way to go to the Small Holding it was beyond the woods, it would take her the best part of the morning to get there.

Stopping to rest her weary legs Sara got out the sandwiches that Martha had given her in a basket and some home- made lemonade.

Sara was grateful, without realising it she was quite hungry. Sitting quietly, looking around at all the natural life in the shape of trees and wild flowers birds singing and flitting from branch to branch. She thought,

"I should feel lonely but strangely I don't, look how nature provides for all the wild

creatures, the bees collecting nectar, Ferns gracefully draped under the canopy of leaves, the earth providing them with all that they need, the sun filtering through to make shadows that seem to highlight the patches of wild flowers."

Sara didn't know the wild flowers names; they were just as pretty without a name. Her mind wandered to the flower book that Vincent had given her.

"When I go home at the weekend I will get that ready for next week I would like to have it with me. I could continue collecting; Maggie will surely know all the names."

This thought refreshed her she was ready again to step forward.

Sara wondered just what these next few weeks would bring. Thinking too of Vincent, admitting there was a warm place for him in her heart.

"Enough of that Sara" she whispered to herself.

Reaching the edge of the wood, she crossed a field, she had reached the cottage, and there was a twirl of smoke coming from the chimney. Getting to the door she could smell bread being baked, a very homely aroma. Lifting the big round knocker she banged it on the thick wooden door. A moment later the door was opened, and there stood Maggie. She was grey haired, pinned up with tendrils escaping from the white mop cap she had on to keep her hair out of the way while baking. They smiled at each other.

"Hello Maggie I am Sara, I think you know of me through Martha.

"Yes of course I do. Martha has given me a glowing report of you; I almost think I know you already come in dear. You find me baking but you won't mind that will you?"

Maggie picked up her apron and wiped her hands, they were covered with flour.

"Of course I don't mind, I will help as soon as I have put my clothes away"

Sara had already taken to Maggie, her generously rounded figure, her rosy cheeks, her willing hands. If her husband was of the same comfortable nature Sara considered herself lucky.

"Just put your things at the bottom of the stairs there's a dear. I will have the kettle boiling in no time. A cup of tea would be welcome eh?

Maggie busied herself tidying and brushing down the table top. Away went the flour sieve and the half bag of flour. The remainder of the baking tins went away. When all was clean on the table Maggie threw over a small *lace tablecloth, and a stand for the teapot. Cups and saucers, and small plates were chosen.*

"The milk is fresh dear I am assuming you take milk?"

Sara sat by the table in front of the fire, logs and flames leaping burnt in the black leaded grate, the welcoming flames dancing up the chimney.

"I will have to disturb you a minute Sara, must get the final batch of bread out of the oven."

Sara moved and the bread was fetched out golden brown. Maggie tapped the bottom of each loaf in an educated manner, she approved of it being cooked and ready to take out of the oven and so stood it on an elevated wire tray for it to cool.

"Will I have a room of my own Maggie?"

"Yes we have a spare room built on to the side of the Cottage. Joe emptied it of rubbish and put a lick of whitewash over it last week when we knew you would be arriving. It should be as good as you can expect. We added it a couple of years ago. It was quite easy to build same stone as the cottage as it is local. It could actually at a push make two rooms but one is what is needed so you have space I think you will like it."

"I am sure I will, it sounds quite special."

"You will be spending a lot of the time with me, to get the hang of things you see. I hope you take to this place Sara it isn't Grand like your last place."

"Grand oh not for me, I worked in the Kitchen, and the housekeeper Miss Olivine was not far from being cruel. The kitchen floor had to be scrubbed that was my first job in the morning, I hated it. The only time I enjoyed being there was when Mr Vincent took me into the garden. He treated me like a true friend. It was that though his Mother didn't like,

Milord and Milady finished me, gave me very little pay in lieu and packed me off without even saying goodbye to Mr Vincent. It was a shock Maggie I have to put it behind me. I only hope Mr Vincent doesn't get the sharp end of their tongues. I couldn't say anything in my own defence for one thing they didn't give me chance. Nothing was wrong in the friendship I had with Mr Vincent. It is over now I only hope I can be what you want me to be."

"Of course you will Sara, life has its twists and turns you will be good with us. Joe should be in soon when you have met him you will feel safe. The only other help we *have is a young man that just comes when the work has piled up and Joe needs a hand. It is teatime now what would you like for tea Sara?"*

"I don't mind I will have what you are having."

"Poached eggs on toast then eh? Here's Joe now. Had a good day my love?"

Joe was very much like Martha and Sara felt instantly at home with him. He had Martha's kind eyes and ready smile, he greeted her.

"So here we are then I have heard a lot about you from our Martha, come to stay for a while then? We shall be pleased to have your company. Helping Maggie is just what she needs, and I can surely give you some cultivating jobs to do. Do you fancy that?"

"I shall do my best in anything you ask of me, although I don't know much about gardening or planting, I can learn though."

"Well said mi' dear, I can see we will get along together, are you happy Maggie?"

"You know me Joe, I will teach Sara a few things too."

They all laughed while the table was set for the poached eggs on toast.

Sara noticed that Maggie had put a cake tin on the table, she wanted to ask what sort of cake was in it but she daren't, not wanting to seem too pushy on her first day.

Now the lid was lifted on the cake to find a raspberry sponge with butter cream. Sara was given a generous slice which she thoroughly enjoyed.

The meal was finished and Sara washed up, with Maggie looking at Joe with a satisfied grin, it was the first time in a very long time the washing up was done by anyone but herself.

Chapter Twenty-six

In the bedroom that now was Sara's an oil lamp had been lit, Sara thought it was lovely. On her bed lay a flock mattress, the bed had wrought iron ends and an Eiderdown. Sheets were folded ready for her to use fresh, in the corner a wicker chair, well worn but still useful, a chest of drawers with a mirror balanced on top and a small dark oak cupboard. Opening the cupboard it smelled a little bit musty, Sara decided to leave it open a day or two before she put her folded clothes into it, soon it would dry the bit of damp that had got trapped inside it, she could line it with some paper and give it a second life. The drawers weren't so bad, just a dry dusty smell in there she would polish them with a good dry duster. She felt very strange in her new room, it was all very nice but she hadn't got Alice and Rosa to talk too, she was going to miss the chit chat of the girls. Sara thought,

"I wonder how Alice is with the baby coming, I would liked to have helped her in the situation, this has all been so sudden. Perhaps one weekend I can arrange to go and see them both. Although the risk of bumping into Mr Vincent is going to put me off. Perhaps Martha will invite them just for a cup of tea yes I am sure she will."

With this talk that she had entirely on her own it was time for bed, she made the bed up and enjoyed the fresh clean sheets that Maggie had so thoughtfully left her.

Sara was a little bewildered, although grateful. This was a room she could do as she alone wanted to do. Sharing had always been difficult, but she always had shared. Keeping her books for pressing flowers and having a special place to stand the candle so that she could watch it flicker on the ceiling. She could lie and remember the happy times with Vincent; although she could hardly say his name without wanting him.

"How silly I am to think a Scullery Maid could be the least bit of interest to Vincent. I was falling in love oh! Dearly Lord no, he could have broken my heart, and in fact that is why I feel so down. Maggie and Joe will occupy my time; there will be no time for tears. I will do my utmost to please them."

Getting up next morning, Sara settling in went into the Kitchen. The rain poured down the window panes, and splattered on the ledges, the heavy sky looked ominous.

"Well dear I would say Good morning but it isn't is it? Not good at all."

Joe came in wringing wet through, making puddles on the Kitchen floor.

"Eh Maggie, it is a wet one, can't do much outdoors today. Ross has been and we have seen to the animals. He has gone straight home, he is a good help with the heavy things. He knows when to stay and when to leave, I count that important. We don't have to pay him for hours of waiting. He gets the job done, and gets paid for the hours he has actually worked. His hands are occupied all the time he is here. Today is as dead as a Dodo as regards the field work, I shall go out and deliver the customer's sacks of potatoes, also trays of eggs, and then it will be one job less when the weekend comes. First though Maggie I will have a cup of tea and some toast, get something warm in my stomach eh?"

"We will join you Joe, Sara has just come in we'll sit together and shut out the rain. Sara and me can fill our time easily enough I can discover what you are good at Sara, and we will get to know each other, won't let a drop of rain put us down eh? They had their tea and toast. Joe got up to put on his Wellington Boots, a Tarpaulin Coat, and a Sou'wester hat.

"You look as though you are well equipped Joe" Maggie said.

"Yes I am throwing a tarpaulin on the old

gels back as well; he was referring to his horse. I know you don't think it is worth it turning out on a day such as this, but comes weekend I will be glad it is a job less to do. Don't worry, I shall be home by teatime, I shan't prolong the trip."

He left leaving Maggie and Sara to sort out just what they could do on this damp day.

"Sara can you make pastry dear?"

"I haven't done much lately, but yes I know how to do it."

"Right then I will get some meat on to cook slowly; we'll have a meat pie this evening. Joe will want a good warming meal after being in the rain all day. I would have tried to stop him but he knows best, he is always confidant in his intentions, it is one of his good points, you always know where you stand with Joe. It was one of the attractions that took him to the altar."

"Have you been married long Maggie?

"For 45yrs dear and no children, we just took it for granted after a while that Children were not going to be part of our union. We have jogged along together very happily; of course we know each other without question. He can tell what is in my mind before I know myself ha ha. Have you got a beau Sara?"

"No I am alone now, Martha helped me when

Bill died, she is more of a Mother to my children than I am, and she certainly cares for the Kids very well. We have talked about her adopting them. The Kids love her to bits. Since Bill died I have had no time, I must earn money, at one stage I thought we would all land up in the Workhouse, this way we can stay afloat, I am very grateful to Martha. I have just thought you can't have children and Martha hasn't had any, so you can't even spoil nieces or nephews, it is very odd."

Sara didn't want to pursue that Avenue any longer, she might say something out of place, and she certainly did not want to offend Maggie or Joe. Best to let sleeping dogs lie, and leave well alone. She would do that which she had come to do and hold her peace.

In Danbury Hall the balloon had gone up. Vincent was appalled, his Mother and Father had no right to dismiss Sara. As soon as he knew Sara was not where he expected her to be he went to the Kitchen to see Rosa and Alice. He pulled no punches anger swallowed him up he demanded,

"Where is Sara? I know she has been dismissed, although it would seem I am the last one to be advised. You must tell me where to find her,"

"Don't rightly know Sir, so we can't tell you,"

"Being cautious are you, one of you must know, I am very angry indeed, dear girl what she must be thinking of me now. Damn nerve not even saying goodbye to me. Where is she I say I shall go to her, it will be your jobs at stake if you don't tell me?"

Fuming he turned on his heel and pounced out. Not trusting his temper to say any more. He loved Sara; she was the first girl he had really wanted, she had moved him to boiling point. Leaving, Vincent then went to find his Mother and Father; he would leave them in no doubt of his feelings.

Storming into the Library where his Mother and Father sat discussing new editions, his face in a red torment. They both looked up sharply at this unannounced intrusion.

"Why? That is what I need to know."

"Why? What Son"

They tried to keep their usual finesse.

"Why did you dismiss Sara?"

"Steady on Son, calm down, sit down and we will discuss what is bothering you."

"I don't want to sit down, and there is nothing to discuss, Sara and me were just getting to know each other. I shall find her, and if you do not accept that I love her, I

shall find a place to live with Sara, you will not stop me." Father looked stern saying,

"She is but a commoner dear boy, you will meet one of the upper class soon and Sara will be forgotten. You are the Heir to Danbury Hall, and must produce in your turn a Son to take on the title. You are aware of the fact."

"If I can't have Sara I don't want anyone. Your desires will not be met with. I won't be chained down to Danbury Hall, unless it includes Sara. She could give me a Son, my future and yours would be decided. How could you have the audacity to dismiss her without reason is beyond me? What she must think of me now is beyond my comprehension. Thanks to both of you I am in despair."

Vincent heavily sat down, his head in his hands, Mother and Father exchanged a knowing look. Had they won this battle? Certainly they had to call a truce, perhaps time would solve things for them all, and time does heal. They had no idea what they would do next. Vincent's outrage had floored them, he was after all their dearest Son, and it was far from what they wanted. Who was going to make the next move? Someone had to step down. It was unthinkable to go along with

Vincent's intentions, but their Son was adamant, and very unhappy.

Vincent got up as briskly as he had sat down saying,

"I can't stay in this room with you a moment longer, I have said all I need to say. I am fervent in my quest. My search for Sara will begin, as soon as this infernal rain goes over I shall saddle my horse Bella she will be my trusty friend. First though I shall go back to Rosa and Alice to ask again of anything that might give me an idea of Sara's whereabouts. You must have an address from the interview that took place between you?"

"The only address she gave us was....a Cottage in the Ford. We didn't ask further as she was only going to be a Scullery maid."

"I shall ride then to the Ford and find someone who knows her. I mean all that I have said, I shall follow my heart. I am sorry we do not see eye to eye there is no other path for me to take. I shall renounce my right to be your heir. Richard can have the title. Now you know just how I feel I must go. I take my leave of you Mother and Father."

He stormed out of the door not giving his parents any chance to reply.

It was a couple of days before Vincent could saddle his horse Bella, a handsome Filly dapple grey, with a lovely mane that was brushed till it shone. A swish of a tail too, she had many hours of grooming in her stable, the evidence of this being apparent. Vincent liked to ride in the grounds of Danbury, he knew his mount very well, and they made a dignified pair. Vincent would fondle and pat Bella, the large eyes of the horse showing she was comfortable with her master.

"Come on Bella dear friend you have to help me find my love. I do not like taking you on to the Cobblestone roads but I must. I will look after you Bella we have this job to do together."

Vincent patted her, and felt the horse understood all he was saying. They trotted off with determination and care.

Chapter Twenty-seven

It wasn't long before Sara had settled in Maggie and Joe being good to her. She did various jobs inside and outside the Cottage. At weekend getting home to Martha was a distance to walk, in fine weather it was just about doable, but when the clouds turned the ground to snow and ice, and the fogs came down Sara was pretty sure she wouldn't make it. Back in the Quarry Yard she spoke to Martha about this.

"I won't be able to see much of you in the Winter Martha are you going to be able to cope?

"Don't you worry Sara the family is growing up so fast and taking on responsibility? They don't bother me much I see that they have at least one good meal a day. The elder boys have jobs of a sort, earning a few pence for their pockets."

"Martha you are much more of a Mother than me, I know it is awful but I sometimes forget the children, I see so little of them. I have thought for a long time you should go a step more and legally adopt them. Am I going a step too far?"

"No Sara, I have thought on the same lines more than once myself, I know exactly what you mean. The thing is Sara I would have to

consult Dick. I ask him about most things these days. He helps a lot with the elder boys too, they get on well together. We'll have to see won't we, as regards coming in the winter, well I had worked that one out for myself.

If you slipped or fell during the journey over here it wouldn't be good for any of us so you must judge for yourself. I will know how things stand when I see what the weather is doing. We will take things in our stride, spring will come then you can come again.

"You are a brick Martha, I am glad you have found Dick, you deserve to be happy."

"By the way I have heard in the Ford there is someone asking about for a Sara, the second name I didn't recognise, it isn't you is it?"

"Well if it is Martha they certainly mustn't find me, it might be from the Hall. I have bitterly regretted not telling them I had been married and that I have children, the only important thing at the time was getting the job. I thought the facts were never going to be bothered about, now I am in a bit of a mess, fancy if it is Vincent looking for me, oh dear God it would be what I wanted in my wildest dream, but he doesn't know anything about me so it is a good job he won't find my whereabouts."

"If it is Vincent he must think something about you Sara, but if you don't want to be found I will steer him out of your way. Living in the Quarry Yard we are tucked away, bet he won't know of these Cottages."

Sara sighed, not wanting him to find her was not the way she really wanted it. That is if it was Vincent?

Rosa was playing a case of avoidance with Richard, yes she went whenever he sent for her but she had her own safety in mind more than most. Alice was a good reminder of how simply things could happen she was still looking for her lost love. As if Miss Olivine could read her thoughts she came striding into the kitchen she said,

"Mr Richard wants to see you at 2pm Rosa, make sure you are presentable girl."

Miss Olivine had the knack of picking out the weak spots; the girls cringed under the picture that was present in Miss Olivine's mind of the low status of the scullery maids. It was all a person could do to muster a little self pride, the situation was almost intolerable but life must go on, so with a shrug of the shoulders, she was never disobeyed. At 2pm as she was duty bound Rosa prepared to see Richard. Going to the medicine chest before she took leave of Alice she put something into *her pocket. Standing outside Richards study door she tapped the door,*

"Come in my dear, nice to see you, prompt too"

The day although September was dismal with a chill in the air unmistakably saying summer was over.

"I have lit the fire Rosa it will take the damp out of the air and make us more comfortable."

"Thank you Sir, you are right the room does want airing. It is always the same even though we have had a pleasant summer the damp in the bones of the Hall always comes to the fore this time of year. Richard replied,

"Now tell me any news I might have missed?"

"I think you know the news better than me Sir,"

"No indeed I do not; I have never felt so isolated in my life."

"Did you know Sara has been dismissed?"

"No I didn't, what is that all about."

"Your Mother and Father found out about Mr Vincent inviting Sara out into the garden, they couldn't allow such familiarity. Dear Sara she had done nothing to be ashamed of, we miss her."

"Oh I said I wanted news but that is

depressing news, how about a round of Whist?"

The cards were brought out and dealt.

After half hour Richard was again looking for something new.

"Come and sit over here Rosa beside me."

Rosa went, sitting side by side Richard who was much taller than Rosa looked down on her face.

"Rosa you are indeed a beautiful woman, your eyes your skin, to put you to work in the Kitchen is utter waste. If you say the right words I can make you my personal Maid how would that suit you?"

"I would have to decline Sir, I am quite happy in the scullery, I have Alice to talk to we get along well,"

Rosa was thinking just what this offer involved and she couldn't leave Alice and her coming baby alone. Time was moving on and although Alice carried well not showing yet for anyone to recognise her being with child. It was fact though, and soon it would have to be dealt with.

"You must think of yourself and your own needs Rosa, Alice is big enough to look after herself, or don't you think so?"

"She isn't very inclined to do that Mr. Richard she needs me to talk through *anything that is worrying her."*

"Well alright then, we will have to make do with the times I am allowed to send for you."

His arm slid around her shoulders, she glanced it away saying she wasn't comfortable,"

"What is the matter with you God damn it! Are you repulsed by me?"

"Not at all Sir, I was just thinking the time has gone so quickly and I don't want Miss Olivine to come looking for me." Richard said,

"Damn the woman, she gets too big for her boots, I will have to keep a check on her she thinks she can rule the roost, and I will open her eyes for her."

"Please Sir I don't want any trouble, it would be better if I left now, I have been here for some time and I still have jobs to finish downstairs."

"Go then get your duties done, it doesn't matter about me."

He sounded child like, but underneath was the man who wanted at this moment more than he could get.

Rosa got up dipped a little courtesy and went, breathing a huge sigh of relief. She still had not used the item from the medicine cabinet, it remained in her pocket.

Getting back to Alice she was flushed Alice noticed and asked,

"Are you alright Rosa? You look as though you could do with a cup of tea, sit down I will put the kettle on. He hasn't abused you has he?"

"No I am just worried because I know he wanted to. Men! They think they can always have their own way, not caring who they hurt; an inbuilt system rings in their brain and requires them to spread their seed of mankind. The woman shoulders all the aftermath it just isn't fair."

"I too Rosa am looking for just such a man but he will have red gold hair, and he will return the love I have for him."

"You are nuts do you know that? He has forgotten you exist it is just typical of the picture I have just painted, they are all alike. Look at yourself Alice and the responsibility you carry, while he is as free as a bird. Let's get off this subject you are hurting enough without me pouring salt in the wound. Mr Richard is going to be very disappointed if he thinks I am going to travel down that road."

"Come on Rosa don't be angry anymore, soon it will be teatime that will calm us down a bit."

"Did cook say what is for tea? It better be

something I can grit my teeth on to get rid of this venom."

Chapter Twenty eight

The days moved on, Alice and Rosa talked about Sara, they missed her. A Sisterly alliance between them that had formed while working together still bonded them. Knowing where Martha lived (of course they hadn't told Mr Vincent) they began to make plans to go and see Sara one weekend. Dick could give them a lift one way and they could walk back. It would have to be Sunday as that was their day off. They would arrange with Dick so that his call at Danbury would be Sunday just for one week. Sara would also have to be informed so that she would also have the same time off and go to Martha's. Plotting this little plan had taken some of the drudge out of their daily work, finding a smile instead of a frown.

Cook remarked about Alice putting on weight, but had left it at that and didn't pursue the matter although there were a few anxious moments. There was Christmas to get through, and the early spring months, something would have to change. Alice would have to prepare for the little one who was kicking her insides like mad, letting Alice know this was really and truly happening. Rosa and Alice in their free time were listing names, not knowing girl or boy. They found it *exciting. Rosa putting her hand flat on to Alice's stomach would feel the movement and the kick. Sometimes they could even watch the undulating movement that involved the whole stomach in a rolling motion. Rosa was going to be Auntie Rosa, she was very proud of it too. There was still a way to go to get to see this baby being born.*

The days went passively by, the nights were drawing in and a chill in the air was apparent. Before it got really cold they planned to see Sara at the cottage in the Quarry Yard. The following Sunday it would be the end of October so that was the day they chose. Sara told Maggie of their plans, Maggie said,

"I hope then it is a fine day, the trees are all in their autumn shades, it will be well worth the walk through the woods, the colour is breath taking at the moment."

It will indeed be a pleasant walk if the sun is out but even if it rains I must go, I really want to see Alice and Rosa, we became good friends at the Hall I miss them."

"Yes you are bound to miss them I suppose they miss you too. It is good of Martha to invite them to the cottage to see you. I know Martha will give them a Sunday dinner they will look forward to that. I bet they don't get

many meals home cooked."

Maggie busied herself around the kitchen then asked Sara to take a pack of sandwiches to Joe who was working alongside Josh in the stable. Sara put on her coat and went.

"Maggie sent these Joe she says there is enough to offer Josh a couple if he would like them."

"There you are Josh, being spoilt again I see."

Joe gave Josh a good humoured smile, handing him two cheese sandwiches.

"You must thank Maggie for me Joe she has a heart of gold."

Joe looking at Sara said,

"I haven't introduced you to Josh have I Sara?" Sara said,

"No I have seen him come and go but we haven't spoken have we Josh?" He replied,

"I feel I know you Sara from Joe talking about you, it is nice to meet you face to face, pleased to meet you Sara."

"You too Josh the only time I have spotted you is by your head bobbing in and out of the sheds. I knew there must be a handsome face underneath that balaclava hat."

"Yes I wear this hat most of my working day, my Mother knitted it for me I am very glad to have a hat that protects me from the early

morning cold. It is a time of day that even if it turns warm later is still a little on the cold side usually worthy of wearing this hat it can be very perky at dawn I would be lost without it. Do you know my nose and my mouth is the only parts that it leaves uncovered, my nose gets so cold it goes quite red and feels like a block of ice ready to drop off."

They all laughed saying his Mother would have to knit him another one that covered his nose, just leaving his lips showing. He jokingly replied,

"I have to have my mouth free to get some grub down me; it is work that builds up the appetite. I shall now have my cheese sandwiches which I am fully ready for." Joe smiled and replied,

"It is only a couple of hours ago since you devoured your breakfast pack from home I don't know where you put it all there isn't an ounce of fat on you Josh."

"I work it off Joe. I am fast and furious when I want to be, got to get the job done. There is none but you that know it is a fact, I need my energy food."

"I am off now, Sara said, see you again sometime Josh."

She walked away back towards the Cottage to find as she entered the door a pungent delicious, aroma. Maggie had jars and pots on the table ready to receive the Blackberry jam she was making.

"That smells lovely Maggie, a true country tang; it has made my mouth water."

"Well there is seed bread in the oven it is just coming to that beautiful glossy brown that you so like. I thought you would be back to help me make it. What took you so long taking the sandwiches?"

"Sorry Maggie to tell you the truth I was introduced to Josh and we talked for a while, if I had known you needed me I wouldn't have stayed so long."

"Don't worry Sara it is of no matter, you can help me fill and label these jars, this is nearly ready. Maggie stirred the jam as it cooked her experienced eye knew when it was setting quality. I want it to stand for a little while then we will jar it up. If the jam is boiling it can be the cause of a bad burn, it sticks to the skin, I know from experience. Come on fill the kettle we will have time for a cup of tea while the jam cools. I just have to test the setting."

Maggie took a little of the jam in one spoon and put it into a second cold spoon. She put her little finger into the jam on the spoon to taste the result. The smile on her face made

Sara smile, such a satisfied Maggie, her cheeks glowing a rosy red a true artist in the culinary profession. The Kitchen was full of her morning's work fit for a Queen Sara thought.

Maggie was satisfied with her life her cooking and her Joe. Simple and right, there was nothing else she wanted.

Sunday had arrived and Sara was leaving to go and see Martha and her friends from the Hall. The day was quiet with very little breeze, the dappled sunlight playing in and out with the trees, the autumn browns and gold, falling the leaves slow and gentle so Sara could see individual ones fall to the mossy ground. Sara's trip was proving pleasant. In a wicker basket she had several jars of jam, homemade pickle, and a freshly baked Cottage loaf. While packing the basket Maggie had said,

"Just a few tempting treats for Martha and Dick I don't think she has a lot of time for extra home baking. The family meals are more than enough to get on with. I won't put too much in Sara I don't want to make the basket too heavy to carry."

"Don't mind me Maggie put in what you like. I shall be only too pleased to take Martha some of your delights."

"Just one more jar then, I know Martha has a weakness for Piccalilli. There you go then." She covered the basket in a red gingham tea towel. Sara thought it looked lovely it would be a nice surprise for Martha. At the last minute Maggie had added a green jar of salted kidney beans, for the family to have with their Christmas dinner, and a bottle of gooseberry wine to toast the Christmas day. The basket was full to overflowing!

As Sara picked her way through the trees a feeling of pleasure came over her, such a contrast from the early days of married life with Bill. She thought of the coal miners and the coal pits which had given them such a meagre existence it was now a million miles away. It was as though it had happened to somebody else. She quickly dismissed these recollections.

Today she would see Martha, Rosa and Alice telling them of the kind of position she had filled, and of Maggie Joe, and Josh her new friend. It was only when she thought of Vincent did she feel sad. Love was such a fickle thing her heart ached too readily, but her heart did ache she could not deny it. How silly could it be, a Maid falling for the Master, a scullery Maid at that!

Arriving at her Cottage Martha greeted her,

"Happy to see you Sara, did you have a nice walk?"

"Yes it was lovely walking through the woods today, dappled sunlight and the leaves crackling beneath my feet, very dry and pleasant. Maggie sent you this basket Martha."

Placing the basket on the table Sara saw Martha's eyes light up.

"Oh what has she sent me?"

Handling the jars one by one and looking at the labels Martha was well pleased saying,

"Very good of Maggie, I must send you back with a note of thanks. Look at this bottle of Gooseberry wine, Dick will like to share that with me. We are making Elderberry wine, but Dick says it will be after the winter before that is anyway near being ready to bottle. Then it will have to stand for a good while before it is ready to drink. He has a few bottles of an earlier brew it has a few years of maturity, so that is a Christmas wine too. It certainly will be a merry Christmas I have never tasted homemade wine. Dick speaks highly of it, and I am dying to try it."

Chapter twenty-nine

A tap came at the door, here was Rosa and Alice.

"Come in dear girls, let me take your coats and hats, isn't this exciting we can have a good girly chat, that is after dinner."

The girl's eyes lit up.

"Are you getting a dinner for us Martha?"

"Of course dears, I hope you have come with an appetite, I have roast pork in the oven to go with roast potatoes Brussels sprouts and carrots, apple pie and custard to follow. How will that suit you?"

Shrugging their coats off their shoulders, taking off hats and scarf they said,

"Appetite oh yes, it is very good of you to include us at your table, and the smell of it cooking would make anyone hungry. Rosa said,

"Alice is always hungry she says it is eating for two that makes the difference don't you Alice?" Alice replied,

"I should say so, I am very much looking forward to your roast pork Martha, Apple pie too my favourite."

Martha did the meal for them at 1pm. The rest of the family would be in at 5pm. It was nice to fetch out what was usually kept in the drawers for special occasions. A table cloth on, some half decent cutlery placed at proper intervals around the table, a pretty cruet set, a small silver server for the apple sauce to go with the pork. Martha was as proud as punch it was a long time since these items had been used. They had been part of her Ma's collection Martha had brought them with her when she closed her own home up, never thinking they would be used again. The meal was nothing short of a feast, they all enjoyed the food the happy banter and exchange of news that went around the table.

"Are you keeping well Alice? Martha said, about three or four months to go isn't it or longer?"

"The due date is in April, with the feel of it I don't think it will be that long, I can feel the movement and the kick in a very lively manner, so I think things are alright."

"That's good maybe one day you will find the baby's Father and be a proper family dear."

"I pray for that day Martha, I know he loves me, but when he left on Open Day I had no idea where to look for him. I shall not give up because I love him."

"That's the spirit Alice what will be will be, there is no use trying to cheat fate. Destiny I believe in that, you only have to cast an eye in my direction, look where destiny has led me. I take care of Sara's children, and I have met Dick, he approves of me what more can I say."

Sara looked across at Martha, after all this time of secrecy her friends now knew the Kids were Sara's brood. There was a very awkward moment, because no-one knew what to say. It wasn't a crime Sara having the family, but the knowledge of this had been a secret well kept and so shocked Rosa and Alice.

"Sorry I didn't confide in you girls Sara said, but I needed a job so badly. It would have meant the Workhouse for the Kids and me if things had gone badly. I have fought tooth and nail to prevent this. Martha has been wonderful about it all she is now more the Mother than ever I would have been she and Dick both are thinking of adoption, I shan't stand in their way."

The whole story of Sara and Bill was tumbling out, how Bill had abused her and used his strap, her black eyes and bruised skin it was a moment of telling the whole sordid story of Bill and his drunken ways, and finally his death. The two girls were astonished, it made Alice's problem look small by comparison. Soon they were all drinking tea and exchanging sympathies.

Rosa addressed Sara saying,

"Did you know Sara Mr. Vincent is looking for you? He had a big row with his Mother and Father over your dismissal he is a very unhappy man. Should we tell him where to contact you?" Sara looked dismayed saying,

"How could I face him and tell him all the things you have learned this afternoon? Never,

I have to keep out of his way please don't tell him where I am. Although my feelings for him are deep I may hurt him, he thinks I am single with no family, I am ashamed to say I have acted out a lie. How can I back track now?"

Rosa looked at Alice in that moment it was decided to keep all that they had learned still as a secret. Perhaps it wasn't the right thing to do but they couldn't forsake their friend, she needed them as much as they needed her. Martha was very apologetic toward Sara. She said,

"It just slipped off my tongue Sara I don't know what came over me. I am really sorry."

"It is alright Martha I knew the truth would come out one day, don't worry." Turning to Rosa Sara continued,

"What about you Rosa? Is your slate as clean as we think it is?" Rosa replied

"I was never going to tell anyone, I too am ashamed of part of my past." Sara asked,

"Is it all that bad Rosa, I have always thought you have spoken very little about when you lived at home?"

"That is because I don't want to remember those days."

Alice and Martha heard what Sara had said to Rosa, they gathered round once more to hear Rosa's story, Martha said,

"Well it looks like a day for confessing, do you want to tell us Rosa? It may ease your burden if you do. Of course we all swear to secrecy, what you say in this room stays in this room." Rosa began,

"It is a sad tale hardly believable now, but at the time there was no escape."

They all sat around the fire in the black lead grate while Rosa told her past.

"I must go back to my early teens, my Ma was a dominant woman, and my Pa had upped and gone many years before. He was always in a state owing to his drinking habits he didn't care where the money came from as long as he had whisky in the house. He was either in the pub, or drinking in the house then sleeping it off. I can see Ma now prodding him sharply with her finger telling the lazy lout to get up and go and find work,

of course he took no notice at all. Ma used to go out at night saying she had friends to meet. My sister and I never saw these friends, until I was fourteen, and my sister thirteen. It was then they started to come back to the house with her. Pa was still there then but it made no difference as he was always stupefied and didn't care a jot. I think just after that time Ma threw him out, he went to live elsewhere. None of us knew or cared what happened to him. This one particular night it all started, Ma came in with this rough looking man, he also being worse for drink I remember his words clearly he said to Ma,

"That's a nice looking girl you've got there, I would pay double to get her between the sheets.

"I saw my mother's eyes light up.

"Make it three times the cost and you can have her. She is a virgin you know, be well worth your money."

"I was terrified although I didn't know clearly what they were saying; it was the way the Man looked at me with his bloodshot eyes. Next thing I knew I was being hustled upstairs

Ma and this Man pushing and shoving me, again icy fingers of shear fear encased my mind and body. Ma got me into the bedroom the man just behind her. Ma told me to undress. I didn't know what was going to happen. I said to my Ma. I shouldn't be undressing with this Man present, I don't know where the response came from it wasn't natural to have the right words at my command. I was fighting. Ma came up to me and swiped me across the face threatening to throw me out into the gutter if I didn't obey her. With a sickly smile on her face she turned to the Man saying,

"Take no notice my dear this should prove to you that Rosa is very new to the game."

The man licked his lips and replied,

"I like em young with a bit of spirit it excites me even more, you go now I will master this one."

Ma turned and went despite my plea and my sobbing, I was alone and I knew I must do as this Man said he had a glassy eyed slobbering face. His stature overpowered me. He took hold of my hands and forced them down to hold his private parts, it reviled me, fleshy and slimy. I pulled away. Next thing I knew he had me on my back lowering his body over me. He was strong he slid down my skirts and knickers. Then I felt the pain of him inside me pushing and throbbing. I was fourteen I had never seen a man's private part before. I was absolutely shocked. I fought him like a trapped animal but to my dismay he had his own way with me. When I finally stood up after much poring and touching, slime ran down my legs, the filthy beast laid with his parts all hanging limp and a satisfied grin on his face. I wanted to get to the closet and scrub until my skin was raw, deep inside me I understood there was no amount of washing that would take away the shame. I heard Ma come in saying,

"Enjoyed that did you? Don't let the word get around and I will keep that one especially for you, how would that suit you my fine friend?" Rosa continued,

"Money was brought from his pocket and Ma was happy about it. I had no chance. My Ma used me in this way saying it was about time I earned my keep, for two years. Now I was growing up and my periods had begun. I fell with child with no knowledge of what love was about, and not knowing which of these vile men had planted his seed in me. Ma went mad saying,

"I told you what to do it is your own fault, now you must suffer the consequences. We will go and see a woman I know she will get rid of the brat, but it won't be easy for you,

and it will cost a pretty penny. You can make up for that by entertaining a few more Male guests." "I sobbed in utter despair. Why couldn't Ma be a little understanding? The money she had coming in from me and now my Sister was too important to her. I was livid! No word of consolation, no tender feeling to ease my burden. Love where was that? I was a money maker for my own Ma. I knew the baby had to go so I went along with the fearsome and painful episode that had to be. As soon as I stopped bleeding I was going to get away, then I would apply for any proper job I had heard of, and that is what brought me to the Scullery of Danbury Hall. I am keeping no contact with my Ma or my Sister. I never want to see them again. They must never know just where I am. We have things in common you and me Alice, and yes you too Sara, and that is why I made such a big fuss about your baby Alice, it brought it all back to me. At least you know who is your baby's Father and it was through an act of love the mite was conceived. So things might just be put right for you. There was no way I could enjoy the seed planted in me, I wanted to rip it out myself."

"My God Rosa, I don't know how you have lived so long without telling a soul"

Martha reached over to Rosa and put her arm around her. The warm comfort of Martha's bulky form went through to Rosa; tears of relief began to fall. Alice and Sara eyes wide at the sheer power that the story had released didn't say anything. What was there to be said?

Reaching for the kettle Martha said,

"I think we all need a cup of tea, I didn't think such Mothers existed, getting away was the best thing you could do my poor dear, I feel sorrow and anger. It is no wonder you wanted to keep up your friendship with Sara and Alice, you three have become a little family in your own right. Again Martha went around the table and dropped a kiss on Rosa's head.

"Come to me whenever you need to talk, count me in as a friend I know I haven't got much but what I have you are welcome to share."

Martha was truly taken aback by this confession.

Alice and Sara had thought Rosa was beyond reproach. Rosa all along had known just what the world was all about.

It had been an afternoon to remember, the four of them had a close bond of friendship. Life had taught each one of them a lesson.

Fact is sometimes stranger than fiction.

Soon enough it became time to leave, Alice and Rosa had been welcomed by Martha and felt better for their intimate talk. Promising Sara they would not disclose her whereabouts.

Putting their coats and outdoor clothing on and contemplating the long walk back to the Hall.

Dick called by, he said,

"I am glad you haven't already left I can give you a lift to the Tower it will be a leg up for you won't it? Otherwise you will be arriving back after dark, the nights are rolling in now, don't want you young Ladies out in the dark." Rosa replied,

"How good of you Dick, I suppose we may call you Dick?"

"Of course, let's be off right now while we can see the road. You will have to find something to hold on to, it is only a cart we are travelling in, a bumpy ride you know"

They arrived at the Hall very tired, the traumatic afternoon had drained them, Alice said,

"I am glad to be back Rosa yet still glad we went. The dinner was lovely and especially enjoyed. Telling your story made my blood run cold, although I feel I know you much

better now. It must have been agony for you."
Rosa replied,

"It was, being so young I didn't know where to go or who to turn to, I hadn't a penny to my name and no skill behind me. I had a fearsome hate of all men. This subsided when I got this job, as the job included getting along with Mr. Richard and Mr. Vincent. Just when they were on school vacations, of course they then were only boys and easy to get along with. I find now the company of Mr Richard puts me ill at ease the boy has become a man and I still hate all Men."

"Don't you think one day you will find the right Man and fall in love with him?"

"I can't see it Alice, I shall finish up a bitter old Spinster just like Miss Olivine."

Alice laughed; Rosa could never be like Miss Olivine her character was not formed that way, she was warm and loving.

Chapter Thirty

Martha and Dick were talking to each other about all three of the girls and the danger they had to accept not of their own doing, Dick saying,

"How a Mother could treat her own Daughter like that is beyond me. The Men want hanging, surely utter despair or drink must be how they get to that state. It certainly makes my blood boil to hear of such things. I know our sort haven't got much money but if we can't do a good turn it is best to leave the problem altogether. What a bitter and cold life eh? Let's end this conversation Martha it is making me feel guilty for my fellow Man that sort want taking off the face of the earth in my opinion, look at the way Bill treated Sara too, and if I was to judge them I would not be in control of the sentence I delivered." Martha replied,

"Rosa was ashen while she told us, in all this time we are the first people she has told, I tell you Dick we were so surprised, it left us speechless. I wanted to take the pain away for her, I know it isn't possible. I have told her if she needs me anytime I will be here for her to talk to." Dick took Martha's hand and said,

"Well Martha you can't say fairer than that my dear. It could mean a lot to Rosa, you *haven't condemned her eventually she will be glad you have listened. I really came to see you for a very different reason altogether. I was thinking of having a bonfire on the night of Halloween, all the neighbours would be welcome and their families, I thought just on the patch of waste ground past the Pig Sties. I don't figure on making it too much work or cost. We could put jacket potatoes into our ovens, and have sausage and stuffing batches, doing gravy from the Pork stock that would go well with the stuffing. The bottom half of the batch being dowsed into the gravy before the filling was put in. I have some benches and some old wooden crates; our friends could sit on. The nights are getting darker now, and it would give the Kids something to look forward to, what do you say Martha?"*

"It sounds like fun Dick, I could make and shape some white masks in cardboard and whitewash them, put a bit of elastic to hold them on they would make good Halloween Scares eh? I would make enough for the all the kids to get one each so no-one would be left out. What would we have to drink Dick?"

"I thought we could make a punch, there are plenty of Apple fallings we could juice, then I have a bottle of Elderberry wine to top it up,

the wine would give us a warmth from within but would not be so strong as to upset anyone, even the kids could have a small glass. They could all bring their own cups. If it was going well we could have a sing song. I know one friend who is good with the mouth organ and another who could bring his accordion."

"It already sounds exciting Martha exclaimed! We would have to pray for good weather. I will order the Moon to be out, and the Stars to shine. We will have a great night Dick.

"Do you know just what I am celebrating Martha?"

"No I don't, except it is Halloween."

"Listen carefully my dear."

Dick took her hand in his, smiling into her lovely open face.

"This is not just any night Martha, tonight I am asking you to marry me, No protests and I know all the if's and butt's, they make no difference to how I feel about you. Dear Martha you can have until the night of Halloween to give me your answer, and as we are having a party on the night of Halloween you will have to say yes."

Dick simply and lovingly kissed her lips, and left her dazed with a lot to think about.

Never imagining she could be married, who would want her? She could cook she gave this to herself as an asset, she could clean, and make bread, but Dick would want much more than that. To be his wife, and share the same bed to be his wife completely, could she do that? Sitting quietly after Dick had left and speaking softly to herself she said,

"This has come into my life without any persuasion or conscious effort; I can't let this chance slip through my fingers. Dick loves me although he hasn't said so in as many words, and yes I love Dick. Until now I haven't allowed myself the knowledge of my own love, I know that is because I was afraid of rejection. I have stopped short of this final emotion because I didn't dare to hope my love was returned. What about the Kids? Has he overlooked I have four juniors to look after?"

This reality tended to dull her emotion she was very near to tears, they had started to run down her nose and face without her noticing. Loving the Kids how could she ever part with them in favour of Dick? Speaking again quietly to herself she said,

"I must see Dick with the sole purpose of wanting to know how he would or wouldn't

want the Kids. It has to be thrashed out. Not until this is done will I be able to make my mind up. This is the deciding factor, another thing do I tell the Kids? I am in a dilemma, has it all come too late for Dick and me? I shall tell Sara perhaps she will help me sort it out, for tonight I must relax there is no rush and Dick would not want me worrying about it."

Martha was not going to jump into anything without much thought it was not in her nature.

She went and got her stone hot water bottle and filled it from the kettle on the hob, took a candle and a holder and lit it to take upstairs with her. There would be plenty to colour her dreams tonight. It was her turn to watch the Candle with its Flicker on the ceiling. Sleep would evade her while she roamed among her choices.

Vincent was still very down he had searched all over the immediate area, especially the Ford. Sara had disappeared into thin air. Mother and Father were in their element, while Vincent could not find Sara their Son could not do anything about it. They hoped it would all simmer down and be forgotten. Vincent was on safe ground just where they wanted him to be.

Vincent had questioned Miss Olivine,

"I still haven't found Sara Miss Olivine, are you sure she didn't leave any hint as to her next position?"

"I really didn't bother to ask Sir, she was dismissed and that was all I needed to know. It is perhaps for the best Sir. She is not one of your breeding, and I feel nothing good could come from your relationship with her. Take the advice of your Mother and Father and settle down. The Christmas festivities will soon be upon us, and there will be more than one pretty Lady attending that you can choose from."

Vincent's face contorted in anger.

"I do not want the choice of pretty girls; you are siding with my Mother and Father. It is a sad state of affairs when a chap can't choose his love. I shall find Sara, and when I do I shall tell her how precious she is to me. You or anyone else that tries to change my mind will be disappointed."

"Sir I was only telling you what I thought was for the best, I wouldn't like to see you hurt."

"Hurt! You positively don't know how I feel. I think you should go now Miss Olivine before I say something I shouldn't. If you truly want the best for me help me to find

Sara, other persuasion is lost on me. I have made up my mind and will not falter."

He waved his hand to dismiss her company. He needed to be on his own to decide his next move. The people around him had been no help at all he began to think there was a strategic plan hatched between them to stop him finding this girl he loved so much. They were making sure Sara could not be found what a mockery they were making of his love.

This was real he could not deny Sara was locked close within his heart. The pomp and display of surrounding decor in the Hall seemed very artificial; his love for Sara was pure.

Sharing his life with her so real Sara was the sanity he clung to, nothing would change that ever.

Below stairs Rosa and Alice were also talking. Alice saying,

"It came as quite a surprise knowing Sara had children and had her husband Bill until his untimely death, he had sounded a mean and miserable cuss didn't he?"

"Yes Alice I think that is why it tempted me to tell my past story. It would appear each one of us has been ill treated by Men, perhaps abused would describe it better."

No Rosa, my encounter was decided the minute I saw my Man, he was all that I desired

I didn't even question myself, it was "hook line and sinker" for me, so natural as though we had been destined for that meeting. I know what you are going to say, look at the mess it landed me in, the truth be known I do not think of it as a mess I really want this child, I am convinced I shall find this man that I love, I shall HIT you if you laugh!"

"I am not really laughing at you Alice, in fact I think the opposite I envy you with your baby and your love, and I have never come even close to that. All my dealings with men have been forced upon me, pleasure? Well I don't know a thing about that! I know this though our talk has brought us a lot closer together, we are bonded now." Alice said,

Mr. Vincent must think a lot of Sara, Cook says he is still questioning everyone as to her whereabouts. When we see her again I think we should ask her if it is time she was found." Rosa looked at Alice with a frown.

"You know what Sara said, we were not to tell Mr. Vincent anything."

I know Rosa but I am thinking of the future, I agree we must keep quiet about it at the moment."

Cook bustled in saying,

"Have you girls got nothing better to do? Get those idle hands occupied."

"Yes Cook we were just talking about where to start for the best."

With that they fetched out the cleaning cloths appropriate to what they would need, gave each other a wry smile and got on with their work.

Alice was thinking as she cleaned,

"Mr Vincent is in the same position as me both looking for the people we love."

Vincent couldn't talk to his Mother and Father without Sara coming into the conversation. This always flared up the anger as before. Vincent still wanted Sara and nothing would persuade him to any different line of thinking. He bounced around the rooms in the Hall.

Displaying his discontent he felt trapped by the position that he held. He spotted Alice coming from her recent duties.

"Have you any further news of Sara Alice?"

His voice was gentle he knew he would not get Alice to tell anything she might know by raising his voice.

"I am sorry Sir I don't know where she has gone it can't be local can it? One of us would have seen her by now."

"Yes you're right Alice; I must cast my net further afield and ask around all the neighbouring farms, thank- you have renewed my hopes. Please if you do see her tell her to get in touch with me."

He smiled, even a little hope was better than the blind search he had been on.

Alice scurried to the kitchen and told Rosa, Rosa said,

"You shouldn't have said anything Alice, Sara will be annoyed to say the least."

"Well I think it is silly if Mr Vincent wants to see her that badly it must be love, and if he genuinely loves Sara he will forgive her past and her children. Of course Milord and Milady will be furious, but what the heck! Sara is a good person her character is beyond reproach Mr Vincent would be hard put to find anyone that comes even close to Sara. I think too Sara loves him otherwise she would not care about hurting him. It all has to change surely?"

Sara was still visiting home at the weekend the October weather had been good. Martha wanted to talk to Sara about Dick she greeted her with a hug Martha said,

"I am glad you could come this week Sara there is something I have to discuss with you."

"Sounds important Martha shall we have dinner first then talk after?"

"Yes there will be no-one around to interrupt us then will there?"

Sara went over to the oven saying,

"What can I smell cooking you darlin genius of the kitchen?"

"It is some of Dick's pork, smells good doesn't it? Alice and Rosa loved it last week so I thought we would have it again." Sara said,

"They were well pleased Martha, they were pleased with the visit altogether. The talk and exchanging secrets did a power of good. There is not anything wrong you want to tell me about today is there Martha?"

"Nothing we can't sort out between us dear, so don't worry."

After dinner settling by the fire Martha told Sara about Dick's proposal of marriage.

"This is the big news I wanted to tell you Sara, Dick has asked me to marry him what do you think about that eh?"

It was true Sara was quite taken aback, she hadn't thought of Dick and Martha in that way.

Love blooming at such a late time in their lives had not occurred to her."

"Oh my goodness Martha that is news I

wasn't expecting, have you accepted?"

"I am thinking of it Sara I have till the 31st October to give him my answer."

Sara's mind went straight to the Kids that Martha looked after for her, she felt a dull pain in the bottom of her stomach. This could only mean more problems but she answered Martha brightly saying,

"Do you love him Martha?"

"Yes I do, I thought it was just a fondness I had for him never dreaming of marriage. I must admit though I am at my happiest when we are together and always sorry when he has to leave. At our age I think that is love! Now Sara I don't want you worrying yourself to death about me looking after the Kids, because if Dick doesn't want me "Lock stock and barrel" he won't have me at all. I do not intend letting you down. I feel sure Dick would have thought this over and won't be intending anything else. He gets on well with the kids, and he is reminded daily I have commitments. I am sure between us being two grown sensitive people we will work it out."

Sara felt so relieved she threw her arms around Martha saying,

"How wonderful of you both to consider my problems, I have to say my heart sank a little

when you told me, selfish of me Martha forgive me you deserve the best."

Sara hurried back to Maggie's she had Martha's news and couldn't wait to tell Maggie and Joe. She hurriedly took off her coat and boots and said,

"I have some real news for you today I can't wait to tell you."

"What's Martha been up to then?"

"It is Dick really, he has asked Martha to marry him."

Well I never! Martha to be married, Joe will be pleased he worries about Martha, I tell him there is no need but it is his way. I am sure I could help I must ask Martha just what I could do for her."

Just like Maggie as soon as she knew there was going to be an event there she was offering her help. Sara said,

"Hold on Maggie Martha hasn't said yes yet, but she is going to. Dick has given her until the 31ˢᵗ October to give him an answer. I am sure she would have answered him right away but there are the Kids to be considered. Martha is going to see that they are included in this marriage proposal, so kind and she has done that at her own cost because she says if Dick doesn't want the Kids he will not have her."

"I don't think for one minute that Dick would have not included the Kids, he loves them they get along so well. Here is Joe he will be surprised."

Joe came in and took off his outdoor attire, and then without more ado Maggie told him just what Sara had told her. Joe said,

"That is the best news I could get, Martha needs a man about the house I have been telling her so for years. I like Dick no airs and graces there I am thinking, good and solid salt of the earth. Well Maggie get the tea poured let us toast my Sister even if it is only with tea."

They all smiled, there was good in this news for them all. Sara said,

"After they have discussed their plans and Martha has said yes, there is a lot we can do. Looks like you will have to make a few extra things that will keep in case Martha needs your help with food Maggie."

"I don't mind that Sara, I will offer to make a Wedding Cake if that is what she would want, I have to be sure of her decision before it is full steam ahead, mind you we could always eat the excess should there be any."

Chapter Thirty-one

Sara being back with Maggie and Joe, this time of year there were many items to prepare in readiness for the Christmas season. Now they had Martha's Wedding to consider as well. There was not going to be many dull moments in Maggie's Kitchen. Sara was learning beside Maggie who was a very good teacher. They had twelve Turkeys ordered, many eggs to deliver, Christmas cakes to bake, Wedding cake to bake, and plum puddings to boil.

Never were they at a loss for something to do. Maggie wanted to get the pickling done, it was best for flavour if they were in their jars a short while before eating, onions, red cabbage, mixed pickle, and Piccalilli. Making sure she had the spices and turmeric in the cupboard. Joe would be selling these on his weekly rounds to his regular customers apart from their own needs. He was very popular Maggie and Joe made enough money to live on with supply to the regular potato and egg customers, plus the extra items bought for the Christmas season money was saved for use all year round. Maggie saved the overflow of Christmas cash this was carefully taken to the bank to use it as it became needed, their needs were very little and they didn't need a *purse full of money to be happy. Of course the work involved meant all of them pulling their weight. Each day was consumed with effort and yes the passion it brought. Although Sara had worked in the Hall Scullery, Cook never let the Skivvy maid see or help in what she was doing, keeping her secrets of the kitchen to herself. It was so different beside Maggie Sara was picking up a few tricks and was eager to try her hand at anything shown to her. It made her feel important, and shared the pride when the end result was fetched out of the oven on to the kitchen table. The fruit they had boiled the week before to make jam was now on top of the dresser, a lovely presentation all labelled with grease proof paper frilled around the top.*

The pickles had the same deserved favour. Very tempting they looked, Joe and Josh remarked at the colour display on the shelves. Apple and Blackberry, Victoria plum, Gooseberry, Red currant jelly and Strawberry jam, all grown in their own garden on the patch outside the back door. Kidney beans were there too salted down for the big day, of course being Christmas day. Because Joe had grown all the fruit and vegetables the flavour was delicious. Joe's customers were well looked after, as were the meals that Maggie turned out daily. Joe also grew magnificent Onions to hang and dry, these would be laid out to dry before stringing them up and placing them on a hook in the Kitchen. Sara threw herself into doing any of the work, it was enjoyable. Although her mind was occupied there were still moments that went back and she remembered what Rosa had told them. Poor Rosa, and poor Alice indeed with her baby coming, how could she possibly help them? Her work took all the time she had. What on earth could she do anyway? Her own conundrums were enough.

Maggie interrupted her line of thought saying,

"We will make the Christmas pudding tomorrow Sara, today I have had enough even my feet hurt and I have only stood in this Kitchen."

"Look at the results though Maggie Sara replied, I know it has took you a week or two but you have supplies to last all winter, besides some to sell you have a very productive life Maggie. I am half your age and I too am tired. Sit down in your cosy chair by the fire, I will do the rest of the tidying up and make a nice pot of tea."

"That would be lovely Sara I really

appreciate your help, I know we pay you but you are always ready to do that extra bit that makes all the difference."

Maggie sat down thinking it was good to rest her weary back, it had started to rain outside the sound of it hitting the window panes funnily enough made the Kitchen more of a haven.

Peace and tranquillity settled around them, the firelight played with the shadows and danced on the ceiling. Both Maggie and Sara were loath to light the paraffin lamp, the dusk with the rain tangible, the kettle singing on the hob ready to make tea, warmth and devotion in the kitchen was not to be disturbed. Joe would not be in for another half hour, all was well.

At breakfast next day Maggie said to Sara, "Joe and I are going into the town next weekend, Joe sees his cousin and I look around the shops. Would you like to join us Sara?"

"That would be lovely Maggie, I expect the shops will have colourful displays in their windows, perhaps we could go into one of those posh tea shops. There are lots of things I would like to window shop for, maybe get a small Christmas gift for Alice and Rosa, I am so excited."

"Well I thought I could get a small wedding present for Martha and Dick, what do you think they would like?"

"Let's go with an open mind Maggie maybe then we will spot just the right thing. I will be counting the days now, thank you so much for asking me. Joe popped his head around the door saying,

"I am off now Maggie it is a nice dry day should get done well into the allotted time so I won't be late for tea."

"That's good Joe it is beginning to get cold when the sun drops so early, by the way I have asked Sara to come with us at the weekend."

"You will be very welcome Sara it will give us all a break from routine."

With that he closed the door and went on his way.

Although the weekend seemed far away it was all too soon upon them.

Looking around to make sure all was safe to leave, trying to do this in quick time as they wanted to get off on their trip to town.

"Ready then Joe called, got your money? You won't be any good without it; you will have an eye opener as to the prices these town people charge. We don't often entertain the idea of town buying, now and again though it

doesn't hurt."

The front bench seat of the cart gave them all a position to sit.

"Come on old girl Joe said giving the reigns a short pull. Take us to town."

All of them smiling, the morning sunshine was bright the day clear.

"Just right" Maggie said for a good sort around,"

Even the horse seemed to gallop sprightly along, as if he knew this was a special day.

Arriving at the Market place they jumped down and tidied hair and clothes, they didn't want to look like ragamuffins. Even Joe pulled his coat down at the back and straightened his cap, he said,

"Now I will go my way you go yours, we will meet here where I have tethered the horse, about four o'clock do you? I will give my horse a drink before I leave. Off with you then time goes all too quick when you are after bargains.

Maggie looked at Sara,

"We are to be let off the leash Sara, come on let's make the most of it."

The town was a good walk around and on this day the market with numerous stalls were open, there were cries from the sales people,

"Three for a tanner you good people, come

and get your bargains before they are all gone."

There was a man doing tricks with hoops, and another man fire eating, it was all very entertaining, Sara said,

"Do have to throw a ha'penny into the hat for them Maggie?"

"You must please yourself Sara, but you might want that ha'penny before the day is through so think on."

Going into the shopping area looking at the items for sale in the windows was almost confusing; Maggie and Sara were used to quiet, without the hustle and bustle.

"I am going to buy Martha and Dick a Copper Kettle said Maggie, She can use it practically or she can shine it up and have it as decoration, I think Martha would like that, there haven't been many things that Martha has had that could be counted as special items. Yes that is what we will look for."

"I am going to buy them a teapot, china if they are not too expensive, the time when Alice and Rosa came to see Martha and me, I noticed the spout of the teapot was slightly chipped and was getting tea stained. Martha remarked that it had seen better days. That it had gone by its useful life she apologised for it, so I know she would be happy to have a new one, and Dick will be sharing many cups of tea from it. Let's look for those two things we won't get buying that which we do not want then will we? We will concentrate and decide together. Try to get the best bargain, I am sure with all that is going on, it would not be hard to get distracted." One more thing though, I need to get a small gift for Rosa and Alice for Christmas.

Chapter Thirty-two

Martha had talked to Dick and as she thought Dick would fondly look after the Kids beside her. They had been talking about the Wine they were making and having a look at the brew.

"Does it still want stirring, Martha asked."

"No not now we must leave it to settle so that the remaining bits drop down to the bottom of the Copper, I have finished feeding it now, and I shan't be putting any more fire under it, the colder it is now the better it will settle."

"I am ever so proud that I have done it with you Dick, can't wait to try it."

"Now you know very well what I said, it must stand and clear for several months, and even then it is not really ready. Now a couple of years ahead we might have some very good wine, which is as long as it takes to mature properly."

"We won't be drinking it at our Wedding then Dick?"

"No but I told a white lie I have more than several bottles from my last brew, in fact I have enough for our Wedding, we are only having a small affair aren't we?"

"I would like it better that way Dick, perhaps we could get the Church at the top of the hill

booked so that it would be a proper Church Wedding, Guests? Well I think Maggie and Joe Sara and her family and I would like to ask Alice and Rosa, they don't get much fun in their dull lives it would maybe cheer them a little. That would be seven of us and the Kids we could come back here to celebrate no need to look for cost. I am sure Maggie will help with the spread." Dick replied,

"That is one of the things I like about you Martha, straight forward I know exactly where I am with you. You are the love I have been waiting for all my life."

"How lovely to hear those words Dick, I never thought of you as romantic but you know how to turn a phrase when need be."

Martha leaned over and kissed Dick's cheek. How fortunate was she to have found such a kind and loving man, age didn't seem to come into it they were as much in love as a couple of youngsters, Martha thought she wouldn't be able to give herself to any man, Dick was not any man, he was her future husband and she would give herself gladly. Dick broke the silence that had descended on them in the past few moments saying,

"Martha I have been leading up to this all night now we are to be man and wife I would like you to wear my ring."

"Yes Dick that would mean a great deal to me, but I don't want you to spend your hard earned cash on a ring dear."

"That is why I have hesitated, I have this ring."

Dick brought out a beautiful three stoned diamond ring boxed, he had opened the lid very carefully and there it was in all its glory.

"Dick what a lovely ring,"

"It was my mother's ring, and I loved my mother, now I want you to wear it simply because I love you."

The ring was gently with reverence taken out of the box and tried on Martha's wedding band finger it fitted perfectly. Martha couldn't believe it and could not take her eyes of the ring. Diamonds for her being kept all these years by Dick, tears welled in her eyes she looked at Dick saying,

"In my wildest dreams I never thought of me owning a diamond ring. Forgive me if I keep looking at it I will treasure it all the days of my life. I will try to be worthy of wearing it, I think as it was your Mothers before me it has twice the love and value. A mere thank you doesn't seem adequate, I will show you as we go through our life together just what this means."

Dick could hardly answer her he too had a

lump in his throat, but he knew without a doubt in his mind this was right for both of them.

Chapter Thirty-three

Martha was anxious to speak to Sara about the wedding and ensure her that all was well about the Kids there would be no alteration in the way they all lived. It was the Wedding Dress that needed to be discussed. The weekend came quick enough so Sara was at home again.

They had the customary meal between them first, and then talking over a cup of tea Martha took the plunge and said,

"I have something to tell you Sara dear,"

"What have you been up to now Martha? I have noticed that look in your eye."

"Well you know all about Dick and me but you haven't seen the ring he has given me."

With that she went over to the dresser draw and pulled out a box.

"Look Sara, isn't it just beautiful?"

Sara took the box from Martha.

"Oh Martha, that is really lovely, what are the stones in it?"

"Diamonds no less, I don't know how I have become worthy of wearing Diamonds, but here they are and Dick says they must stay on my finger forever."

Martha held her hand at an angle so as to admire the ring, it was not hard to see just what this meant to her, a blush came into her cheeks, and her mind was with Dick, all everyday things put to one side while she savoured the magic of the moment.

"You deserve it Martha, Dick is a very lucky man."

Sara picked up Martha's hand to look more closely at the ring.

"It fits you perfectly Martha, do you think I could try it on?"

Martha reluctantly took off the ring and passed it to Sara.

"I can feel the weight in this ring Martha it must have cost a fortune."

"Yes I suppose it is an expensive ring, it was Dick's Mothers ring I am honoured in more ways than one you see, Dick said he loved his Mother and now it was me he loved, to wear it with pride for all the world to see, I must say it brought tears to my eyes when he presented it to me."

"You wear it well Martha, it is too big for me and doesn't look at all right, but on you it jumps to life as though made to measure."

Sara gave the ring back to Martha and she slipped it back on her finger.

"Why did you put it in the drawer Martha, it belongs where it is now." Martha replied,

"I am afraid of getting it spoilt, so while doing the cooking and housework I pop it

into the drawer, it is safe from harm there."

"It would be safe on your finger Martha, it is made to take everyday wear, don't let Dick catch you while the ring is in the drawer, he wants it where we all can see it, he is proud of giving it to you, so you must be proud of wearing it."

"Oh! Indeed I am it is the loveliest ring, so if what you say is true and the durability as strong I will wear it all the time. I must ask Dick so as to be sure."

Sara sat before the fire her mind wandering to her love Vincent. Again she had to stop herself before she had dug a pit to fall into. It wasn't as though this was a matter of time, Sara could never belong to Vincent she was removed by class his family would never accept such a union.

Martha broke her daydream saying,

"I have to get a dress for my Wedding Day Sara, what do you suggest?"

Hardly wanting to reply because disappointment about Vincent still overwhelmed her, Sara took up the challenge saying,

"You could wear white Martha you have never been married even though a few years have passed you by, why not?"

"People would think I was daft an old girl

like me wearing white."

"No not at all Martha, well if you think white is too daring wear cream perhaps you would be happier doing that?"

"Yes cream would be more toned in with my years wouldn't it?"

"You would look lovely in cream Martha or indeed any colour you choose, you have a heart of pure gold Dick has found this out for himself your Wedding Day will be all that is to be desired. I don't mind saying Martha I envy you, in the nicest way of course."
Martha replied

"This is the once in my life I am enviable, no-one wanted the burden of my parents that is why I stayed at home to look after them. I don't suppose any-one envies me looking after your Kids Sara, although I do that quite willingly, now you say you envy me? Yes now having found my Dick I am enviable and I must say very content."

"You are entering a new way of life Martha with a good man you deserve all that is to come which I sincerely hope will be nothing but the best."

Both ladies by now had a tear spring into their eye they had respect for each other and an unsaid camaraderie not to be denied and not to be taken lightly.

Chapter Thirty-four

Vincent was getting despondent the search for Sara had been fruitless she had disappeared into thin air much to his parents delight. Still there was that longing in his heart and he would never dismiss this quest. He would talk it over with his Brother Richard. Vincent went to find his Brother, he was in his room. Vincent immediately brought Sara into the conversation. Richard's face turned quite sour saying,

"Oh Vincent come on, the way you talk about this Sara is stupid ten a penny in the village her sort, go and find one and have a good time with her, you don't have to marry these girls they are there for our entertainment there isn't any need to kick up so much fuss. I quite like the challenge of picking up just such a girl, it is like dibbing into a bag of assorted sweets and seeing which one you have pulled out. Hoping it is a good and juicy one to enjoy."

Vincent nearly jumped upon Richard, he was very angry saying,

"You are despicable Richard, what I am talking about and what you are explaining are two very different things. I do not want what you seem to think is fun, my feelings for Sara are real and true I wouldn't hurt a hair

on her dear head. Don't you know the feeling of love in all its glory? It consumes me day and night if I could I would be with Sara for all time. I have no desire to play the field you are pathetic in your estimation of love." Richard said,

"Look here old chap I didn't say anything about love, when I think of girls in the Scullery love does not come into it. I can still have a good time without talking about love. Why take it all so seriously?"

"Because I feel it is serious and I do want to marry Sara, I have never met anyone like Sara

She is supreme among woman. I shall go on till I find her, this conversation has gone far enough I don't want to discuss it any more with you. I thought you above all would either help me in my search or discuss the point rationally with me as you are not doing either I will take my leave of you." Richard was indignant,

"Vincent it doesn't have to be like that perhaps I haven't chosen my words as carefully as you would have liked but facts are facts and Mother and Father will never let you marry this girl. Having overheard their conversation the other day they are only too pleased you can't find Sara. Why don't

you face it Sara is not for you?"

Vincent went off with a flurry and an indignant air of discontent, about Sara he knew he was right there was no-one like her. He would find her. Where could she have gone? He

was not going to let his Mother and Father's disapproval get in his way he was to be Lord.

It was part of his inheritance, NO he would give up his title and let Richard take his place, his own values lay elsewhere this was not a game he was playing. Richard called after Vincent,

"If you see Rosa on your way down send her up to me."

It was like a red rag to a bull! Vincent called back,

"I shall not, you do your own dirty work I respect the staff yes all of them, leave Rosa alone

I shall not throw her at your feet to get trodden on she deserves better."

Richard's face reddened, he was his own master no-one could tell him what to do he was not going to change his ways for Vincent or anyone else for that matter. The Scullery Maids and the upstairs Maids knew quite well how to provide him with a playmate, why shouldn't he indulge himself it was expected of him.

Richard sent for Miss Olivine,

"Go and ask Rosa to come to my room."

Richard's discussion with Vincent had fired his blood he went about his room like a caged tiger. Vincent must be mad not to take advantage and get all he could out of these girls dismissing Miss Olivine now, he would wait for Rosa.

In the kitchen Rosa and Alice had just planned to take a tea break.

"Oh drat Rosa said, now Mr Richard wants me, he and Mr Vincent are acting like spoiled brats what excuse will he find this time? I shall get away as soon as I can Alice, so wait just a little while for your cup of tea and I will be back."

Going over to the medicine cupboard again she put something in her pocket.

Tapping Richard's door he called "Enter,"

"Miss Olivine says you wanted me Sir, she dipped a little curtsey."

"Yes Rosa, I don't seem to see very much of you so I thought we could have an hour together?

There was a feeling in the room, Rosa couldn't decide what it was but it made her wary.

"Sit down Rosa you and me know each other

enough over the years don't stand on ceremony come and sit beside me."

His glance indicating the chosen spot, it was too close for Rosa's likes but she was duty bound to comply.

"There that's better, a glass of wine maybe?" He went across the room to fetch the decanter and two glasses. Speaking to Rosa he said,

"This is a splendid little wine I am sure you will like it,"

"Please don't pour me any yet Sir you have some if you desire."

Richard talked small talk for what seemed ages taking little sips of wine. He kept nudging

closer to Rosa, he stroked her face with the back of his hand, she felt herself stiffen.

His breath was hot and the alcohol in the wine made it offensive. Now his hand was on her knee, No! She silently said to herself, trying at the same time to alter the position he had cornered her into.

"Come on Rosa you weren't born yesterday give a chap a good time"

Rosa shot up from her seat beside him, walking across the room tried to make an immediate change of subject.

"I am sure there are better looking girls than me attracting your attention Mr Richard."

Richard replied,

"You and me we know each other very well you played with me as a boy why shouldn't we indulge in a few grown up games?"

"Sorry Mr Richard I don't see it as you see it, I would have thought knowing you so long you would by now have respect for me."

"I do respect you Rosa I wouldn't let any harm come to you. You can trust me,"

He got up from the settee and walked towards her, he pulled her to him in a clumsy manner. Now she really had to say an out and out "NO." She pushed him away as hard as she could. He stumbled and almost fell flat on his face the wine he had drank making him unsteady. Rosa flew for the door as soon as she could, he would get over it men always did it was no big deal for them. She heard him laugh but didn't look back, going down the stairs holding on to the banister so that her speed did not trip her up. Shaking all over she had panicked he was not going to make a downright fool of her. She had to be aware now.

Chapter Thirty-five

Sara was back at Maggie's; being adept in her response to anything that was asked of her this made all three of them comfortable. Sara had loved doing the winter preparation of Jams and Pickles, the cooking of the Christmas fare, the daily baking of Bread and Scones, fetching the eggs newly laid, the colour of the yolks when cracked to fry made the plate look scrumptious, with the deep colour contained in the yolk also with the tomato, bacon, sausage a feast fit for a King no less! Very often she wondered at the meals she used to prepare when Bill was with her. These would be sparse and usually finished up with scraggy end of meat with any vegetables that she could find thrown in to make a stew. There were too many of them to feed on one poor wage to even think of anything else. Bill used to thump the table and demand he wanted meat on his plate, perhaps if Sara had found the money for his meat he would not have gone down the pub to drown his sorrows. In fact if he had given her the money that he took down the pub she could have provided him with meat, what a mix up of intentions. It had evolved into Bill's death and her family split, she still thanked God she had lost the baby she had been *carrying when Bill died. At that moment in time she was desolate, the Workhouse loomed ever closer and if it hadn't have been for Martha that is where they would have all finished up. Sara couldn't deny she had been so lucky. These comparisons made her life with Maggie very special, now she knew how to cook and prepare food, how to store it for winter and how to enjoy the table set before her. Her feelings for Vincent still deep in her heart had to be left quietly and referred to as a memory she would always treasure Maggie said,*

"You have gone very quiet Sara, deep in thought were you?"

"Sorry Maggie yes I was thinking about Martha and what she would wear to get married in."

It wasn't the truth well indirectly perhaps, Sara needed Maggie's jolt to get her out of the web she was weaving it was a web too, of deception and poverty the lowly state of life she had been accustomed to living when married to Bill. Her feet had been certainly glued to the ground, for toeing the line became the normal thing to be done. The bedtime activities too, no thought for her or her needs, it was always his own self he had to please. Why couldn't she get him out of her mind forever he was like that stubborn stain you could not shift no matter what. Then in which case the item stained had to be thrown out, and she would throw him out of her mind he had no place in there, this she had promised herself many times. Again Maggie interrupted,

"Has Martha chosen the colour she is going to wear Sara?"

"Yes Maggie I said she could wear white but she thinks White is not the colour for her age, so Cream was chosen, with Coffee coloured hat and gloves."

"What I was asking for I thought of making her the dress, she won't want too many frills if I know Martha. I could get some nice material we could shop for it all three of us then discuss style. I don't think this Wedding is going to happen before Christmas so I would make the dress in the dark days of January."

"Have you got a machine then Maggie? I have never seen you stitch anything."

"I have a treadle machine hidden away under a pretty pink cloth in my bedroom, you are right it doesn't see the light of day from one year to the next I would have to oil it and get it running well before I make my offer, do you think Martha would want me to make her

dress?"

"I am sure she would, have it precisely the way she wanted would hide her lumps and bumps as she calls them, and she wants to look nice for Dick. I will ask her when I go at the weekend if that is alright Maggie,"

"Yes you have been lucky with the weather so far it hasn't stopped you going home at weekend has it? Let's hope this weekend is not the exception you could relay my message and arrange some sort of time to go to get the cloth. You know things are getting exciting in my old age; I will get a thrill out of making the dress as Martha will get out of wearing it. We always see eye to eye I have been Martha's friend for many Moons although she is more than a friend now being Joe's Sister brings her dear to me."

"Martha wants Joe or I to be Best Man does that entail a lot Maggie"?

"No not really there would be some responsibility like seeing to the rings and making sure Dick shows up on time,"

"No fear of that I assure you, it is Dick that will want assurance from Martha,"

They laughed things were shaping up this was going to be a very happy occasion.

"I think I shall wear cream as accessories only my suit will have to be a smart looking brown, I have said to Martha a Cream Rose Court-age would be better than a posy, and then Dick could have a smart button hole of cream Rose, and so could I. We have been talking to the folks in the Quarry Yard. They have been very helpful saying that the table in Martha's house will be spread by them, and all will be ready when the couple come back from Church It all fits together very well, Dick has some Elderberry wine he made a couple of year ago, and you are making the Wedding cake. All we want is fine weather, as no fixed date has been set as yet I am thinking this will happen in the spring. We are too close to Christmas now and the Jan. Feb weather can be cold and nasty, when the snowdrops show their faces and the daffodils bloom we will have the whole thing arranged."

"Sounds like a plan to me Maggie said, I have yet to see Martha's ring, fancy Martha having Diamonds she is a very proud lady at the moment and she deserves to be. It is so strange how life works out and finally has all the answers.

Chapter Thirty-six

The October celebration had gone down a treat, Martha had now officially accepted Dick as her future husband they were both very happy. Martha was still wary about wearing her ring all day, what if it came off in a bowl full of suds? It was far too precious to lose. Dick now was a frequent visitor at Martha's cottage, staying for meals, doing odd jobs that needed a Man's hand, their bond was growing the Kids didn't take a bit of notice about Dick being almost part of the family they all liked Dick, he treated them with respect, and gentle persuasion was his way of getting the best out of them. Martha bustled around quietly approving of Dick's gentle ways. He had a powerful physic but used that part of himself to tackle the many jobs that were thrown his way.

"I saw Alice and Rosa when I went to take the goods to the Hall" Dick said,

"Did you Dick? How are they both?"

"Well in general health they seem alright, but I am afraid Alice will not be able to keep her secret much longer I bet already there are a few tongues wagging She is beginning to show her condition. I noticed she had adopted a very lose dress and apron. The other staff must think she is putting on a lot

of weight as yet she is getting away with it, she looks well but the time has come to face the music or it will be shortly."

"I suppose she wants to get over Christmas, poor girl I know she doesn't know who to turn to. I usually have got a trick up my sleeve but this time I am stumped."

"You help enough people as it is Martha I do know what you mean though. I will keep my eyes and ears open see if anything turns up, life has a way of sorting things out you have only to look at the natural world outside to see that, we get the seasons and we cannot stop them coming year after year, new births occur in all species nature deals with them. Let us hope in Alice's case nature will look after her."

"Oh Dick you make things so uncomplicated I find myself worrying and after we have talked it over the worries drift away, I love you in so many different ways Dick."

Dick leaned over and took her hand confidant that Martha would be glad to hold his hand,

he gave it a gentle squeeze saying,

"I love you too Martha you are going to be my wife and I am so very proud,"

They had each other, never wanting to go out to various parks or places of interest. It didn't enter their minds, all they wanted was spread out before them and was theirs in an instant if asked for.

Martha broke the silence that had spread across the room asking,

"How is our wine coming along Dick? Is it still clearing?

"Hark at you, still clearing! Asking in such a professional way I am blessed! You will be making the next lot alongside me and you will know as well as I what to do."

"I must say I am a little proud of myself and pleased because now I can follow the process without keep bothering you to tell me what to do. Well is it still clearing?"

"Yes it is doing a treat, next time you are round to see me I will draw off a tiny drop and you will see for yourself. Of course it will still be strong in flavour, Elderberry takes maturity time.

"I know Dick but I would just like to see the progress it is making."

"No fear about that my dear it will be like port wine when it finally matures, and there will be quite an abundance of it, the berries were so good this year and with your help we picked a good harvest. The Blackberries that we found also will add to the flavour, and strengthen

The colour I have high hopes for this one. We will be known for it in the future everyone will want a bottle. I am already collecting the empty wine bottles from the Hall, washing them when I get them home, I shall sterilise them finally before our wine goes into them. There will be no infection then, the one thing you do have to be clear about is the cleanliness in the making of wine, so far so good eh? Just another job that takes a lot of patience Martha, we will get our rewards you'll see."

"My rewards are already coming just being beside you, and the talks we have give me so much pleasure. Hey come on look at the time I will have a hungry crew coming in shortly with no dinner on the table, are you eating with us today? No I have a couple of calls I want to make so I'll make myself scarce and get going."

Getting up from his chair he went and kissed Martha's cheek, the warm glow that spread over her when he did this went from head to toe.

"When will you be by again Dick?"

"Shouldn't have to ask that Martha I will be by every minute I am not working, I look forward to finishing my tasks because I know you are waiting for me."

He gave her a lingering fond look and went out of the door.

Martha went around the kitchen with purpose she wouldn't want the kids to find no tea on the table.

"Sausage and mash, that is what I will do it is quick and easy as well as being tummy filling."

She picked up her well used paring knife and got on with the bowl full of potatoes, she thought of how many sacks of potatoes she had peeled in her time and she still did them with a purpose not leaving a single mark on them when finished, a little salt and on the fire in a saucepan to boil. Having some of Dicks homemade pork sausages made the meal nutritious and tasty. A huge frying pan was brought out of the cupboard, a little lard and a swish around to melt the fat and the sausage was popped in, Martha rolled them from side to side of the pan to get an overall baked finish, the smell was so appetising, Martha had baked bread that morning, so a large crusty loaf was put at the centre of the table, cutting it first into thick slices.

One by one the kids appeared at the door.

"Hmmm that smells good Auntie Martha, I'm hungry." This was Sara's eldest boy.

"You are always hungry, sit down and wait

for the others they will be here in a minute.
Have they found you much to do today
dear?"
"Yes I have been busy, the shop keeper says
he is keeping his eye on me, reckons he will
give me a full time job when I am old enough.
That would be right up my street Martha.

Chapter Thirty-seven

Sara and Maggie now November had arrived were even busier than in October. Maggie wanted everything spruced up as she called it ready to entertain family and friends. They would be all grown up's. Maggie had a couple of cousins living not so far away and she was hoping Martha and Dick would come too. Maggie was looking forward to seeing Martha's Diamond Ring and to get to know Dick a bit better. So the heat was on and all through the cottage was polished and cleaned till it shone. Maggie held up a pair of brass candlesticks saying,

"Look Sara these have polished up a treat when we next go into the village I want some tall red candles to go in them they will look lovely on the table, I have a deep green tablecloth I keep especially for the Christmas period, I shall enhance it with red, like a holly berry.

I am really excited this year, there is Martha's wedding dress to discuss and her ring to see. Joe says he can get us a small real Christmas tree. It would have to be small I just haven't got room for a big one. I have a few baubles and tree ornaments that we have collected over the years we won't have to buy those unless there is something new that takes our eye. Joe is equally as interested in buying at least one bauble to dedicate to this particular year. It will be good to get the stored ones down from the closet and look at them again."

Sara found she was carried along with Maggie's enthusiasm she was full of the coming season Maggie carried on saying,

"Joe is going to the woods today. There are a few small Fir trees to look at, he will pick one out and then bring it home just as December comes in. I like the tree up early it brings a glow to the cottage, heart warming that is what it is. He was only telling me last week there are a couple gone over with the strong winds we had last week. So he is going to take the horse and cart to the edge of the woods and with his special saw he will fill a few sacks of logs for the fire, leaving the best tree for Christmas so we can decorate it. He will do this several times and fill up the wood shed for winter, there is nothing like a log fire, the smell of it burning and bright flames licking up the chimney there is no place on this earth I would rather be than right here by my own fire there is magic in the glow. You being here with us Sara is making the preparation and the planning doubly exciting are you enjoying it dear?"

"Yes thank you Maggie. It certainly beats any Christmas I have shared."

Sara was thinking about Bill and his drinking. Christmas brought that to the fore. It was a good excuse to get drunk, and take his pick of the pub maids, who willingly gave Bill all the liberty he wanted. Christmas presents for the kids? There were none. Bill would want all his money to spend over the bar. Sara had tried to make a few items for a Christmas stocking. Keeping small things that her friends gave her second hand that their kids had tired off, she would mend and polish them up. Sara would carefully wrap them up in the thinnest Christmas paper just for the element of surprise. She did her best what more could she do, the weeks previously she had hounded her Butcher to save any meat he could, hoping a small chicken would be left over from his orders, hoping that he would sell it very cheaply to her. It was always a hand to mouth existence scraping her way by, ignoring Bills request for meat on his plate, she needed money to get meat. On seeing Christmas stockings being filled Bill would taunt her.

"Spending my bloody hard earned cash on Christmas presents, get some bloody meat on the table woman he moaned, I need my food"

Bill needed his drink also he always chose drink instead of food. The kid's cowered away from him in this mood they knew only too well what the buckle end of his strap felt like. Running over to their Mother clinging on to her skirts They were only little then, they gathered for protection but often they all had a hiding with Mum finishing up with black eyes and a bruised body as she took the blows intended for the kids. A shudder passed through her entire body as she recalled the scene. Why? Just lately had she thought of Bill and her disastrous life with him, when she was at the Hall she had been able to dismiss herself from that time, yet now it came back with such clarity as the thought passed through her mind she at once knew the answer? It was because her eldest two boys were now growing up into young men and the resemblance to Bill was striking. Their faces needed shaving and as the dark stubble grew they were becoming their Father all over again She sighed and made a silent prayer

"Please dear Lord let their temperament be like my own, placid and understanding"

The pub that is where they would be drawn in I must have words with Martha and tell her of my fears. Sara still felt the belittling back hand swipe across her face Bill had delivered it so often. Her hand went up to her cheek as if to comfort the spot, after all these years the sting was still there impossible to erase.

"This must be why I don't feel worth anything, Bill put me down and I can't shake off this feeling of degradation, the confidence in me is easily cut back to nil when I remember the dark side of my life. I must teach myself to bury it in a dark place with a solid door never to find the key."

Time after time she went through the awful degradation that Bill had marked her mind with. Promising to herself never would she think of it again but it still persisted raising its head and she went through it all over again.

Chapter Thirty -eight

Maggie came back into the room breaking Sara's thought saying,

"Here we are Sara."

She placed a box full of Christmas baubles on the table, Sara was at once returned to the present.

"Oh Maggie Christmas jewels!"

"Now handle these with care Sara some of them are as much as forty years old and a bit fragile. Joe and me we looked every year at the small wooden tree decorations and the new baubles, buying two pieces each year and as the years have gone on they have collected into quite a few. In fact that is what is placed before you now. This year when the Village has its Christmas fare we will buy two more it has become like a Calendar of years and our life together. Each of us could tell you where and when we bought that particular item. It is like a box of happy memories to savour once again each year,"

Sara thought how the dark memories had run through her mind just a while ago, Joe and Maggie yes that's just what they were no pretence believing in each other as they did and never failing to walk side by side as they trod gently on the path of life.

Sara found her hands in the box with a

caressing touch, wanting to look at each item as they revealed their splendour, the tissue paper they were wrapped in carefully straightened out to use again in January when they were again stored. Sara and Maggie had a piece of soft cloth to shine each piece as revealed. Absorbed in their task the day grew darker and the firelight grew brighter. The flames danced their reflection on the shiny baubles making Sara and Maggie very content with their labour of love.

"Here's Joe with the tree Sara" Joe came in saying,

"What are you two up to it is getting dark in here, it is a wonder you can see to do anything"

Maggie gave one of her knowing smiles and said,

"We are getting the baubles ready for the tree, after tea we will dress it and put it in pride of place. Sara felt like an intruder when she saw Joe lean the tree on the inside of the door and put a gentle arm around Maggie to give her a squeeze.

"That's enough of that Joe it is time for the kettle to go on for tea,"

Joe reluctantly dropped his arm and said,

"There's your tree then, small but a fine tree with good colour and firm needles."

After tea Maggie said to Sara,

"Can you smell the lovely pine needles from the tree?"

"Yes a special pine fresh from the forest, it has scented the whole room,"

They sat together in the evening, having dressed the tree which was now looking splendid. "I think I am going to get to bed early tonight Maggie if you don't mind I expect there will be a full day again tomorrow and I want to be fresh for you."

"That's good Sara dear, I won't be long following you I am too feeling the extra work and I am used to it. There is never a dull moment this time of year,"

"Goodnight then both of you see you in the morning."

Sara went to her stone walled bedroom it was cold in there so she had a small log burner right in the corner which Maggie had thoughtfully lit earlier on.

"Hmm this is so cosy,"

Her eiderdown snuggled her in and once more she was at peace. Sleep as fast as her head touched the pillow.

At breakfast Maggie was sorting out the day.

"Joe wants me to go to the village to order some Pork for Christmas, we already have

Chicken and Turkey, but as we have visitors I want there to be plenty to offer. Would you like to come with me Sara?"

"That would be very nice Maggie I perhaps would be able to get just a couple of things for the kids stockings, they never have had much, so they won't be expecting great things it would be nice though to surprise them with something."

"Oh I am sure it would Sara, do you miss them very much?"

"I have to be honest Maggie, they are far better off with Martha, I have sort of lost contact with them, they now look to Maggie as they should look to me, but none of us are upset by that, it is all working very well."

"I am glad to hear that Sara, it means if you found the right man you could marry again,"

"Don't be daft Maggie, no-one would want me, what could I have to offer,"

"You would make some-one a lovely wife don't even think like that, your life is still ongoing you have time even to have another family,"

This did not appeal to Sara she dropped her eyes and didn't answer.

"Get my coat then, Joe let's be off see what we can find, put a scarf on Sara it is rather cold today"

Sara went back to her room and chose a woolly brown scarf, it was old but it was warm and she liked the feeling around her neck, she also found gloves a bit tatty but they would do.

"That's better Maggie said when she saw Sara dressed. Don't want you catching a chill do we. The cart is outside ready for us, yes Joe is coming too we shan't stay as long as we did when we went to Town, the Village is only small but the Christmas stalls will be set out and they always bring something new."

Sara was feeling excited now, the stalls would be something new to look at.

"Do the stalls bring Christmas gift ideas? Or are they mostly vegetables?"

"There are both sorts Sara, many a time I have picked up some lovely knitting wool for a very good price. It is certainly worth rummaging through the second hand stall too, the things people throw out unbelievable.

Sara now all ears could not wait to get there.

The atmosphere in the pretty Christmas market was all aglow, the vendors shouting their wares, the mistletoe hanging on the canopy for Sale, Holly wreathed with berries, hot chestnuts from the man with a fire in a grid roasting. Even the pungent smell as they walked along was Christmas. A stall selling *pork batches with stuffing. The holder calling,*

"Come on Ladies let your Christmas start here, hot and very tasty, and only tuppence each."

His cheerful face helped his sales, everyone was there for Christmas cheer and he was throwing plenty of that into the crowd, the pork roasting indeed tempting.

"Would you like pork and stuffing batch Sara?"

Maggie with an enquiring eye looked towards Sara, but Sara was absorbed with other things.

"No I won't Maggie I will get my hands all greasy and I want to pick up items I intend to buy, I must say though they do smell good."

"You won't mind if I do then?"

"Don't be daft Maggie enjoy a treat that is what we have come here for."

Maggie walked along eating her pork and stuffing batch, saying she would wipe her hands clean on her handkerchief. The air was brisk, the sky was bright a sunshine without the heat, pallor but just right for this excursion, dry underfoot so they could stroll along.

"It is a big market Maggie I wasn't expecting it to be, I am enjoying it immensely,"

"That's good to hear Sara, have you spotted the Hurdy Gurdy man over there?"

Martha pointed her finger to the spot where there was a Merry Go Round the man was getting the children into each seat and putting a safety strap across the front of them. Then he would take his place in the centre start the music off and with strong arms wind the large red wheel. This with squeals of delight from the children sent the chairs spinning around.

"A proper market delight" said Maggie,

Sara agreed it was obviously well sort after, a queue formed as soon as the last children had emptied the seats. Going on a little further Sara said,

"Is that what you were telling me about Maggie?"

"Where? What are you looking at dear?"

"Over there Maggie, is that the second hand stall?"

"Ah yes it is, we will come to it eventually."

"There are lots of scents here Maggie I think the girls would like some Cologne. I will have two please one Old Rose, and the other Lavender."

This lady as round as an apple with a simple Shawl around her shoulders put the items into a pink bag.

"Can I interest you in some bath salts too? I have the matching perfume,"

"No thank you, but I will have talcum powder, the one with the powder puff included,"

Off they set again with more treasures to look for.

"What can I get my boys Maggie? Boys are so hard to please."

"You say they are growing up fast perhaps a shaving brush and soap would please them"

"Oh Maggie you are a treasure that will be what I will get,"

They went over to the other side of the stall.

"Yes please I will have two of those, and how much is the mirror?"

This was a shaving mirror special for the purpose.

"They will feel quite the young Gent when they use these Maggie,"

"I am sure they will, better save a bit of cash for the next stall though, we are coming to the second hand you have been dying to find."

Where to start? All sorts of clothes from the everyday wear into the classier wear.

"What do you think of this Sara?"

Maggie was holding up to her neck a dress, it was ankle length, with a floral pattern.

"No Maggie it is far too gaudy for you we can find something better than that it depends where you wish to wear it. I like to see you in a quieter material, with your piny over the top."

"Are you looking for anything special Sara?"

"Well at the back of my mind I was thinking about Martha's wedding, I don't suppose there will be anything as grand as I want on here."

"Hark at you grand is it you want? Then it is the other side of the stall you need to go,"

Maggie went before Sara leading her to the more expensive clothes.

"There you are then sort yourself out from that,"

A wide range of dresses and suits ladies style appeared these were placed on hangers and treated with more care. Sara was delighted and taken aback at the choice of both style and colour. Some looked as though they had barely been out of the wardrobe.

"Look Maggie at this pretty blue dress isn't it lovely?"

Maggie went over to Sara,

"Powder blue I call that, yes it is pretty but you say you want something for Martha's Wedding and she will be wearing cream. It would be better to find a suit that would go *alongside Martha's cream wouldn't it? You said you thought brown would go."*

The clothes hangers were shuffled stopping here and there to pull an item out so to look at it fully.

"This is a nice style Maggie,"

Sara was holding up an ankle length skirt with a matching flared jacket in a deep coffee colour. The blouse it had with it much paler in shade with a ruffled inlet at the top.

"Can I try these on Maggie?"

"I think so the lady will let you go into her cabin over there, you will be able to look into a mirror."

Sara hesitated then went over to ask.

"Is it possible to go into your cabin to see how this suit fits me?"

"Of course my dear, but I should choose more than one to try on, once you have got your own clothes off it is always better to have several items to try."

"Thank you I will carry on with my search then and come to you when I am ready,"

Sara knew Maggie had overheard so they both started to look again. Finally Sara had her three choices. The powder blue that she had spotted first, and the coffee coloured suit, and last but not least, a suit much the same style as the coffee one only this one was deep apricot. Sara was so excited she couldn't remember one time in her entire life she had been able to choose her own clothes and try them on, she felt a shiver of delight as she stepped into the cabin Maggie behind her holding some of the pieces. There was a mirror so Sara looked all around her to see that no-one was able to peek at her state of undress. She didn't mind Maggie being with her she needed her opinion.

"Which shall I try on first Maggie?"

"I should leave the blue till last because being a dress and that colour I don't think it will do for the Wedding. Try the coffee suit on first."

Trembling with delight as she pulled the skirt over her head it dropped down to the waist and done up at the back.

"It fits well Maggie, well the skirt does let's see about the blouse and jacket."

Putting on the blouse Sara noticed a small seam ragged under the arm she showed Maggie.

"Well dear it will mend you can't expect it to be perfect, they are second hand you know."

Sara replied,

"Well otherwise it doesn't look too bad does it?"

"I will tell you which one I like when I have

seen all of them on you. Do you want me to help you get out of that one Sara? We don't want that rip in the sleeve going further do we?"

Sara with Maggie's help carefully removed the suit.

"I want to try the blue dress next Maggie it took my eye when I first saw it."

"Alright dear,"

Maggie passed Sara the blue dress this one had frills and buttons on it. Sara slipped it over her head wriggling it down passed her thigh to her ankles the skirt was pencil slim it hugged Sara's slim figure and made the frills around the neckline stand out, they both stood in awe Maggie looking at Sara and Sara looking into the mirror.

"Well it won't do for the Wedding but it is so pretty on you, and brings out the colour of your eyes in balance. We must ask how much it is maybe we could afford the two outfits. I must say if you wanted to go to the Hall on its Open Day this powder blue in the summer would look charming."

"Yes I think so too Maggie it feels right just like I have had it made for me and yes the colour is perfect for a summer outside. Will you ask how much it is? I can't see a price label."

"First before I do Sara try the Apricot Suit on, with cream button boots and a cream blouse it would be just the job with Martha all in cream and cream roses for sprays on the suit coat."

"I don't think I can afford both of them Maggie it depends what she wants for the blue dress,"

"Just get on with it Sara I have a feeling this apricot suit is going to look good, we will haggle with her about price when we know what we are buying."

Sara took off the blue dress and put on the Apricot Suit.

"That's done it they are both a good fit, what does this look like at the back Maggie?"

"Very well indeed Sara, the flare of the jacket from the waistline makes your figure enhanced you would only need a light blouse as there is a lot of trimming in the suit. We must get you dressed and have a look at the blouses I think they are separately hung around the other side of the stall. Might as well look for a hat and some high button boots while we are about it Look Sara don't worry about the cost because Joe and me wanted to get you something for Christmas and we just couldn't think what to get so we will half the cost of this package and that will be your Christmas present settled."

"Oh Maggie would you, how lovely I would certainly like that."

"Just as long as you know when Christmas day comes there will be nothing to unwrap."

"I will know what I have already had Maggie I am sure I won't forget."

"Right then pick up the items you want to buy and I will take this coffee one to go back on the rail. We will tell the lady what our intentions are and see if we can get a good price."

Showing the stall holder what they had chosen she was well pleased it was always good to make a multiple sale rather than the odd item so she took them to where the hats and boots were displayed.

"Try the boots first Sara they will be difficult to get a good fit."

Picking up and trying on several high buttoned boots Sara didn't seem to be having much luck. Some too high up the calf, some not fitting at all, and some that should never have been offered for sale they were ready for the rag bag. The stall lady was keeping her distance but had an eye on them to see how they were getting along.

"Can't you find anything me darlin's? Would you like me to look with you?"

Sara looked up saying,
"We are alright thank you I don't think there
is anything for me here"
"Now said the assistant that is where I can
help you. I keep the best till last so to speak. I
like my customers to sort out the old stuff
before I bring out the new, yes I know they
are not really new but very close mi dears,"
Maggie and Sara looked at each other in a
knowing kind of way. Maggie whispered.
"What has she got up her sleeve then" and
gave Sara a wink.
Into the changing hut the Lady disappeared
bringing out with her an armful of boot
boxes.
"Here ya are then sort that lot out, these are
me specials I only have them a short while
they sell out very quickly. Luck would have it
I only had these bought in this morning. Use
this wooden crate to sit on dearie it is better
than balancing on one foot."
Sara although these were not new could see
they had only the slightest wear. Pair by pair
Maggie helped Sara try them on. Then they
came to a white box, undoing it the tissue
revealed cream boots with the fastening of
cream pearl buttons to one side of them. Sara
felt her heart quicken its beat, these were
lovely she had never dreamed of owning a

pair of boots as grand as these and filling all the requirements, but here they were in her hand. Maggie's eyes lit up too, thinking these were meant for Sara.

"Try them on Sara I do hope they fit they would be the icing on the cake."

Sara slipped her foot into the right one first wriggling her toes so that the shoe could fit the foot correctly.

"Well that one is a decent fit I hope the left one is as comfortable,"

Leaving the right one on and slipping her foot into the left one,

"How is it Sara?"

"The right one is a better fit than the left, I think though if I wore them a few evenings they would stretch that bit."

"Now don't have them if you are not going to wear them in comfort Maggie said, at a push I suppose we could pack the left one with some dampened brown paper that would widen them a bit."

"Yes Maggie I think my left foot must be a little larger than my right, it is such a little bit I think I am going to risk it and buy them."
Maggie replied,

"You won't get any better than those for style and colour, you also have the bonus of pearl buttons and they come up high at the ankle

real elegant. We now have the hat to sort out."

The stall lady smiled taking the shoes from Sara and placing them with the other clothes she had chosen.

"What style head wear would you like Sara?" Maggie asked,

"I have never had occasion to wear a hat before Maggie, but the wide brim that slants over the eye at one side appeals. It has to be cream so that narrows the choice down a bit doesn't it?"

One by one the hats were tried on while the lady held a brown framed mirror so that Sara could see the effect.

"I rather like this one Sara said it is not too overwhelming."

The choice of hat was cream with apricot coloured ribbon around the crown next to the wide brim. It finished to one side with a small spray of apricot rosebuds. It was the colour and very near to the hat she had pictured in her mind. Now to count the cost the stall lady didn't price each item separately she picked each item up in her hand and her mind was totting up the final price.

"Right then dearie you have chosen top end stuff, the price reflects that, how will thirty bob do you for the lot?"

"What do you think Sara?" Maggie enquired, wondering if Sara could find half of the total. Sara said,

"Well I am not taking home rubbish am I? These are all quality items, so I think the price is about right."

"That's it then" said Maggie opening her handbag and taking out of her purse a White Five Pound Note.

This fascinated Sara, who had never seen a white Five pound note in her life.

"Let me look at that, Sara said I have never seen a White bank note like that."

Sara took it from Maggie it was very grand looking with the writing in black using a fancy scroll to say "Five Pounds" It opened the stall Ladies eyes too, she said,

"I can't say I see many of those either Ladies, thank you very much."She held the bank note up for the light to show the water mark so as to know it was genuine. Always happy to oblige."

With that she put the Five Pound note down her bosom, and fetched out three one pound notes and a ten shilling note as the change from the leather pouch she had strapped to her.

Tired now Maggie and Sara had reached that moment when no matter how much stuff there was left to buy, home and a cup of tea was the best option. Sara saying she would square up moneywise with Maggie when they got home. Maggie looked up at the Church clock.

"Goodness me it is a good job we have done shopping, Joe will be waiting for us."

The time as always when you are engrossed in what you are doing had simply flown away. Picking up all their parcels they headed for their meeting place. On the way Sara and Maggie passed a flower seller, Sara stopped and bought a pretty bunch of violets giving them to Maggie.

"Just a thank you Maggie for all your patience this day,"

"How kind of you Sara" and put them into the top of her basket.

"Here you are at last Joe said I can see you have bought up half of the town."

Good humouredly he got the parcels into the cart and made them secure. Then he helped Maggie and Sara up to sit beside him, he jolted the reigns to signal the horse to set off at a trot. Clip clop the sound of the horse's hooves on the Cobblestoned Street strangely easy on the ears. Sara was thinking how secure she felt with these two good people beside her.

Chapter Thirty-nine

The days to Christmas passed quickly always finding things to do. Sitting beside the fire to talk Maggie and Sara talked together, Sara always talking about Rosa and Alice, and wondering when she would see them again. Maggie knew Sara was missing the company of those girls.

"When is Alice's baby due Sara?"

"In April I think, I wonder how she is disguising the fact at the Hall, pity she couldn't find the Father it was love at first sight for her. Funnily enough although it has left her with a problem she has no regrets. Perhaps it will all work out I do hope so she is a lovely girl."

Maggie gave her opinion,

"Trouble is, lovely girl or not, the problem as you put it will not go away, she needs the Lord and Lady of the Hall to take her under their wing is that an impossibility?"

"I wouldn't like to say Maggie people in the upper class have no idea how it is to be poor. Nevertheless you are right she has no-one, she really needs to go to them and tell of her predicament maybe they would listen. I will suggest it when I see her again but I don't know when that will be, the weather will be closing in on us any day now, and I can't get

through the woods over to Martha's when that happens. I find myself worrying about her at the oddest times I have to stop myself, if I can't do anything what is the good to come out of worrying about it. Tea Maggie that is what we need."

Sara moved around the kitchen putting cups and saucers out and the tea in the pot.

"You are right dear a cup of tea will solve all our problems" Maggie said with a laugh.

"Have you started Martha's wedding clothes yet Maggie?"

"No the season has taken up all of my time when we get to January that will be time enough to get the old treadle out."

"I have never used a treadle machine, is it easy Maggie?"

"Well all things have to be learned Sara, I will show you how if you would like me to, but again it has to be after Christmas when the days are dark and the time in home needs filling with things to do. I like Joe to drag the old machine out for me so I can sit in the warmth of this room while I stitch. Stone wall cottages are not the best of places, unless the heat inside is adequate then they are cosy so get the fire roaring up the chimney, and something good in the oven then we can forget the fierce winds and the snow. Joe has

to brave the elements I must say I feel for him especially in winter, Josh too, you can't see Josh for the clothes he has to wear his balaclava, barely let's his nose out to breathe. Scarves, gloves, winter boots

The pair of them being unrecognisable when they come in the cottage it takes a while to peel all their clothes off. They have to go into the kitchen to dry. You will soon see for yourself what a winter here is like."

Thinking about what Maggie had said, Sara was glad she had her small log burner in her bedroom, she could go into her own space and write or read, and still be warm. She could even make herself a hot drink if it pleased her to do so. Her imagination working overtime had produced a vivid picture of winter. A shiver ran down her back at the thought. Her life before had always been close to other people, here there was just themselves to be relied on. Winter would be here very soon.

Chapter Forty

There had been talk at the Hall Cook had spoken to Milord and Milady going out of her way to do so she said,

"I am sorry to bother you Madam, but I think there is something you should know."

"What is it Cook have you found some-one pilfering?"

"No Madam I am worried about Alice the Kitchen Maid, I thought she was putting on weight but now I fear she is pregnant, so I thought a word in your ear would be appropriate."

"Are you sure Cook, how long has it been since this was noticeable?"

"About a fortnight ago, I was giving her the benefit of the doubt but now to me it is obvious,"

"I will see if you are right Cook and talk to her later this afternoon is there anything else?"

"No Madam."

Cook bobbed a courtesy and left the room feeling the tension she had left behind. Milady said

"Well that is a turn up isn't it dear? How do you think that has happened?"

"In the usual way my love no doubt about that more to the point who is the Father?"

"You are not thinking what I am thinking are you?" Milady said distressed,

"What are you thinking then, the worst I expect?" Milord replied

"We will have to see her and ask outright how this has come about, shall I send for her right now?" Milady looked worried.

"Best get it over with I think and went over to the bell cord to summon Alice."

"You sent for me Milady, Milord, Alice dipped a little courtesy."

"Yes Alice I will come straight to the point Cook says she thinks you are pregnant is this right or not?"

Alice decided as soon as she heard the question it was useless lying so she made a clean straight reply.

"Yes I am, but I am not sorry when I find the man that fathered my child he will surely marry me."

"Oh so you don't know who the Father is?" Milady thinking Richard or Vincent hadn't been named.

"Yes of course I know I am not a bad girl Milady. It happened very suddenly, nature flung us into each other's arms, this is a very private matter between the two of us."

"What is his name does he work in these grounds?" It was Milady wanting to know

detail,

Alice knew she was cornered, she didn't even know her lover's name.

"No Milady it was a romantic encounter we saw each other and immediately the bond was there. I have tried to find him again but as yet he hasn't shown up."

"It gets better! You really don't know this man at all Alice, how you could behave without thought is beyond me." Milady felt relieved Alice still hadn't named her Sons. It softened her a little. Alice jumped in and said, "I am sorry Madam; I will leave first thing in the morning."

"Who said anything about leaving? We have discussed this predicament between us. You have served us well Alice; we haven't the heart to turn you out on to the Streets."

"If I could stay on Milady I would make sure there wouldn't be anything to disturb you. The baby wouldn't ever come into your sight. I would look after him or her below stairs; I would eat less to make up for the babies keep. I wouldn't get a job in this condition then it would be the Workhouse for us both I have been losing sleep worrying about it."

"We wouldn't be worried about feeding the baby, but we would be worried if you neglected this child in any way." Milady

replied.

"I already love this baby and I would never neglect the child, I know one day I shall find my love and he will set the pattern correct and marry me."

"Then if that is the case you may stay on. When is the baby due?"

Alice by now had fallen into a tearful state between her broken sobs she replied,

"In April sob, her breath caught in her throat, I do still have a way to go."

"Come on now dear girl you have just been delivered good news surely? You now know you can stay at the Hall."

"Yes, sob, thank you so much. This is pent up emotion I am crying with relief I will never be able to thank you enough."

"You just keep true to yourself and let things slowly come to full circle. You may go now Alice.

Tomorrow another day her heart would be quiet and she could wait for her baby to arrive without the torment of worry. Alice couldn't wait to tell Rosa.

In the room Alice had just left, there was still the subject on their minds to be discussed.

"What did you think of that dear? Milord looked anxious for a reply. Milady replied

"I am very glad it is over, I meant it when I

said we will look after her, poor dear she was torn apart with guilt. It was such a relief when Vincent or Richard's name didn't get mentioned it could have so easily have been one of them. You know what these Kitchen Maids are like. It is not unusual for them to name the nearest man with money. I find it quite a relief to know our Sons are not involved. Our support will help Alice and of course the real Father may come forward. We can leave it at that for the moment and breathe a sigh of relief."

"My dear you are an old softy at heart I would like you to reveal that side of you to our Son's sometimes, I think they do not know their own Mother as well as they should. That is what comes of sending them away to boarding School. They have lost contact with you and me for that matter. We shall have to open up our hearts and let them see just who their Mother and Father are. For instance I hate being at logger heads with Vincent over this Kitchen Maid called Sara. I don't want to lose Vincent and his trust and love. Maybe there will be a way we can accept his wishes?" Milady baulked at that!

"My dear Sir, do you mean to say you can contemplate a former Maid to eventually fill

my shoes?" Milord knew he had to tread carefully and said,

"Times are changing dear and we must change with them, we could have hoped for a better outcome but the love I have for my Sons dictates to me, we must learn to bend or else we will break."

"We'll see dear, we will see." Milady closed that conversation she didn't want to be cornered into giving an answer.

Chapter Forty-one

The closing of this conversation left lots of room for doubt. They looked at each other and quietly they were left to thoughts each of their own. Life was too short to waste it arguing.

Alice reached the Kitchen with her tear stained face saying,

"Oh Rosa it was awful I thought they were going to dismiss me."

"Well didn't they?"

"No I am to stay on they will actually help me when it becomes time for the delivery. I was stunned it was their kindness that brought about the tears I never expected them to understand as they did."

Rosa pulled a chair out for Alice to sit down Alice's legs were trembling with the deep emotion that the encounter had brought about.

"I will make us a cup of tea" Rosa said going over to Alice and giving her a gentle hug.

This occasion they had both been dreading had been met and dealt with, the relief for both of them was paramount. Even Miss Olivine and her sharp tongue wouldn't destroy the relief that both of them felt. Together they could cope now, they had nothing to hide. A quiet moment for sincere

thought, if they hadn't got each other they would have no-one
who really cared, call it what you will they had a bond not often found.
"Feeling a bit better now Alice?"
Alice sipped her tea and replied,
"What would I do without you Rosa? Yes, I will feel better now that I can think straight. I have been dreading the time when all this came to light. I have been losing sleep and feeling down, but I still want my baby and wish with all my heart to find my love. Rosa and Alice knew they could depend on each other.

Sara and Maggie were also sitting by the fire, this time to make a list of things that would be offered on the Christmas table.
"Do you like turkey Sara?"
"Yes of course I do it wouldn't be Christmas without one, although I can remember many Christmas's that I just couldn't afford one, we compromised and had a chicken from Dick
I knew he would find me one and always said it was one of his cheap ones, we both knew darned well it was one of his best. He even tried to protect me from my poverty, and brought all sorts of things for me and the kids to have on Christmas day. He knew Bill

would be too drunk to care. Here I go again I don't want to even think about those days leave the past where it belongs, buried."

"I know you like pork, so they are the two meats I shall have for Christmas dinner followed by a plum pudding eh? We will have custard too, and a glass of wine to wash it all down with."

"Yummy that sounds a feast it is making my mouth water. I know you made the puddings but have you made the Christmas cake?"

"You know I have, can't leave that to the last minute it is better matured and fed with a little brandy to keep it moist I sometimes use an apple cut into quarters and placed in the air tight tin with the cake, that will also keep it moist."

"I shall never be able to store all the tips you teach me Maggie."

"You will, it is surprising just how much our minds will keep for further use, I remember the way my Mother taught me, and it is so good that I can pass it on to you,"

"What time is Joe coming in tonight Maggie?"

"He won't be long now, I suppose we had better get the tea set, and the butter spread, it is boiled eggs tonight, I always recon to famish before the feast, it is one of my

personal things, always did even when a child getting myself prepared so to speak ha ha. I still have mince pies to make but I leave them a little nearer the day, they do keep, but once made I like to see them all ate not wasted. I soak raisons in some red wine and add to the mincemeat at the point of putting the mix all together sometimes I will put glazed cherries in too. If they do get left there is always custard to add and have them as a pudding. I never waste anything if I can possibly help it. Here is Joe now that will stop our nattering he will be hungry, put the kettle on Sara and set the table. I shall go and see what eggs have been laid today."

"Hello Sara, my, it is a cold wind out there today goes straight through you I am not sorry to be finished, happy to say all the live stock is now undercover and fed. What's for tea dear?

"It is boiled eggs tonight Joe, Maggie has gone to collect some. Shall I wait to make the tea until she comes in?"

"Ah that would be best, I can get out of these soggy clothes and change my boots while I wait I will be good and ready to eat then."

Joe cluttered about pushing his boots into a cupboard alongside the fire, they would slowly dry out there and be ready for morning.

Maggie came in with the bluster of wind that drove the curtain at the door into a sail.

"Brr don't want to be out there long, it is freezing, had a good day Joe?"

"Apart from the cold yes I have seen to everything that needs immediate attention and I am ready to sit down by the fire. Get some good eggs Maggie?"

"Yes the Hens never let me down good food that is what it is, you reap as you sow, and these eggs show it." Maggie placed half a dozen large brown eggs into a bowl and gently washed them off.

"Will boiled eggs suit you both? I can poach or scramble if you like."

"I like boiled" Sara said with plenty of bread and butter to make soldiers."

"That won't take long mi dears."

Maggie lifted a saucepan down and put in the six eggs. Sara cut the bread and buttered it. The fire flamed, the cottage cosy, the tea cosy on the pot, a jar of homemade jam on the table, the clock on the mantelpiece struck five, and all was well in their small world.

Getting up next morning there was a hint of snow in the air.

"Get something extra warm on today Sara, it is bitterly cold,"

"Well I thought I had but now that I am out of my warm bedroom I can feel the extra chill, I will go and put a jumper on top that should keep me warm."

Sara noticed Maggie had her slipper boots on with lamb's wool lining, when it was as cold as this she needed them. Joe came in his nose was blue.

"I think it is too cold for snow, it is freezing hard I had to break thick ice from the horse trough. Good job I lagged all those outdoor water pipes, if you prepare for winter it is half the battle, of course Mother Nature will have her way and very often finds the spot you have missed, can't help that though can we?"

Sara and Maggie were busying themselves around so that the work of the day would be done by dinner time, this afternoon they had planned to put some bright wrapping paper around their small gifts, these would then be placed under the tree to make the mystery of Christmas. Most times the gift would be small and simple but the unwrapping of it was no less exciting. Maggie said,

"I have got some brown paper and some red crepe paper left over from last year, I was thinking we could make a few paper roses with the red, and get a bit more when we are in the village to replace it"

"I have never heard of paper roses Maggie, how do you make those?"

"It is best to show you dear, they are quite effective in a small bowl, a candle in the middle and Holly around it topped off with red Rosebuds. Let's get this work out of the way then we can do just what we want to do."

So while Sara black leaded the grate while the fire was low. Maggie was at the kitchen sink washing net curtains she wanted them fresh and white for when her guests came, saying,

"These nets seem to catch all the dirt, probably the open fire with its smoke does it; they seem to be always in the wash. Trouble is I like to see the nets it makes the room feel cosy,

I had better just get on with it then."

By this time Maggie was talking to herself, by this time she didn't need an answer.

Sara thought though Maggie was right it did seem cosier with the nets up.

"I have done the grate Maggie shall I build the fire back up now?"

Yes let's get the old place cosy as quick as we can, Joe hates to see things disorderly he thinks things should stay put forever, men don't seem to see when a spruce up is necessary

Just hate to be disturbed, but things don't stay like that, he must think I wave a magic wand and all is done. That is why I like to get it out of the way when he has gone to the barns."

"No wonder he thinks you have a magic touch if he never sees you do the jobs, oh Maggie you should let him know how you work to keep everything spick and span, I shall tell him if I get the chance"

"Don't you worry your pretty head about that I have a sneaky feeling he does know but doesn't want to admit it, just a man's way dear."

They both smiled and got on with the task in hand.

After tea Sara and Maggie set about making crepe paper Roses. Maggie cut the red crepe into strips then one side of them were cut into the shape of rose petals, so now she had a strip with one side plain and one side rounded in a wavy pattern. Next she opened the scissors wide and pulled the sharp edge on the crepe making it curl like a Rose petal. She carefully took hold of the bottom of the red crepe and turned it round and around, forming a rose like look, tweaking the petals as she went. From a centre tight bud and so on to make the full Rose, when it was satisfactory to the eye, and looking like a rose she tied fine cotton around the base to hold it in the required position.

"Pass me one of those twigs Sara"

Sara passed the twig gathered from the hedgerow outside. Finally Maggie tied the Rose she had made on to an appealing part of the twig.

"There we go then here is your rose Sara,"

"That's lovely Maggie can I try to do one?"

"Of course you can your fingers are nimbler than mine you will be good at doing the dainty buds.

So the two of them spent the evening, materials on the table sitting before a warm fire making their Roses, Joe was content smoking his pipe.

"I am going down to the Ford this weekend, I could drop you off Sara to see Martha you would be able to take the gifts from you for the Kids stockings. Better take the opportunity never know what weather will turn up, could be snow soon, and when we get snow here we get stuck sometimes for weeks, we get used to it don't we Maggie?"

"Oh yes that is why my store cupboard is stocked so well I like to be prepared. Look at our Roses Joe, mingled with a spray of natural green either Pine or Holly they will *look a treat in the centre of our table."*

"You certainly know how to make the place cosy Maggie, I think I sensed that even before we were married. You could make a shilling go where oil wouldn't run."

"It wasn't my pretty face then Joe?" Maggie said with a smile knowing exactly what Joe meant.

Saturday morning and Sara with her parcels all wrapped prettily was off with Joe to see Martha.

"It's a bitter wind this morning Joe, I have piled on my jumpers but the wind is still cutting like a knife."

"We'll soon have you there mi dear, Martha will be pleased to see you."

Waving goodbye to Maggie the horse was set off at a trot. Joe treated his horse with gentle persuasion getting the best from him as they galloped along.

Sara pulled her coat collar up to cover her ears although she had a woolly hat on; her mittens were also up holding the coat lapel tight. They couldn't converse with each other their voices wouldn't be adequate to keep up a sensible exchange of words. So they clip clopped along, the wheels of the cart giving them great jolts as they hit the rough stony frozen ground.

Soon they would be at Martha's, and the kettle would be put on the fire for a warming cup of tea.

Sara knocked the door, it seemed strange to her to be in the Quarry Yard again and it brought back vivid recollections of Bill and her fear of him. The many times he had slapped her to the floor, and his brutal way with her in bed. Yes it all flooded back, how had she lived like that for so long? A shudder went down her spine. Her whole personality had changed since then. The deep regard she had for Vincent. She couldn't call it love, she DARE not call it love, it was not her place to admit to such a deep feeling, yet it was there and she couldn't deny it. Living too away from this unhappy place had changed her. Never would she return the visit was more than enough. Sara and Joe waited on the doorstep.

"Come on Martha, Joe said stamping his feet up and down don't keep us waiting in this cold wind."

The door opened, it was Sara's eldest son who opened it. Shock spread over Sara's face, it was more like looking at his Dad even his manner.

"Oh it's you Ma come in; Martha is bringing in the clothes off the line."

There was no affection in his eyes, no contact only the straight "Oh it's you Ma" she could sense he couldn't care less.

Martha bundled in with her full basket of clothes hardly being able to see over the top of the huge mound

"Martha it is Mam and Joe come to see you." He scurried away as if to be in their presence was the last thing he wanted.

"Well this is a surprise Sara just a minute let me get organised," Martha put down her clothes basket making sure nothing dropped to the floor. She swept her hair back with her hand the wind had blown it into a thousand tangles and reddened her cheeks.

"What brings you here then?" Martha asked.

"I am not stopping Martha Joe said, Just here to drop Sara off for an hour while I do some deliveries. I know it will have to be a short visit but Sara has a few stocking fillers to leave."

"Surely you have time for a cup of tea Joe?"

"Aw go on then it would warm my insides up,"

"Sit down then the two of you tea won't take but a few minutes."

The warmth of the kitchen began to fold around them, so Sara took off her coat and hat, and Joe loosened his neck scarf, knowing he would be tightening it up again to go back outside very shortly.

After pouring the tea Martha fetched a tin down from the top shelf.

"Here ya ar I baked a few early mince pies, I put them on the top shelf so that enquiring fingers would not dip in too soon, this brood are always hungry."

She laughed and conveyed she wasn't as serious as she made out to be. Joe and Sara took a mince pie and sipped their tea."

"Everything alright up at the farm Joe? I know this is your busiest time, is Maggie well?"

"Everything is being taken care of Martha, Maggie has spent lots of time preserving for the cold weather and my! It is telling us now today it is well and truly on its way, it is a bitter wind."

"Yes I felt it bringing in the washing, I must say though it has dried all my sheets as well as clothes so I mustn't grumble. I may even have to damp down a few things before I iron them, more tea Joe?"

"No thanks must get my deliveries done I will pick you up Sara in about an hour, don't want to be too late getting back."

"Bye then Joe" the Ladies chorused, the rush of the wind as the door was opened caught the mat and scurried it along the red brick floor, bringing in a flurry of snow that was lightly coming down and had settled on to the doorstep.

"Get the door shut Sara, brrr it is so cold, go and sit beside the fire and tell me how you are getting on at Maggie's."

"I like what I am doing Martha but I very often feel guilty when I think of the load I have left you to deal with."

"Think nothing of it dear I am happy with my lot, Dick helps and is content in doing so I wouldn't have it any other way so don't you fret yourself."

"I have a few bits and pieces for the Kid's stockings Christmas morning, Joe said bring them now because the weather is closing in, we have got through this light fall of snow but Joe says this is nothing compared with how it can be."

"Take them upstairs then Sara, lay them on the bed I will put them out of sight later."

Sara opened the door at the bottom of the stairs and tried to edge round the spot where Bill had lay dead. On her way upstairs her mind her mind filled again with the events of that fatal night.

"Dear God! I don't want to remember."

She almost ran to the top landing dropping

one of her parcels in her haste. Now she must stop and pick it up, the odour of death seemed to still linger in the air, was it the musty smell of the well worn carpet ugh! It overpowered her senses. She arrived at the bedroom, went in and hastily put the parcels on the bed for Martha to sort out they all had labels on them so they wouldn't get mixed. Strange but the bedside candle had been left burning, in the gloom and the darkness of the winter afternoon it caught the draft from the open door and flickered, she was tormented, so as quickly as she could she left the room ran downstairs opened the door at the bottom of the stairs went into the kitchen standing first with her back against the door, and her hands spread eagled behind her as if to stop someone who was chasing her.

"What on earth is the matter with you Sara? You look as though you had seen a ghost,"

"I feel as though I have Martha, I am trembling all over,"

"Sit down I will make more tea you are as white as a sheet."

"Martha sob…sob I am never going to live a natural life, my past is always looming up before me."

Martha took hold of her shaking body and gently steered it towards the fireside chair, sitting her down with purpose.

"You must pull yourself together Sara, Joe will be back before you know it, you don't want him to see you so alarmed it will worry him."

Sniffing up her tears Sara realised what a scene she was making also how she was burdening Martha with her own troubles.

"I am sorry Martha I came with Joe intending to have a pleasant talk with you about Christmas, and you're Spring Wedding. Now look what I have done, upset you. I really didn't mean to it just swept over me when I went upstairs and into the bedroom. Forgive me, I promise I won't let you down next time. I am tutoring myself every day to get rid of the guilt, then before I know it I am snatched into the depths of despair and it happens all over again, the events as though they were yesterday. I am then dropped into that black hole of despair."

"Come now dear tell me you are feeling a bit better."

Martha pushed a steaming cup of tea into Sara's hands trying her best to be positive and stand firm. She hated seeing Sara so distraught it was time the past was buried, and left buried.

A tap came on the front door. Martha

went and opened it.

"You haven't been long Joe we have hardly had any time at all."

"If you had been on that open cart seat you would know why I haven't been long it is enough to freeze you as you sit. I just want to get back to Maggie and my fireside. Not getting any younger you know."

He emphasised the fact by putting both his arms around his body and giving himself a hug. Sara quickly put on her outdoor clothes and followed Joe to the door, she was careful he couldn't see her tearstained face. Martha followed them then put her arms around Sara and said,

"Don't you worry anymore Sara live your life we are quite happy and content, it will soon be Christmas and you will be here with your friends Rosa and Alice on Boxing Day look forward to it, there will also be Dick, and Maggie with Joe, we will all have a lot to talk about then won't we, cos the next event will be my Wedding. How time flies."

Turning to Joe she added,

"Go safely now Joe it is almost dark keep happy and give Maggie my love."

Martha waved them off, hoping Sara had gained her self control by the time she arrived back at the cottage.

Chapter Forty-two

Christmas Eve, and Maggie Sara and Joe had smartened themselves up to go and sing Carols in the Church Hall. To get into the spirit of things they all wore a bit of red. Scarf and wool hat for Maggie. Sara sported a red and green tweed coat with green mittens and hat. Joe had on his red plaid scarf and decided that was as far as he was going to stretch his imagination.

On the way out of the cottage Joe had insisted on drinking a toast with the red wine they had made and stored.

"It'll warm the cockles of your hearts mi bonnie wee Ladies"

Sara and Maggie giggled, and lifted their glasses in a toast to the Season Sara spluttered on hers she hadn't expected it to be that strong. It warmed the throat as it went down and gave her a nice light feeling.

There was a good gathering of people from outlying farms and the evening went on without incident everyone in good spirit shaking hands and wishing each other a "Merry Christmas" an atmosphere of congeniality. The Carol singers were bright and sincere, the evening stayed dry, and on the way back to the Cottage they all remarked at the brightness of the Moon and Stars.

Home and tired, Maggie quickly made them a hot drink and ushered them off to bed, tomorrow was Christmas Day, a big day in all families.

Christmas morning and all was well in their world, smiles and happy laughter, along with the preparing of the Christmas dinner, and the gathering of parcels around the Christmas tree.

"When shall we open the gifts Maggie?"

"I think after Christmas dinner, now you know Sara you had the money to pay for half of the clothes you chose from the market, so don't get excited there is only one small thing wrapped for you under the tree."

"Of course I know Maggie, now is the time to say a very big thank you to you and Joe."

Maggie said,

"It is a pity I haven't got a wardrobe for you to hang your clothes in, I have always thought a wardrobe would take up too much room in there, space is not exactly abundant."   Sara   replied,

"The Hall Stand you have given me is quite adequate. The clothes are all on hangers and draped with brown paper to keep them dust free. I can't wait to wear them."

"Now then, you can't wear them until Martha and Dick gets married. You have to *look your best standing beside Martha, you are giving her away, it is usual for a Man to do that job but Martha has chosen you, you should be highly honoured."*

"Oh I am Maggie, I will do my best to fit the part and do my duty, and I thought she would choose Joe, but as she has chosen me so I am duty bound. It is my deep regard for Martha and Dick that moves me to be upright and conscientious it is a big day for them I don't want anything to spoil it."

Joe broke the conversation by sidling up to Maggie putting his arm around her waist saying,

"Hmmm, it is all starting to smell very good, I didn't have much breakfast I am good and ready for my Christmas dinner, his arm tightened its grip and he dropped a kiss on Maggie's grey hair.

"I have never known you not to be ready to eat Joe, about like your help Josh, he will have anything you offer him, is he coming to see to the animals today?"

"He has been and gone mi dear. All the stock is fed and watered so you don't have to worry about that. You just concentrate on looking after Sara and me, and we in turn will help you"

Maggie said,

"For one thing Joe get a couple more logs on the fire, must have the heat up today the oven has a lot to do."

The table was set, the red Crepe Paper Roses circling the candle holder alongside the Holly looked pretty, a single lighted candle throwing its light around the green table cloth which was dressed with red place mats and best cutlery all looked very inviting. Sara said,

"Maggie, thank you so much for your care and thought shown to me today."

Sara felt a lump in her throat so kept her words short, there was so much more she could have added but she had to keep peace, knowing that Maggie and Joe didn't need words to convey just what she thought of them both.

"I think it is about ready now Joe dear, you can lift the Turkey from the oven, mind you be careful it is heavy and very hot."

Joe took the oven cloth from Sara, and as told carefully lifted the Turkey on to a side table ready to get it on to the huge serving plate ready for carving at the table. The vegetables were served on the three plates selected, all ready for the carving of the Turkey to take place, Joe's eyes were gleaming.

"You Ladies want breast meat I assume? I will have a leg and then I can pick it up in my hands and devour it like an Ogre."

Sara and Maggie laughed at his suggestion, but knew exactly what he meant.

"Who's for Pork then? Joe said having served the Turkey. They all wanted Pork, it was Dick's own breeding and would be without a doubt good and tasty meat. So they settled down to eat the feast, there was not much said they were too busy swallowing the sumptuous food. After dinner there were the parcels to open.

"Look what I have got" said Joe entering into the spirit of the parcel opening.

"My goodness I will see you coming in that Joe"

Sara had knitted Joe a red Balaclava. Sara smiled and said,

"Best new wool Joe you will have to wear it."

"It will keep me good and warm thank you Sara and I don't think Josh will mind the colour, so there is no one else to worry about."

He pulled it over his head, the base acted as a scarf to tuck into his coat he was well pleased.

"What is in your parcel Maggie? All eyes went to Maggie as she pulled the string off

her gift. *A very pretty apron was revealed it had a pattern of tiny roses all over it.*

"You can serve tea outside in the summer wearing that Maggie," Sara said.

"Did you make this Sara?" Maggie asked,

"Yes I did, when you had gone to the market with Joe" Maggie inspected the stitching saying,

"As you say for summer use when the Sun is blazing down, it is very neat dear thank you very much"

It was Sara's turn carefully she unwound the paper, it seemed like two items in the parcel and she didn't want to break anything. Her eyes shone as she took the contents into her hands Eau-de-cologne in a very attractive bottle, and the talcum powder to match the fragrance.

"Thank you so very much I have never had any scent or talcum before. I have stood gazing into windows where they were displayed but I thought that was as near as I would ever come to actually having my own."

"Well Sara you had received your gift with the money for your clothes, we thought the perfume to wear when you put on those clothes would be just right, we are so glad that you like it."

"Like it? I love it I am very lucky and I love

you both."

Sara went to each of them and kissed their cheek, she was thinking this was how life should be, not waking up and dreading what the day would hold.

All cleared away, they sat by the fire.

"Shall we play cards for an hour Joe said or dominoes? Which do you like best?

"I like dominoes I know better how to play that." Sara said.

"Dominoes it is then."

Joe lifted down a well worn cardboard box, the card curling at the edges and brown with age, it had seen some use over the years. When the dominoes were tipped out they too looked worn, they had been black and white many moons ago now they had a distinctive yellow tinge the black spots were still evident and made ready for the game. They played for an hour, Sara giggling when she won, a sweet from the Chocolate box her prize.

"Let's just relax now Joe said, I will wind up the old Gramophone, I have a Christmas Carol record I haven't played yet.

Joe lovingly slid the large black record from the paper packet, then lifted the arm with the steel needle attached, looked at the needle to see that it was secure, and free of fluff then gently placed the needle on to the revolving

record, and there it was like magic the soft chorus of Christmas Carols floated in the air.
"Is it double sided Joe? Sara asked,
"Yes it has "In a Monastery Garden" on the other side. I will play that after this if you would like. That is if I don't drop off in the chair as I am likely to do."
"I think I know how to turn the record over said Maggie, and I don't drop off as quickly as you Joe."

They all laughed each knowing what the other was thinking a satisfied and happy three individuals. They sat back to listen. The glass of wine that they had during the meal had gone straight down to Sara's toes, it was a pleasant feeling. She was offered more but declined she too would have been asleep as well as Joe.
"I have a mince pie before we settle down if you would like one"
"We are full to the brim Maggie said Sara, perhaps later on we will have one."
The warmth of the log fire the flame leaping up the chimney the half dark of the room the candles as they flickered and dripped tallow down the sides. The peace and tranquillity
shared by them all made the outside world seem far away, a place where dreams are made a place that all men envy.

Chapter Forty- three

"Off we go then said Joe, helping Sara and Maggie up to get into the cart beside him saying to Maggie,

"Glad that wind has dropped it was cruel. Maggie replied,

"It is not too bad at all today."

"Even early morning there was no frost Sara joined in. I have still put on some warm things". She flung her scarf over her shoulder, and pulled her hat well down over her ears, and off they trotted.

They were having a cold spread at Martha's, that way the Kids could eat their fill as well as the visitors. There was a knock on the door Martha went.

"Come in mi dears I thought it would be you, go and put your hats and coats on my bed,"

Sara felt her heart sink she didn't want to go up those stairs ever again. Joe saw her hesitate and said,

"Give me your clothes and you Maggie, you can have a natter with Martha before Rosa and Alice arrives."

Piled high with the burden of coats hats and scarves Joe went upstairs.

"Have a good day yesterday Martha?" Maggie asked, Martha replied,

"Quiet and the dinner was lovely, the Kids

were pleased with the gifts they had, we played cards using farthings to play "Banker" I must say it made the boys pay a bit more attention than if we used matchsticks as money, all in fun you know Maggie. The Kids had a prize out of the Chocolate assortment along with the odd farthing or two Very competitive and we all enjoyed the banter that went with the game." Maggie said,

"We did much the same only we had Dominoes Joe is too good for Sara and me, although I must say Sara was a good player and took one or two rounds. We had about ten different shuffles then decided we had used up all our energy and enough was enough."

They laughed together, Martha putting glasses on the table to have wine. She poured three small ones Maggie wouldn't let her fill the glasses saying,

"Hey! That is enough, don't want to get tipsy do we?"

Yet another knock at the door, and Rosa with Alice stood there.

"Merry Christmas Martha they chimed in together,"

"A merry Christmas to you mi dears, we have a lovely fire and a spread fit for a Queen."

They bundled in unbuttoning their coats as they did so.

"The Candles on the table look lovely Martha, said Alice and Rosa, and the spread has so many choices ready we won't know where to begin,"

Martha smiled and said "You will begin right here," and put a glass of wine in their hand.

Martha took their clothes and told them to feast their eyes on the table in front of them, noticing they had both made the most of what they could wear. Rosa was elegant, just a plain black dress with a long string of artificial pearls draped around her neck and falling down on to the black material of the dress. The contrast was good without being showy. Alice had a very loose dress on, gathered from under the bodice to tumble down over her bump, (yes the baby was now showing) the dress finished at the ankle, as did Rosa's. They had spent days going over what they would wear and their choice showed it had been well worth the while.

Dick came in they all exchanged greetings then Martha passed around the plates so they could chose what they wanted to eat. Maggie noticed one or two of her old favourites and knew Martha had been very busy indeed.

A quiet day followed their visit to Martha

and Dick it felt good to just relax now that all the pressure had gone. Sara had been presented with a romantic book so with the Chocolate that she had been given she asked if Joe and Maggie would mind if she went to her own room. So lighting a few candles to read by she lay on top of her eiderdown, opened her Chocolate box and felt at one with the world and all that was in it. The book was called "Enchanted" and she couldn't wait to read the first chapter. The title had already made her want to read the story.

Getting up next day gave them all a shock, it had snowed in the night and all was blanketed in the fresh white glitter. Sara said, "We were lucky to get to Martha's yesterday weren't we? Although it doesn't look very deep it looks treacherous. There are icicles dripping from the gutters still frozen, so the ground will be icy too. I am glad we are indoors."

"Speak for yourself mi dear, I must go and tend to the stock, but I won't be out there one minute more than I have to. Josh will be here early tomorrow, I shall be glad to see him. The trouble is with these holidays the routine is set aside and it is a job to get back to normal again. Maggie was listening and said, "Now Joe don't get spoiling the last few days

with a grumpy tone you know we have all enjoyed it, the change will have done us all good. While you are out Sara and me will take down the trimmings and the tree. You'll be home as fast as your legs will carry you, so get off, the sooner you go the sooner you'll be home. With a gust of whippy wind carrying snow Joe went out of the door.

"Sara we will put the Christmas trimmings in the box ready for next year."

The box was brought down and placed on the table one by one each item was carefully wrapped into the tissue paper that they had come out of, gently dusting as they went. Maggie was talking to Sara in between the packing of the items.

"I know how it is with Joe he is not getting any younger and the years are starting to take their toll. Winter must be endured we must do the best we can, spring will be around again soon although it is hard to imagine that at the moment."

Next day piles of Snow had been carried by the strong wind, there were huge drifts and the rooftops were layered, almost too laden to hold the deep Snow that had settled upon them.

It was frozen snow and it defied the laws of gravity. This was the time when Maggie was glad she had filled her store cupboard, it was evident that they had to stay put for the moment, and how long that moment stretched out was any ones guess. Getting to outlying districts was impossible. They were marooned and that was that! Maggie said,

"You can't argue with the weather Joe you must do your best, is Josh getting through the snow?"

"Yes but he is having to walk it is too treacherous for his Horse, he is finding it a job just getting here, let alone the work he has to do when he arrives. He is more muffled up than ever. I can just see his eyes all the rest of his head is mightily covered. It must take him best part of an hour just to get here he says there are drifts of 4ft and more deep in the lanes it is hard going. Before he leaves to go home I want to bring him across to see you and Sara. He hasn't had as much as a mince pie or a glass of wine with us this season. It would warm him up and get him prepared for his journey home."

"I wondered why you hadn't done that before Joe, I will expect you to bring him today, don't do anything you can safely leave, then you will be done sooner. Take great care, I don't want you slipping and breaking those old bones. Josh too I want to see you both in

one piece."

"Alright Alright, I hear you, see you later Maggie."

"The door opened and Joe was gone into the freezing landscape.

"What will we be doing today Maggie?"

"I want to make some fresh bread, I thought I had made enough but Joe likes to take a pack of sandwiches for Josh as well as his own and it soon takes up the bread, we have the odd slice of toast as well, not that I am saying we shouldn't it just uses the bread quickly."

Maggie stripped the table of cloths and crockery, carefully folding the chenille afternoon cloth, the posh cloth as Sara called it. Now to discover the scrubbed table top of white wood that was kept clean just for the purpose of making bread or other cooking that took space. There was plenty of room to knead bread, or make pastry, or fill jars with fruit preserves, or jams. This table was sturdy and ready to take all the knocks that it was dealt.

The hub of the Cottage it seemed.

"Get the large Jowl out Sara, and some yeast from the cold meat safe just outside the back door. I will make a warm mix of milk and water with a touch of sugar, the yeast will

soon start to thrive in that."

The Jowl was placed in the preferred position it was a large wide bowl cream on the inside and light brown on the outside, made of heavy pot, just the thing for bread making as Maggie got her hands and half way up her arms involved in the process.

"Give your hands a good scrub Sara there is some carbolic soap under the sink."

Sara slid the gathered curtain that covered the gap under the sink carefully the curtain was only on a wire spring pushed through the top hem stretched with a hook at both ends. She could see the soap it had gone a bit gooey sitting in its damp container it was the one that was in use so she had to use it. Doing as Maggie had said, her hands were now nice and clean.

"Here you have a turn Sara,"

Maggie showed Sara how to knead bread.

"Not like that, like this."

Maggie got hold of the bread dough and slapped it down on the table folding sides to middle, kneading again, punching spreading folding sides to middle again making the little bubbles in the dough evident and even popping one or two of them.

"Whew! Now come and have a go Sara."

Sara went forward and this time had a lot

more determination strength and persuasion, it was now beginning to look like bread.

"Move over I will finish it off," Maggie said holding her floury hands up in front of her.

She floured the table once more, and pulled the dough this way and that, then made a nice round pile of dough in front of her ready to set aside to rise, the aroma of the yeast working with the flour was pungent soon it would be in the oven and the smell of the crust as it browned would give the whole Cottage a warm and welcoming delight.

"Could you wash the Jowl for me Sara?"

Sara did saying,

"Here you are Maggie,"

"Is it fully dry dear?"

Sara gave the vessel an extra rub with the tea towel.

"Yes Maggie it is dry"

Maggie sprinkled flour over the base of the jowl and placed the dough inside it and draped a clean towel over the top.

"That will take a while to rise Sara, then I shall punch it down and let it rise a second time, while we wait put the kettle on and make tea, what would I do without my tea."

She sighed.

The bread now had risen twice and been put into baking tins, into the oven it went and soon there was that glorious aroma that baking bread delivers.

Sara looked outside as she drew over the heavy curtains to stop the draft, the light was quickly fading. The Candles would have to be lit early today.

"Have you noticed Maggie? The snow is falling heavily; the mounds on the window ledge must be at least four inches deep?"

Maggie went to look.

"My word that has settled quickly, I hope Joe and Josh can get back home alright. I must make a good substantial tea tonight they will both be very hungry. I have a rabbit hanging waiting to be used; this is about the right time to put it in the pot."

A cauldron type cooking vessel, black with a handle over the top of it so that it could be put on the hook over the fire to cook, then swung back from the centre to the side of the fire to keep simmering and be out of the way. Now was the time it was going to be used so Maggie fetched in the rabbit. She would have to take off the fur it still was dressed in, then chopping the legs off dispensing with the head cutting out the rib bones although they would still be put into the stew, there was not much meat on these but added to the nutritional value of the broth. All were washed and then dropped into the pot then the vegetables were added, Onion Carrots Parsnips and with a few green Beans that Maggie had salted down for winter use.

Added salt and pepper, and liquid topped up it being now ready to cook.

"Give me a hand with this Sara I must be getting old can't lift my own pot on to the fire."

"As I am here Maggie there is no need for you to fret I will do the lifting."

Together they did the job, Maggie putting the high black lid on the top. They stepped back with a sigh,

"Did you put in the potatoes Maggie?"

I have them already but don't want to put them in for a while, let the rabbit stew with the other vegetables for a start. Potatoes only take about twenty minutes so we have plenty of time. They would go into a mush if put in too soon."

The pot now full was too heavy for one to lift to serve, so it would be served after thickening, straight to the plate from its Cauldron pot over the fire. Plates that were chosen were more like dishes deep in the centre this allowed the broth to settle in the centre well away from eager hands. Soon the broth added to the sumptuous aroma of the baking bread. The men folk would come into a heaven made on earth that was specially made for their delight. It was just rewards for the cold desolate work that had taken place between them that day.

"Josh can stay and have some with us, Maggie said. Joe will bring him in tonight for a glass of wine. I am sure on a cold night such as this a plate of rabbit stew would be just the thing to offer him. In fact I think Sara when the Potatoes are added we could leave all of it to simmer and go over to the barns to lend a hand. Joe and Josh would get done that bit earlier. Hessian will have to be put over all the sacks of Potatoes to keep the frost out, they will be no good if the frost gets to them, Joe will leave an oil lamp burning too just to keep the temperature just above freezing. If they haven't got round to doing that, it is certainly a job we could do."

"Of course Maggie, I would like to think we could help, they will be dying to be finished won't they?"

"Maggie laughed, I am sure they will and when you have been out in this cold so will you and me it is an important job, if Joes potatoes go frosted he will have none to sell until the new crop. He has regular customers he wouldn't want to let down. Apart from the

drain on our livelihood, so get you well wrapped up and we will go."

They trudged through the Snow which was still falling, hitting their faces as they walked along, there was no sign of it letting up the Snow fell as flakes as large as half crown pieces. The land was frozen so the Snow was settling and mounding into drifts where the harsh wind was blowing it. Joe greeted them,

"Come in quickly don't want the Snow drifting in with you, a dark and hard evening this is and no mistake, you should have stayed where it is warm we would have managed."

"Now Joe don't lecture us just show us what you want us to do and we will get on with it."

Joe showed them how to cover the Potatoes for the best effect and then left them to it. Between them they soon had the job done and was asking what else could they do?

"Just get the blankets for the Horses, and see that they are tied on tight it is going to be a cold night for us all we can only do our best can't we?"

Josh appeared his face what you could see of it was bright red, his nose especially.

"Hello you two, I am coming back with Joe tonight so what are we eating?"

"Cheeky monkey" Maggie said in a pleasant

tone. Sara joined in saying,
"We are having fresh homemade bread and
rabbit stew. The bread is cooling from the
oven and the rabbit is simmering in a pot on
the fire as we speak."
"Now that is what I call a welcoming meal I
can hardly wait, much more to do" he called
across to Joe.
"No I think we are about finished Josh, see to
it that our Ladies are on the way home we
will follow very shortly."
"Right you are Joe, come on now you two get
going you have two hungry men to satisfy
tonight. Maggie smiled and tried to leave the
barn with Sara, but it took the two Ladies and
Josh to open the barn door, the wind was
strong and cutting. Sara said,
"What a night this is going to be Maggie I
will be glad to be by the fire again."
"Me too Sara the Snow has deepened since
we came and it is still coming down with a
vengeance."
Back to the Cottage was heavy going they had
to pick up their boots in a queer fashion to
enable them to walk. The Cottage came into
view. "Phew! Said Maggie Here we are at
last, leave your wet clothes in the shed for
now, hanging in there they can drip and get
most of the wet out of them, we will dry them

tomorrow Sara."

Chapter Forty-four

"Did you hear what Josh was talking about in the barn?" said Sara,

"No I didn't, but let's get inside in the warm then you can tell me, was it important?"

"It could be Maggie I had my thoughts going in all directions." They were inside now with the smell of the Rabbit cooking permeating the cottage all around. Maggie first stirred the rabbit stew and was then was ready to listen.

"What did Josh say then Sara?

"I asked him if he had a regular girl" he replied,

"No I don't have a girlfriend. I am not particularly bothered at the moment. I have never felt deeply for any girl. Well perhaps I tell a lie, there was this one girl I met at Danbury Hall on open day, she knocked me off my feet. Sort of love at first sight but I only knew her briefly, a whirlwind romance if you like. I have been meaning to contact her again, but have felt unsure of myself, I am biding my time. Pretty little thing she keeps returning to my mind."

"I tell you Maggie, my ears pricked up, could this possibly be Alice's lost love. I felt myself tingle with goose pimples all over me. When he comes in tonight I shall raise the subject

again, perhaps I am totally wrong but I must pursue this matter." Maggie replied,

"Now then Sara you let that lad settle from his hard day's work it is his meal he will be wanting not a questioning."

"Yes I know that Maggie but I have to get to the truth. I couldn't let this chance slip by, Alice is desperate to find her lover, what sort of friend does it make me if I am not bothered. Alice would be elated if I was right, that is when I could get to tell her. I am so excited I can't wait to speak to Josh." Sara's eyes were shining with exuberance.

"You do know Sara that you are most likely entirely wrong so don't go jumping in at the deep end, try to be subtle and keep accusations well away from your line of conversation. Remember Josh knows nothing yet."

"Alright Maggie I promise to tread carefully but you must see the importance of all this?"

"Yes dear yes, but first things first they will be in very shortly I must get the rest of these potatoes into the stew, it is nearly done and smelling good isn't it."

It did, Maggie had only to thicken and brown the liquid in the pot to finish with a very tempting and tasty meal.

"Here is Joe and Josh Maggie I can hear

them in the shed taking boots and top clothes off. The Snow is still falling heavily bet they are freezing cold shall I put the kettle on for a nice hot cup of tea?"

"Yes Sara but it won't be long before we sit down to eat, so make the tea now if you are going to, it will relax them." Joe came in,

"Brrr it is very cold out there now Maggie mi dear."

Joe went to his armchair by the fire saying,

"Here ya ar Josh take Maggie's armchair and get thawed out,"

Josh came forward into the room and Sara caught her breath, he had taken off his balaclava and his hair was just as Alice had described it unmistakably red with a glow to it that made it very attractive. Sara felt disturbed it was now to fall on her to identify Josh as Alice's lover. Could he have a Brother she thought? There would be time after they had eaten to find a way to broach the subject. Maggie said

"Here we are then, get your feet under the table and let us see what Rabbit stew will do for you"

Joe and Josh didn't need any special bidding they were sat at the table straight away. Maggie had lit a Candle in the centre of the table and brought out her large white plates she liked these to serve a stew on because she said they were dippy in the middle, meaning they held the gravy of the stew better than flat ones. They all appreciated the rabbit stew, the men having second helpings. Maggie said,

"I only have Mince Pies to offer you for afters you can have custard with it if you want it."

"I love custard Josh remarked but don't make it just for me." Sara joined in saying

"I will have some too, Maggie makes lovely creamy custard."

So they waited while fresh custard was made, Maggie putting six mince pies in the oven to get hot quickly. She said,

"Good job I made more mince pies Sara I don't think I have wasted one in all the years."

The wine was served with the sweet dish and very nice too. Sara had a small glass and sipped it very gently she could feel the warmth in her throat as it went down. After clearing up they sat around the fire generally chatting. Josh had made one attempt to take his leave and go home, but the awful weather had got worse so they decided he should stay. Maggie telling him he could sleep on the worn Settee that was placed along the side of

the wall. That was the best she could do.
"That will suit me fine Maggie thank you."
Now they had time for a hand of cards, using
matchsticks for money. Sitting quietly now
Sara spoke to Josh,
"Do you live far from here Josh?"
"Far enough on a night like this, on a good
day I would say it was about half hours walk,
on Horseback ten to fifteen minutes. I don't
mind walking my legs being long and strong
so I soon stride it out."
"Live with your Ma and Pa do you?"
"Well yes and no, I have all my meals with
them but I have a small stone built Cottage
attached to the main building. They are easy
to build on when the dwelling is erected in
stone. A bit like the room you have here with
Maggie and Joe. But mine has more rooms it
provides me with privacy; I don't get in the
way living on my own. It has two bedrooms
and a Kitchen that I can cook in when I want
to cook, which I must admit is not very often.
It suits me anyway. I have no rent to pay and
I am there to help Ma and Pa. We have a
couple of fields that grow mainly Potatoes.
Joe buys from us to take on his rounds. It
seems to work for all of us. I help Joe as well,
that gives me a regular spending money of
my own."

"Did you say you met an attractive girl on the open day at Danbury Hall Josh?"

Sara was careful with her words it was none of her business after all. The thing is she knew first hand of was Alice's dilemma and felt it her duty towards her friend to get a few facts right Josh replied,

"Now that girl was attractive, I could have run off with her the moment I saw her."

"Have you ever tried to pay her a visit Josh?"

"No, I have very little to offer a girl, and she was I believe a Kitchen Maid at the Hall, I didn't want her to lose her job over my intrusion she may have got dismissed if they found me hanging around."

How close he was to what had really happened but how little he knew of Alice herself and her coming baby.

"I know that girl Josh."

He looked startled,

"Oh how do you know her Sara? Is she a relative of yours?"

"No I worked with her at the Hall before I came to help Maggie and Joe out. I was dismissed because Mi Lord and Mi Lady thought their Son was paying me too much attention. They were wrong. I did have a friendship with Mr Vincent but that is all, they blew it up out of all proportion so I had

to leave."

"Do you see her now Sara?"

"I spent Boxing Day at Martha's, and Alice and Rosa were there, I intend to keep in touch." Josh said,

"So maybe I will see my lovely girl again someday eh?"

"When I next see her I will tell her you were asking after her, I think you are very much in her mind Josh."

Sara turned the subject of the conversation around now thinking she had said enough. Next move was to go to Alice and tell her what she had found out. Sara thought,

"If I push too far now I might upset the Apple cart, leave things be and as soon as I can go to the Hall and see Alice" Maggie broke her line of thought. Yawning and getting up from her armchair she said,

"Time for bed I think I will give you a pillow and a blanket Josh, you won't be cold in here as we keep the fire in all night, banking it up with slack and tealeaves, it keeps the place comfortable."

They all went their separate ways, and left Josh to bed down on the Settee. Josh was settling down before sleep his mind going over what Sara had said about knowing

Alice. Deeply thinking and mouthing the words to himself he said,

"So that was her name was it Alice, he had her picture painted in the back of his mind and was thinking back. A lovely girl and what is more she still remembered him. He almost blushed with the thought of how he had made love to her in that one bright moment. He hadn't been able to stop himself. The beautiful blue eyes with dark hair, her trim little figure, the way she held herself with confidence. Why haven't I gone to visit her, and get

to know her? Because I didn't want a broken heart, what had happened was in the heat and excitement of an Open Day when spirits were high and the mood carefree. If Sara thinks I have just half a chance I would follow the idea through and make a visit to see Alice. The thought excited him and he imagined her warm body pressed close to his. In this cloud of high expectations he fell asleep."

Sara too was devising a plan to get these two together her thoughts were more on a practical line.

"How soon will I be able to get to see Alice, if it wasn't for this awful weather I would go tomorrow, but even the post isn't getting

through I am forced to wait. I have known Josh all this time and never connected him as being Alice's lover. Josh didn't even know Alice was pregnant. He never had an inclination of anything amiss. All the months of agonising wait for Alice with uncertainty carrying the baby. Josh didn't even know he had been the cause of Alice's tears. All this must be put to rights. Right now though it was another waiting game until the weather changed and the Snow went away. Sara had to stay put. At least I have found out that Josh still thinks about Alice, more than that I can't do, will Josh right this wrong, what will Alice think?" The thoughts drifted through her mind. "Will Josh be pleased or shocked?" Sara's eyes blinked they were getting heavy she could hardly stay awake. Tomorrow another day, she would talk again to Maggie and get some straight forward advice. She turned over onto her other side pulled the sheets and cosy feather eiderdown around her shoulders and granted permission for her to sleep.

Morning came bleak and bitter cold freezing icicles that had dripped hung like weapons pointed and sharp. No-one would be moving out of the Cottage yet. The skies were heavy and darkly laden with the prospect of more Snow. Joe had been to see his horse and to throw yet another blanket over him. The water in the trough had frozen to an inch deep so Joe had to get a pick and free it so that his Horse could get to the drinking water. Coming to the Cottage he did the same in the tank and in the butt. He came in perished.

"This is a winter we won't forget Maggie mi dear," Maggie was getting Joe a mug of hot tea.

"You are right Joe looks as though we are stuck until there is a let up, good job we are well stocked up eh?"

"I am sorry Maggie but it looks as though Josh will be staying for a while longer, I am sure his Ma and Pa will have guessed where he is. In any case there is no way we can let them know. We will be lucky to get as far as the barns today everything is at a standstill Josh is out there now trying to clear a path just to get to the shed. I asked him to after the struggle I had seeing to the Horse and the water trough. We should to be prepared for this weather but we never are. We are optimistic in our view about just what the winter will bring. Ah well he sighed we'll get by."

It was weeks before things became

normal; the glint of sunlight through the cloud was very welcome. Sara had held her peace as regards telling Josh about Alice, and not being able to go to see Alice meant things had been left in square one. Now she hoped any day Joe would go out with the cart and take her to the Hall. It was arranged for the next day that the weather would permit and Sara was jubilant.

It had been a cold and not enjoyable ride with Joe, the air was still very sharp and sitting on the front of the cart blasted it right through clothes no matter how padded they were.

Seeing Alice and Rosa together in the kitchen was just what Sara needed.

"Fancy you being out in this cold Sara" Rosa was quick to notice Sara shivering.

"Come over here to the fire you look frozen."

One look at Alice told Sara she was doing the right thing so they sat around the fire while the kettle boiled for a hot drink.

"What if Miss Olivine catches us" Sara said,

"No she won't venture down here in this cold it is one thing we have to be thankful for."

Rosa edged her chair nearer the fire, Alice by her side,

"What brings you here Sara?"

"I have what I think is the most wonderful news Alice."

Both Rosa and Alice leaned forward so they didn't miss anything Sara was about to say.

"This is important Alice I have found your red haired man. Yes, just like that."

Alice found she was trembling and her voice faltered.

"Where and how? When was this Sara?"

Sara went on to tell the whole story also saying she hadn't told Josh about the baby and all that it had entailed.

Tears began to fall down Alice's face it was the shock as much as anything, this was serious news for her it could change her whole life.

A cup of soothing hot chocolate in their hands they went over it all again and again.

"You must let me arrange for you to meet him now Alice, he talks fondly about you, he is a good man and reliable as you will see for yourself." Alice looked worried and said,

"What if he doesn't like me as I am? I certainly am not the snippet of a girl he made love to behind the Oak tree, I hardly dare encounter him."

"Don't be silly Alice all this time you have been searching and waiting to find him of course you must talk to him."

Running through Alice's mind was what she would look like, and how she could make her middle look six sizes smaller!

"Joe will be back for me very soon so please tell me what it is I must do to get you and Josh together, so that you can talk it all over and go forward, it is what you have so desperately wanted Alice."

"I know but I am afraid, I care for him deeply but does he care for me? And will he think I am just palming myself on to him?"

Rosa said "Well you won't ever know if you don't find out will you Alice, tell Sara what do you want to do and how do you figure on meeting him, this is a lifetime we are talking about not a roll in the hay"

"Sunday is my day off do you think I could meet him at Martha's Cottage Sara?"

"I expect so, poor Martha I feel we sometimes put on her, but yes it does seem sensible."

"You can tell him about the baby Sara, in fact I would be glad if you did I don't know where I would start. Alice was full of dismay feelings of guilt were not nice.

"Right! Four- o'clock Sunday afternoon, I will call in and tell Martha on the way back."

Chapter Forty-five

Sara had to choose the right moment to talk to Josh, this was a delicate subject and it was none of her business, she had promised Alice so she must do it.

The weather had improved and jobs were being done as normal, although it was still very cold outside. Sara went a stroll over to the barns Maggie had given her extra sandwiches to take to Joe and Josh just so she could get her foot in the door. Now she was talking light-hearted to Josh finishing on asking him to come to the Cottage after work as she had something important to talk to him about. He obviously wondered what that could be but didn't push to know right away. When his work was finished he would go and see Sara then if it was an important item to be discussed he would then have time to listen properly.

Sara went back to the Cottage and told Maggie she had paved the way and was seeing Josh when his work was done.

"It will be so much better when it is all out in the open, Maggie said, and Alice will be like a different person. As you say it is amazing that only now you have come to recognise Josh in connection with Alice. I really hope all will be well soon."

Josh accepted the tea offered by Maggie and sat drinking it while Sara told her unbelievable story. At first he had his mind set on this not being the truth and that his encounter on the Open Day was too brief, it had done the job and that in a nutshell summed it up. He was shocked. His tea mug was filled again as he floundered trying to keep his self control. He quietly said,

"I will see Alice as you suggest on Sunday, by then I should have come to grips with the situation."

Sunday arrived the weather was cold but bright so Josh borrowed the Horse and cart to go with Sara to Martha's to at last see Alice. They arrived Josh was very fidgety Sara introduced him to Martha who as she always did made him feel at home.

"Hello Josh so you are the fine young Gentleman Alice has been telling us about for months How she has been trying to find you and couldn't. There you were all the time working with my Brother Joe. Strange how these things happen I am sure all will be for the best now and I wish you two happiness" A knock came on the door,

"Come in mi dears it is too cold to stand on doorsteps for long. Josh had all his thoughts on Alice, looking her up and down, seeing if

he had remembered her face correctly. Alice knew at a glance this was her man and her heart thudded.

"Please she prayed let him know and like me, I don't want to accuse him he has done nothing we merely fell in love, well I know I did, hook line and sinker."

"So you are Alice? I have thought about you many times and promised myself I would go to the Hall and visit you, but I was afraid I may lose you your job I didn't want to do that. Of course I didn't know about the baby or that would have been different, sorry seems such a feeble word to say to you, I know the anguish you must have been in."

He sidled up to her side saying "but I am sorry Alice I had no idea of the truth. Is there anything I can say that will make my apology ring true?"

"You don't have to apologise Josh, the fault lies between us, and my realisation at first when I knew for sure there was a baby on the way was total disbelief, this happened to other girls not me I said to myself. Then the time went on and I knew I loved this child, I was tempted by friends to have an abortion, but as luck would have it the time for aborting had gone I can't tell you how pleased I was, and how ashamed too at even thinking along

those lines."

Josh looked deeply into her shining blue eyes saying,

"All that time and I was totally unaware of anything that had happened because of me. The day at the Hall in the grounds I held as a tender memory savouring the thought of you when I had a private moment. We fell in love didn't we Alice? Yes just like that, and it was with innocence I held you in my fondest thoughts."

He gently kissed her for head and said,

"We must start all over again and take all the joy that the Baby will bring between us. Just think Alice I might have a son!"

"No, we might have a Son, and by the way I have felt the kicking I would say that it is most likely. The unaffected laugh that passed between them softened the atmosphere."

He was here. He was standing beside her. He loved her. Her mind did a turn around all in those few minutes at last she knew her way and that was beside Josh. She turned to Sara,

"Oh Sara you have made me so happy, I never thought there could be a happiness such as this." Tears welled in her eyes and finally spilled down her cheeks. None of them knew just what she had been going through, and yet they all had cared. Martha stepped in

and said,

"It is nothing short of a Miracle, come on Josh kiss the girl and get this new chapter started.

A Baby to look forward to and not long to go! You are two very lucky people. Why don't you get married when Dick and I get married? We could have a double Wedding and Alice and Josh could share the reception with us. There would be no cost, well except for the licence, but where would you live?" Josh readily replied,

"I have that sorted Martha, I already have a small dwelling of my own it is next to Ma and Pa. but they are used to my independence we would be all set up wouldn't we Alice?"

Alice looked bewildered everything was going a mite too fast for her to take it all in.

It seemed Sara and Rosa had taken it upon themselves to see to all the detail, Martha and Dick would be married in the Church at the top of the hill and now so would Alice and Josh.

"How can I marry in the Church I will be seven months pregnant exclaimed Alice."

"Don't you worry about that Martha said, we know the Vicar, been friends for years I will explain your circumstance he will surely comply.

There you have it, having found the missing entity in the name of Josh all had been sorted, Alice could jubilantly go to Mi Lord and Mi Lady and tell them all was planned and that she had found her lost love. No tears this time. Not that she had to, no proudly with dignity holding her head up high and loving Josh with all her heart and him loving her. She could have said that one million times…..he loves me, he loves me.

Chapter Forty -six

Time had passed the Wedding day drawing close Sara helped Alice get a suitable Wedding dress that flounced from under the bust line into a gathered long skirt, this gave her quite a regal look, she would have a spray of cream Roses on one shoulder and cream gloves giving the biscuit coloured dress a deeper tone. Josh's Ma and Pa would be there, they had taken the news without any fuss, Josh had to find a wife one day and they liked Alice. This had been a real milestone for Josh their attitude towards the whole affair had been open minded and attentive. It was for all to see how the Baby would be received making them Grand ma and Grand dad they were delighted. Many was the hour they had sat discussing names for the new arrival, at the moment it was to be Lydia for a girl and Timothy for a boy. Secretly they wished for a boy, so did Josh, a Son he would be proud as a peacock teaching him many ways of living, and the use of many tools. Wait they must, after the Wedding April would soon arrive, and like the others Alice could hardly wait, her waiting entailed the huge weight that would become her stature in the last few weeks.

All dressed up the Wedding Day had

arrived everyone had done their best to wear the right thing for this day. Sara looked a picture she had a double job to do as Alice had asked her to perform the best man duties for her as well as Martha. The day was fair with patchy sunshine breaking through the cloud. The time for the Ceremony at the Church was two o'clock the Church was filling up with well wishers and family. Martha had done her bit before going to Church by getting two tables together and starting to lay the fine homemade produce upon them. It looked very pretty, all in white and yellow with vases of Daffodils as centre pieces. The Quarry Yard Cottages were filled with anticipation and welcome; all the neighbours had chipped in to make this reception a right Royal feast, tables spilling out on to the Cobblestone yard, weighed down with food and drink. Blackie who played the Accordion had brought the instrument to leave at Martha's while he attended the Church. This couple were very popular, and the overflow included Alice and Josh and their parents. Martha's friends didn't turn a hair at Alice and her little bundle of love this pair were getting married and would be welcoming a child, very natural in anyone's say so.

Not having Bells or Organ playing didn't detract from the Ceremony. The gathering of those who were going to be saying their Vows were made reverent although simple. Clean cut and precise with love in their hearts. The Church being full was not out of written invitation it was because the people who had turned up wanted to see Martha and Dick happy, Alice and Josh had an abundance of left over love which was not in short supply. Many smiles hands shaken and confetti (home made from coloured paper) were thrown over the couples as they left Church. There was no transport, "for goodness sake said Martha, we only have to walk down the hill."

She was right and all the people present in Church walked down after them, as they went down Church Road curtains were not peeped through they were drawn back so that all could be seen to wish them well. The Sun came out and the warm spring day was just what was needed to complete the scene. The Cobbles on the Quarry Yard's space being used as a dance floor, benches and chairs had been fetched out now that they knew the day was dry and bright. Every lad had got him his lass Blackie played any requested melody.

Evening came too soon, yet perhaps not soon enough for the newlyweds, it was goodbyes and well wishes all around, one or two of the men seemed more than a little inebriated, it didn't matter it was all part of the day. Alice and Josh crept away a little sooner than the party end, Josh saying they had the little un to think about and wanting to get Alice in a warm and safe place, it was done quite without fuss and the party went on. Until Martha and Dick called it a day, saying thanks to all for the part they had played, and would they please return in the morning to clear up all the mess they had made, and indeed they would this was just the sort of common sense they used between them, it worked.

Alone at last Martha looked at Dick, now her Husband and felt proud he was a fine Man she was so lucky. Dick approached Martha saying,

"Well it is all over now we can be with each other all the time, I love you Martha." he put his arm around Martha's ample figure.

"I wish I had more to offer you Dick I can but be myself I love you too."

"That is all I ask, you are the one I have chosen and in my eyes there is no-one better."

"I give you my heart Dick, and my time, my cooking skills, and my patience, my feeling for you will last our lifetime."

In bed they cuddled, and it was as if they had been Man and Wife forever, nothing was shameful, more pure delight as they realised the closeness they had betrothed together.

Simple love is the best kind they were to discover that as time went by.

"Well we made a mess of that lot didn't we? It was Martha standing now looking at the debris the party had left behind. She was soon joined by her friends and Dick clearing it all up, once they got going it wasn't a problem, and they had a few laughs on the way. Lovely people enjoying each other as nature intended, nothing too much trouble, and whisking the broom around the yard with great intent, tea cloths off for washing, Candle stubs kept for melting down to make new ones, nothing was wasted even Dick's pigs got a look in with the left over's in truth there were not many of those. All decent meats and bread had been taken for use in the Cottages next day. Cake too, they would feed for a week now and eat it all as intended. Being homemade it was fresh as a daisy, and had been covered with fresh cloths so to keep it that way. Dick said it was enough to feed

the entire Ford that had been laid out, but then again it felt like the whole Ford had attended this Wedding. His Elderberry wine had gone down a treat with many compliments, he was proud of that, it was just what he had been storing it for and had played it's roll very well. The huge cake that Maggie had made for Martha and Dick was to be cut up today and passed around to all that wanted it, it was too big a task to do it last night, anyway it would keep forever the amount of richness that had been put in it. Dick was also proud of the many things that Martha his wife had made, his wife, and he had to say it again to believe it.

Sara had stayed overnight as well and had her hands deep in the washing up bowl now she was so pleased that all had been achieved so well, Alice of course had gone with Josh and then Sara thought of Rosa, who was now at the Hall all by herself. Sara made a promise to Rosa although she wasn't there,
"I will come and see you Rosa, don't be sad as soon as I can I promise."
Sara was to keep that promise with an unexpected result.

Chapter forty-seven

Through March already, spring flowers all in bloom gladdened the heart. Rosa's heart though was so lonely and her work seemed doubled. Alice had shared the load and no-one as yet had been hired to replace her. More than that she had no company and couldn't air her complaints as she went along her day. The thought of Alice having her baby kept her sane, soon she would hear from them and then she would go on a visit and see this brand new individual. As she worked going over in her mind was the time that Alice very nearly lost this infant, and how she had insisted she was going to keep it, for Sara to find Josh was a chance in a million and it had all worked out. Now instead of pity for Alice, Rosa envied her, in her own place with Josh who lavished affection for his wife.

"What will my life turn out to be? Who would want me? It is likely that I won't want to be married. All that went on in my mother's care has put me off men altogether. Then again I do not want to be skivvy at this Hall forever; oh I suppose something will turn up" she sighed."

It was not usual for Rosa to give in to self pity she had a positive outlook when it came to anyone else's problem, now it seemed she was scraping the bottom of the barrel and her own future looked bleak. Mr Richard still sent for her and the truth be known she was almost glad he did it broke up the monotony in a long day. She still had to watch his moves he was devious and could swing things his own way with little problem. Mr Vincent she hardly ever seen, and when she did he would always ask if there was any news of Sara. Rosa as a person was invisible to him. Of course Rosa knew where Sara was, but she had promised her friend she would not tell, so she always answered with a negative reply.

Day in day out, on and on until this perfect day in April when she was informed that Alice and Josh had a baby Son. Jubilant Rosa had to tell Milord and Milady, saying when in the room where she had been received,

"Milady, Milord, lovely news for us all, Alice and Josh have a Son, he is to be called Timothy. I will ask right now for time to go and see them all, I can't wait to see this baby Boy. I feel in a way related I went through all the first signs with Alice, she has cried on my shoulder many times. This outcome is wonderful."

Milord, and Milady, had to smile at Rosa's

enthusiasm, of course they were pleased that all had turned out well, but Rosa took on a new look to them a smiling and happy person, so pleased she knew she was going to be called Aunt Rosa, that alone had thrilled her whole being. She would be able to buy this little one a few nice things and take them to him at the same time enhancing her closeness to Alice. The loneliness she had been enduring slipped from her outlook straight away. Now she had told Milord, and Milady, she could tell all the upstairs Maids, and the Footman, and everyone she came into contact with. She would be able to give them bulletins about how the Baby was coming along Alice would bring the little boy to visit so that Rosa could take him into the grounds and teach him about natural things.

Auntie! She was to be Timothy's Auntie, a beautiful Boy who she would love and cherish.

Next thing to do was to go and actually see Alice and Josh with their Baby, wanting to go while the Baby was in its first light of day. Seeing who it resembled and holding baby in her own arms. This had swallowed Rosa up completely. Could it be that this was maternal instinct? A feeling she had thought was lost to her from her Mother's behaviour when at her Mother's command. As the thought travelled through her mind she shuddered. She knew if it became her chance a baby would not be served as she had been. Dismissing the thought as quickly as it came and pouring a cup of tea, her way to celebrate this happy news.

Now she must plan the very earliest time she could visit, everything all of a sudden was possible. This weekend, she could not see herself waiting longer than that. Miss Olivine came to check the day's work she said,

"I have heard about Alice and her baby boy, she is indeed a lucky girl to have come out of the situation as readily as she did. Have you seen her yet?"

"No I am just thinking of going this Sunday, I have the time off and I don't want the Baby to be weeks old before I see him. I am so excited I am to be his Aunt."

"Are you indeed" Miss Olivine took on her usual haughty look which was never far away.

"I can't say I am that interested in Babies, they take a lot of looking after, you can tell me how things are with Alice when you have been to see her."

She turned on her heel and went back to her domain.

Rosa smiled to herself knowing Miss Olivine had stretched herself as far as she could asking about Alice, it was not in her person to enquire into anyone's private life. Staunch and rigid, to her only one world existed inside this Hall where she reigned supreme.

So it was to be this Sunday Rosa would see Timothy, her work seemed as nothing as she had only one thought in her mind. It was Saturday afternoon when Mr Vincent came to see her saying,

"Hello Rosa I hear you are going to see Alice's Baby Boy tomorrow, I would like to take the pony and trap and go with you myself. Pay our respects with my Mother and Father's blessing." Rosa replied,

"I think Alice would very much like that, she has been through enough, I for one am happy to see her now getting settled, do you think it would be possible? I am sure Alice would be thrilled at your visit Mr Vincent it is very kind of you to take me, it is a bit out of the way but with the pony and trap the narrow lanes would be no trouble." Rosa was very excited and said,

"Perhaps there would be room to pick up Sara on the way there?"

As soon as the words had left her tongue she realised just what she had said.

Silence fell between them, both of them transfixed to the spot. Rosa waited until Mr Vincent replied.

"So you know where Sara is Rosa?"

The air in between them was like a solid blank wall, what could Rosa say? After all this time she had slipped her guard and in her enthusiasm spurted out her dear friend's secret.

Her face went white there was no way she could retract what she had said.

"I am so sorry Mr. Vincent Sara made us solemnly swear we would keep her whereabouts to ourselves. Now I have let her down, what more can I say?"

"I will be the sole of discretion Rosa you don't know the weight you have taken off my mind. Yes we will pick up Sara as something as normal as breathing, I will make no comment. We three will go to where Alice and Josh live, during that time I will gently break the news to Sara of my search for her, and how I want our friendship to resume. Don't worry you will find that I take a very back seat, the visit will be the very best way of not making a great fuss between Sara and me, the Baby will take up all the conversation. I will just be standing by, and in that mode it will be natural for me to talk to Sara, and let

her know I want to see her. I will be very casual and quiet I do not wish to alarm her in any way. Now I too can't wait until tomorrow afternoon."

With that he left Rosa to her own thoughts. Perhaps after all it could turn out well Mr. Vincent was bound to find out where Sara was eventually and this was as good a time as any.

Chapter Forty -eight

Sara was also getting excited saying to Maggie,

"What should I wear for my visit to Alice, I am undecided Maggie, I don't want to go dressed up to the nines, I shall be waiting to hold little Timothy so I don't want to worry about my dress."

"If it is warm enough Sara wear a pretty summer dress, you can always put a cardigan over the top for warmth. I have seen your blue and white one amongst your dresses, yes the one you recently bought at the Market and blue would be appropriate wouldn't it?"

"Yes it does have long sleeves I will see if it needs ironing I have some white boots too. I don't know what to take for Timothy I haven't been to Market so I think it has to be a Half Crown in his hand."

"That would be better than taking an item to wear, it could go into a Bank for him, and you or anyone giving a gift of money could add to it over the years. There would come a time when he would be most grateful about his Bank money, yes it is a long way away but time doesn't stand still."

The dress was fetched out and ironed, it wasn't showy it was just pretty and suited Sara very well bringing out the blue in her eyes and the slant of her shoulders. Maggie said,

"I have a delicate necklace that would look lovely with that dress Sara; she fetched it and put it on Sara's neck. They agreed that was just what the entire outfit needed. It was set aside for tomorrow.

The day dawned bright and sunshine came just before Sara was due to go to see Alice. Dick had said he was going to pick her up at two thirty pm. Sara and Maggie both were looking out of the window and listening for the sound and sight of his cart. Now coming into view was a Pony and Trap. Sara said,

Dick is taking me in style Maggie, a posh Pony and Traps no less. I am glad I took pains with how I look, washing my hair and ironing my dress, wonder whose rig this is?"

"We will soon know they are here." said Maggie looking out of the window.

"Brace yourself Sara, it is Mr. Vincent."

Sara didn't know what to do although it was obvious there was nothing she could do but act normal. It wasn't how she felt though, this was the Vincent she dreamed about who was never far from her thoughts now he was standing before her.

"Hello Sara, I have come instead of Dick as I wanted to convey my Parents regards to Alice

and Josh".

It was natural, the words broke the ice and Sara was relieved. She climbed into the front seat saying hello to Rosa. It was quite a tight fit but as the girls were dainty a good space was made for Mr Vincent to drive his Pony. Small talk passed between the three saying,

It was a nice warm afternoon, and how they were looking forward to seeing Alice and baby.

Arriving Mr Vincent helped first Rosa and then Sara down from their seats. As his hand touched Sara's hand there was an immediate response, and Sara shivered at his touch.

Alice was still in her Birthing Bed, and hadn't been allowed up as yet. The cot right beside her whickered like basket wear, and on a rocker to sway to and fro. The Baby in it swathed in white with blue ribbon threads here and there, a patchwork quilt loosely covering for warmth. Sara looked in and said, "He is a lovely Baby Alice and so like his Father his hair is already golden red just as you said it would be. This is such a happy conclusion Alice you have Josh and you have Josh's

Son how lucky you are."

"I told you didn't I right from the very beginning my love of that day would be my

love for life. I still wonder how it all came to pass but as we are so very happy it is of no matter. Josh is wonderful and his Parents have welcomed me with open arms. Alice picked up Timothy saying to Rosa,

"You are going to be his Auntie." Rosa came forward saying this was truly a privilege, and oh how the Baby was so bonnie, and then speaking to all who wanted to listen,

"A miniature of Josh no less, he is handsome and not yet a week old."

She sat down with Baby on her knee, he burbled and spluttered and then gave a weak smile his eyes open looking as though he was finding out his new surroundings.

Mr Vincent had let the Ladies have the space; he knew what that meant to them. He could wait, talking to Josh he congratulated him on such a fine Boy and to Josh's surprise gave him a cheque for £25 as his parents had told him to do. Josh went to Alice and told her, she was very pleased. Feeling forgiven for the upset she had caused at the Hall that meant a lot to her she said to Josh,

"We must go to the Hall and thank them in person all in due time Josh." He agreed.

Sara fetched from her pocket her Half Crown piece, and asked if she could put it in the Babies hand for luck. Rosa was holding the

Baby and had only a shilling to give him, Alice said to them both,

"It is so kind of you I know how scarce money is with the allowance you get paid. I will put it with the Cheque money and Josh will open a Bank account for our little Son, won't you Josh?

"Yes I will be happy to, even a few days old and look how lucky he is I am so very proud, I only wish I could have saved you the anguish Alice in the beginning, but it is never too late to make amends is it?"

Cups of tea were passed all around Josh's Ma and Pa joining in the gathering a very happy affair for all. Mr Vincent was taken aback by the wealth of congeniality that was in the company. How he wished his own life could include Sara and be as loving and free.

Riding home Rosa tried to keep the conversation going, but it was stretched and Sara had very little to say. Arriving at Maggie's Mr Vincent jumped down and offered his hand to help Sara down.

"Thank you Sara for a lovely afternoon"

Sara felt herself shiver the touch of his hand on hers had made her legs go weak.

"Now that I have found you dear girl I will not let you go. Would you like to come to the Hall? Or perhaps a ride out, we could discuss

*over a cup of coffee in the Village if it would
suit you?"*

"Mr Vincent what is there to discuss?"

*"My name is Vincent, Sara please don't call
me Mr. surely you and I have a better
understanding than that."*

*His eyes had a pleading look that she could
not deny.*

*"I couldn't come to the Hall Vincent I am out
of my place there."*

*"Nonsense if I invite you your place would be
as my guest."*

*"No you come here I have a small room of
my own so we would be private."*

*"If you are sure Maggie wouldn't mind."
Vincent was secretly pleased. Sara said,*

*"Joe and Maggie only want the best for me,
you would be welcome."*

*They made a time and date and Vincent felt
he had won that round at least she was going
to talk to him.*

"Home then Rosa"

*Setting the horse at a gallop and smiling to
himself he was lighter hearted than he had
been for a long time. Could he say he was a
happy man? No not yet he still had to win
Sara, was that going to be easy? No he had to
remember all the right things to say and he
knew Sara was a proud woman.*

Chapter Forty-nine

It was a week later when Vincent went to see Sara she had been looking forward to and also loathing his visit. The truth must come out she must tell him about Bill and her background, it would probably put him off for good but it must be said. Sara had practised how to say it and never did it come out how she intended it to. Not as though this confession was a small thing she knew it had impact it did matter, how she wished it wasn't true, this was fact, he must realise the Sara he knew had a past and that past wasn't pretty.

He was here Sara let him in, he spoke to Maggie saying,

"It is kind of you to let me come to see Sara, I am much obliged."

"You two go and sort yourselves out I am going to help Joe for an hour so I will be out of your way. No need to go into your room Sara, make your young man a cup of tea and sit where there is more room."

"Thank you Maggie and thank you for giving us our Privacy too"

Vincent sat down all the time looking at Sara, the kettle went on and the familiar motion of making tea seemed to ease the tension.

"I have so much to tell you Vincent I don't

know where to begin" Sara said pouring tea. Vincent replied,

"Some I know, yes I have been making many enquiries Sara, and you already have children don't you? So it follows you must have been Married, now you go on from there you want to explain don't you?"

"Well the hardest thing to explain is the Children although Martha looks after them now I have very little to do for them. Vincent why do you want me? There are lots of aristocratic Ladies that would fall at your feet?" Vincent looked at Sara with tenderness saying,

"Why? Because I love you Sara there is only one girl in this entire world that could make me happy and that is you."

"Do you want me to tell you about Bill and how this whole sorry matter became the story of my life?"

"Yes I do because if you don't it is always going to come between us, I want nothing between us but our love and I know you do love me Sara."

It was a statement not a question she couldn't deny him with all her heart she loved him.

Telling him about Bill and his drinking ways choked her, not wanting even the memory to soil her thoughts but Vincent was right he must know so that they had a chance of happiness. He came over from his chair and put his arm around Sara as the tears escaped down her face, letting her cry out all these pent up feelings, glad he was able to be there for her to trust. Letting nothing come between them except the love they had for each other.

She was quieting now and said,

"What are your parents to think of all this Vincent?"

"They will know just as much as you want to tell them, I know the facts and that is all that matters. I shall give up my Title and Richard can be the next Lord of Danbury. Yes I am ready to do that Sara, you and I could have a cottage on the grounds of the Hall, there would be no pretence. My Mother and Father would agree to that, they know how I have tried to find you even though they have put every good looking girl into my pathway. No-one else matters to me you are my dearest love Sara."

His kiss held the world and all that Sara wanted in it. This was her dear loving Vincent the man she thought could only be hers in dreams, fate at last had dealt her a winning hand and she was going to play that hand to its fullest meaning. Soon Maggie would be back with her Joe. Sara would have Vincent beside her to let them be the first to know of their love. Now she could tell the world shout it from the hilltops and bathe in its glory. This was real and all the previous encounters were as if they had never been. Held in Vincent's arms wanting to be there, and holding him in the same manner. He had made her his equal. Through good times and bad times she would be his. Nothing in God's earth could now separate the love they had, it would finally bind them.

Sylvia Jackson Clark.

32096119R00221

Made in the USA
Charleston, SC
08 August 2014